ANDREW O'CONNOR was born in 1978 in Warragul, Victoria. He studied Arts at Melbourne University before travelling and working in central and northern Australia. For the past four years, Andrew has divided his time between stints teaching English (ESL) in various regions of Japan and writing in Australia.

Andrew O'Connor

ALLEN&UNWIN

First published in 2006

Allen & Unwin
83 Alexander Street
Crows Nest NSW 2065
Australia
Phone: (61 2) 8425 0100
Fax: (61 2) 9906 2218
Email: info@allenandunwin.com
Web: www.allenandunwin.com

National Library of Australia
Cataloguing-in-Publication entry:

O'Connor, Andrew, 1978–.
  Tuvalu.

  ISBN 978 1 74114 871 8.

  ISBN 1 74114 871 5.

  I. Title.

A823.4

Set in 11.5/14pt Adobe Garamond by Asset Typesetting Pty Ltd
Printed in Australia by McPherson's Printing Group

10 9 8 7 6 5 4 3 2 1

For my parents, brother and sister,
who always believed.

For Toshiko, who made it possible.

Mami Kaketa
Can Have This

Early on a Tuesday morning, two weeks after we met in a bar, Mami Kaketa appeared beneath my bedroom window.

'Noah?' she called. 'Noah?'

It was an icy morning and there was a cold burn in my toes. I rubbed them together, one clenched foot atop the other, and watched white breath plume towards the low, mildew-stained ceiling. In the distance, engines fired and faded as motorised carts hauled the day's catch around Tokyo's Tsukiji fish market—frosty tuna, writhing squid, octopuses, eel and seaweed. A dog was yapping mechanically somewhere and, across the alley that ran below my room, Nakamura-san, the owner of my hostel, was grimly beating her futon as she did every morning at ten past seven.

I staggered to my window, wrenched it up and peered down groggily. Was this another dream? It was difficult to say, though Mami appeared real enough. She was shifting her weight from foot to foot to keep warm and biting at her bottom lip. Even from two floors up her eyes, the irises dark, the whites far larger and rounder than on most Japanese, jumped out and demanded admiration. A stray cat rubbed against her shin and she gave it a sharp, un-thinking kick.

'What are you doing here?' I asked uneasily.

She shrugged, shielding her eyes from the sun with one hand. 'Visiting you. You look tired.'

'I didn't sleep well.'

'From what you've told me, you never do.'

A rock dove, perched on a level powerline outside my window, eyed me suspiciously, first with its left eye, then with its right. Below it another bird—a large black crow—marched arrogantly up and down a neatly trimmed hedge, pruning it for bugs. Both were oblivious to the January cold, and to Nakamura-san's din.

Mami was not.

'That's loud,' she said, pointing up at Nakamura-san. I followed her gaze. The old woman's thin bedding, stained yellow by sweat and other secretions, was slung over a lime-green balcony rail. She used a broad, straw paddle to beat it, pausing for air between each wallop, then raising the paddle and bringing it down with a whoosh. Despite the cold she had broken a slight sweat, and her usually pelt-dry skin glistened in the morning sun.

'Good morning, Nakamura-san,' I called to be polite. Nakamura-san looked from me to Mami, then back to me. Her thin, wispy white hair fluttered in the breeze like a tattered flag. In reply she straightened from her usual awkward hunch and brought the paddle down with unaccustomed force.

'Does she understand English?' Mami asked.

'Not much.'

'How do you know for sure?'

'She's my landlady. She runs this hostel.'

Mami nodded and yawned, covering her mouth with an elegant, long-fingered hand. She was one of those girls whose body gave an impression of immense athleticism—lithe, agile and decisive—but who, I felt sure, could not have sprinted more than a few hundred metres without collapsing.

'Once, she—'

'Enough about her,' Mami said, finishing her yawn and cutting me off. 'Stick your head out so I can see you properly.'

Doing as instructed, I discovered other residents also had their heads out, interested to see who it was yelling up from the narrow, normally quiet alley. One grizzly middle-aged Englishman, a newcomer to Nakamura's, drummed on the hostel's rusty iron exterior.

'Some peace!' he demanded, but Mami ignored him. Only the rock dove took offence, launching itself into the air where it hung precariously for a moment before steadily rising. I watched it dip and peel away.

'I can only count four clouds in the whole sky,' Mami said. She pointed to each in turn, arm up and out and spinning in stages like a lawn sprinkler. 'There, there, there and … there. Four. Or is that last one just smoke from a factory? I can't tell.' She stared up at me, one eye clamped shut, waiting for my verdict. The alley around her was cluttered. It was full of pot plants and colourful plastic crates, the latter full to bursting with cans and bottles ready for recycling. A little distance from where she stood a bearded old man, bent double with a trowel, was waiting for an even older dog to do its business. It strained unsteadily, looking set to topple sideways, and when it finished he flicked the shit towards an open drain.

Reluctantly, I peered up into the early morning sky. 'It's a cloud,' I said. 'Maybe. I don't know.' I wanted her to go away; visits like this were out of the question.

'What's with all the corrugated iron?' she asked.

'It covers half the windows.'

'But you don't know why? You don't know very much, Noah.'

'No.'

I surveyed Nakamura-san's lifeless concrete balcony with its antiquated aircon unit and pale blue rope for laundry. It looked drab and depressing. There were no plants as on balconies below—nothing at all had been done to soften the grey. Nakamura-san, now hanging out under-wear, caught my eye and frowned.

Looking back into my room, I tried to think of a polite way to get rid of Mami but nothing came to mind. My head was sluggish with sleep—or, more accurately, with lack of it. I had again given up my sleeping pills, flushing them, and with them the groggy days and nights they struggled to stake out.

Seeing Mami open her mouth to speak, the middle-aged Englishman once again drummed on the iron beneath his window.

'Shut the fuck up!' he shouted.

'I'm not talking to you, idiot,' Mami snapped. 'Go toss off!' She stamped her foot and it echoed loudly in the alley, like a handclap. The man shook his head, muttering. But something made him pull his creaky window shut, sliding the lock into place. Nakamura-san, suffering a piercing coughing fit, hurriedly lit a cigarette. She pulled back her glass sliding door and retreated into darkness.

'I'm coming up,' Mami said. 'There's too much going on down here.'

'It's a mess.'

'I don't care. Messy is more interesting. What number?'

'I don't think you—'

'I think I should. What number?'

'The second floor, 211.'

Quickly, I tried to hide everything that belonged to my girlfriend, Tilly. I rolled up her things in bedsheets—framed photos, jewellery, perfume, magazines, candles, a hairbrush full of long auburn hair. But there was simply too much, too many things. I was terrified. I had never cheated on a girlfriend before and dreaded above all else being revealed as just another cad. Then the absurdity of my actions struck me; I flung the whole pile onto the floor and sat on the bed. Glumly, fretfully, I waited for Mami.

But she did not come. Three minutes became five, then ten. I thought about the hostel, specifically about how it must have appeared to this most unexpected guest—like some sort of sinister carcinogenic lump probably. Most of the corrugated iron on the building's exterior had been painted black and had turned brown with rust over time. Any sheets which had been left silver (like the one covering my window) had fared worse; their rust was orange and dribbled from rotting nails like glacial sewerage. The rear of the building was constructed with smashed-in weatherboards. The roof was a collection of semi-dislodged tiles. And across all of this hung red, green and white wiring, like a string of forgotten Christmas lights. It was clearly a building with more years behind it than ahead, and I wondered if Mami had simply thought better of entering, had turned on her heel.

I stood and inspected my reflection in a small mirror sticky-taped to the inside of my wardrobe. As always it was a fairly depressing sight. My russet hair glinted red in the sunlight and needed a cut. It fell languidly around my pasty face. My chin was dotted with white-headed, angry acne, and my eyes were bloodshot from lack of sleep. I was contemplating picking at my face when Mami knocked on my door, startling me.

I half opened it, anticipating a searing slap. Instead I was greeted by feathers. This plumage was arranged in lush, navy blue balls at her temples, and in seductive, fiery red fingers around her neck, sliding towards her throat lustfully to entice and possess and strangle her all at once. Beneath them was a beige leather necklace, also tight. Its pale beads reminded me of macadamias.

'Good,' she said lazily, before I could say a word about the feathers. 'It is you.' If Mami noticed the mess on the floor or my mounting discomfort she said nothing about either, only, 'I got lost.'

'Like I said, it's a mess, sorry.'

She stepped in, faintly amused. Her eyes, the top lids a vivid blue, were narrowed, and her orange-red lips curled in a half-smile, accentuating angular cheekbones. She circled the pile of feminine knick-knacks on the floor without concern. When she removed her cashmere coat, her long, glossy black hair slid over it like oil. Underneath she had on a light satin print dress with small feathers, all in muted whites, blues, reds and an understated gold. She touched her finger to an inky strand of hair placed diagonally across her forehead, as if to make sure it was still in place, then crossed to my window and determinedly stuck her head out, checking left and right.

'I always forget things if I don't stop to check,' she said. 'But I don't think I had anything with me. Don't you hate days when you have nothing with you? I always step off trains and panic, thinking I've left my bag on a seat or something. It feels wrong to have nothing, wouldn't you say?' She turned, caught my eyes on her slender, shapely bottom and smiled. I averted my gaze and began toying with a long red hair on my bed until it occurred to me what it was—what I was drawing attention to. I brushed it aside. Mami set her coat on my desk and returned to the window.

'It's a dull coat, isn't it?' she said, looking not at the coat, but at the discarded hair. I could see thin, grey, smoke-like rings at the outermost edges of her irises. These, I knew, came and went depending on the light and her mood. 'It's the bit that won't fit. The rest is Zandra Rhodes, British *Vogue*, December 1970.'

She returned to my desk and sat on the edge. She removed the blue feathers but left the red where they were, tenderly choking her. I tried not to glance at the magazines or tampons, at anything belonging to Tilly. But it was all there in the middle of the room like a police haul, impossible to ignore. It seemed the more I tried to avert my gaze, the more my eyes drifted to it.

'I told myself,' Mami said, setting the blue feathers atop the coat, 'that I didn't want this coat. It's not that I don't like it. Actually, no, that is it.'

'I like it.'

Mami frowned. 'The coat? You don't. Or you shouldn't. I've worn it in public now though, so I can throw it in the bin with a clear conscience.' She sucked in air. 'God I'm talking a lot. And about nothing. Were you really sleeping when I arrived?'

'I was.'

She looked around my room, confused. 'This is it? This is everything?'

'What do you mean?'

'There are no other rooms?'

'No, this is it.' I was embarrassed. I had never been embarrassed by my hostel room before. Everyone in Nakamura's inhabited the same cramped quarters, after all. Had the same splotchy yellow carpet, the same faded green curtains, the same bed with hundreds of lewd messages chiselled into its cheap pine frame. If anything, my room was a notch up on most. It had a wardrobe, cast-iron desk and antique lamp. But looking at Mami's amazed face I felt like a bum. I suppose it had to do with knowing she lived on the top floor of a plush Tokyo hotel, with knowing her father was a prominent Japanese hotelier. I picked up a few magazines and straightened them ineffectually, as though this might lend the room a certain elegance.

'You know,' Mami said, as if the idea had only just occurred to her, 'it's a good day to get out—a good day for Odaiba.'

'What's odaiba?'

'Traditional Japanese wig-making,' she said, face deadpan. When I nodded she groaned. 'Foreigners! A place, idiot. Odaiba's a place. A fun place, as it happens. But we'll have to go now or we won't have time. Actually, no, that's a lie—we'll have plenty of time. But let's go.'

'I can't. I have plans, sorry.'

'What plans?'

But I could not conjure a single plausible engagement.

'Nothing?' Mami asked, amused. 'Of course not. You're too shy to have plans.'

'Can you at least give me a minute to get changed?'

Mami pretended to think this over, then rolled her eyes and nodded.

'With you outside,' I added.

She tilted her head. 'I've already seen it, remember? Don't be such a prude.'

In the end I changed just my T-shirt while Mami made a point of staring out the window. My body tingled at the suggestion of sexual familiarity. It willed me to act until I caught sight of my bony shoulders, ribs and soup-white skin in the mirror. I hurriedly covered myself. I was a coward. Only drink—for which I had a genetic frailty— had facilitated the encounter leading to Mami's present visit. And now, paradoxically, I despised myself as much for having succumbed in the first place as I did for not attempting to do so again.

'Can I smoke in here?' Mami asked, rummaging

through her coat. 'I have cigarettes somewhere. Normally I don't smoke, but your stress is making me want to. You look like you are about to do everything incredibly quickly—finish dressing, brush your teeth, eat a cereal bar. Like Superman. One colourful blur. Except you're too stressed so you've stalled. I need a cigarette.'

'Go ahead.'

'Don't worry, I'll smoke out the window.'

'You don't have to.'

But Mami did anyway, drawn perhaps by a clinking of bottles and down-shifting of gears as the recycling truck came to a halt. I noticed a packet of tampons on the sill.

'I really like this area,' she said, sitting beside the tampons, body half in, half out of the room. 'It's nowhere at all.' She puffed a long cigarette ineffectually until her body stiffened. 'Is that gospel music?'

'I can't hear anything.'

'It is. Ugh! Down there somewhere.' She pointed along the exterior of the hostel.

'That's probably Catalina,' I said. 'Is it Portuguese? She's here with a church. Don't let her see you or—' I stopped.

'Or?'

'She hates smokers.'

Mami burst out laughing. 'You're a terrible liar, Noah. Do you know that? You're lucky. That's what first appealed to me about you in that horrible dark bar.' She picked up the packet of tampons and dropped them on my desk. Then she swung her long legs around and dangled them out the window, so that only her bottom was left inside. She showed no regard for the satin dress. I strained to hear her voice.

'You were given a five thousand yen note and coins, remember? Change for drinks you never bought. I would have shot out of the place, never looked back. Anyone would have. But not you. You couldn't keep a hold of it. Dropping the coins, then chasing them round. "Excuse, exc—, excuse me? This note, this isn't ... This isn't mine."' Laughter, possibly forced, took a hold of Mami. She coughed and waved off smoke. 'I was charmed though, Noah, really. You have to understand, I learnt to lie from liars. Every liar does. Learns from watching others lie, or worse, from being lied to—from believing.'

'Charmed?'

'You were something new to me.'

'How so?'

'It didn't enter your head to steal that money, did it?'

'No.'

'See. I'd reached a point where I didn't believe people like you existed.' Mami again began to laugh. 'Sorry, I shouldn't laugh, I know. I don't even know why I'm like this. I've been doing it all morning and for no reason. Always at the stupidest things. But I loved that stammer of yours. I heard it and I thought, Mami, here's someone who won't ever lie to you.'

'Because I can't?'

'Exactly.'

Then, as if Mami had seen something awful in the alleyway—a car crash or murder—her laugh cut out. When she faced me again her eyes narrowed. I had the sensation that all fun, all warmth had flooded from her.

'So tell me again,' she said, 'why you don't want this Catalina girl to see me?'

'Because she's a friend of my girlfriend, Matilda.'

Mami nodded, threw her still-lit cigarette into the street and rolled her legs back into my room. The very edges of the feathers at her throat flashed white in the sunlight. I thought she was angry—leaving. But I glimpsed amusement in her face, and she flopped casually onto my bed.

'Matilda's the girl you share this room with?'

'Yes.'

'And where's she?'

'In Australia, visiting her father.'

Mami smiled—a full, beautiful smile revealing straight, white teeth, teeth with a confidence all of their own. I shifted uneasily.

'To Odaiba,' she said.

Our train trip out to sleek Odaiba was unremarkable, except for the fact that Mami stole her ticket. While I was slotting change into the ticket machine she set her face in a pout and strode up to the stationmaster. I had no inkling of what it was she was doing or why she was upset. Nor could I understand a word she was saying. But her pleading tone was clear. There was something she wanted from this fat, balding man, something she was not meant to have. He peered through his window with the tired, resigned look of a harangued civil servant. Only when Mami shot him an awful look did he shrug, print a ticket and slide it under the screen. He looked unhappy with the whole affair but nevertheless bowed his head when thanked.

Mami found me at a newsstand reading an English

newspaper which featured, among other things, the weather and a photo of a schoolboy, hand in his mother's, glossy red backpack strapped tightly on, returning to school for the winter term. I held up my ticket. Mami took an excessively firm hold of my wrist and flung me through a ticket gate.

'Hurry up,' she said. 'You're too slow.' She dragged me through clumps of people, up stairs, around rubbish bins and into a train.

'What was that all about?' I asked.

'What?'

'Before, with the ticket guy.'

'Oh, that. I lost my ticket.'

'Lost it? You had a ticket?'

Mami thought for a moment, chewing at the inside of her lip. A number of commuters glanced at her, at her dress and the red feathers. She had dropped her cashmere coat in the bin outside the hostel. 'No. Not really. But I told him I did.'

'So you stole this ride?'

She recoiled playfully. 'What are you talking about?'

'You stole your ticket.'

'Stole? So I'm a common thief now? Is that what you're saying?' Still smiling, Mami jutted out her jaw. 'Okay. For how long then? Exactly?'

'How long what?'

'How long will I be a thief?'

I shrugged. 'Until the end of this trip?'

Mami swivelled to look out the window, thinking. 'I can live with that,' she said finally.

We sat in silence after this. Mami pulled a rubber band from somewhere, stretched it, then curled it on her fingers.

Around us, commuters typed messages into phones, did make-up with hand mirrors, slept, drank and exchanged furtive sexual glances. People's lives spilling into trains uninterrupted. The train as bathroom, bedroom and bar.

We somehow changed climates in the space of this fifteen-minute train trip, because when we stepped onto the platform in Odaiba it was snowing big, cumbersome flakes. I had never seen it snow in Tokyo. I watched as Mami held out her hands, trying to catch whatever flakes she could, but they swirled around her open palms and down onto wet concrete.

'To hell with snow,' she mumbled, wrapping her arms around her body, hunching her head and marching me on. Outside the station two young girls in bright pink parkas jumped excitedly, hands up as if snatching fruit from an unseen tree.

'Which way?' I asked.

'No idea,' said Mami. 'Actually, no, that's another lie. This way.' She started off without the slightest regard for a man about to photograph his smiling wife. I watched him frown, pull his phone back to let her pass, then hold it out again as Mami started to talk about what she called 'matters of much significance'.

'You see, Noah, I don't accept rules like most people. That's what you've got to understand about me. I think it's so strange the way people just accept rules. We're supposedly free to do whatever we want, but then there are all these rules—things we can't do.'

'Like stealing a ticket?'

'Exactly. Only I can hear from your voice you think I learnt something from that, something that'll make me less inclined to steal in future.'

'Do you often steal?'

'That's not the point. Keep up. The point is, I don't think it's entirely wrong.'

'And what if everyone did it?'

'That's not the point either. I'm taking a completely different angle here, a far more personal one.'

Mami paused to think. We were nearing a slight bottleneck, unusual in Odaiba. There was a pair of schoolgirls vying to peer at the one mobile phone, a yakuza-looking type with a toothpick, children, mopey husbands and more than a few plump, middle-aged women with fixed fuck-the-world glares. I felt I was trying to follow a string of pebbles while ahead Mami weaved a dexterous, devil-may-care line through it all. As we stepped clear, a red feather, riding the bay breeze, whipped back past me and was lost.

'Let me try and be clear,' she said, twisting her upper body to face me but maintaining the same almost belligerent pace. 'The government says we are free to do whatever—'

'I've heard that but—'

'Let me finish.' Mami halted. Two people collided into and bounced off her.

'I'm saying,' she said, elongating the words, 'a truly free society would be a society without rules—not so much as one rule. Nothing written down.' She made a gesture (possibly tossing out the Japanese constitution).

'That would be chaos.'

'You would think.' She frowned and started walking again. 'But things have a funny way of working themselves out. Criminals live outside the law and therefore have a code. This code is just as effective as any government law. If you don't follow the code, you have to be prepared for the consequences. Why can't everything be like that? Why can't all society be left to sort itself out? Imagine what a different place it'd be.'

'I imagine,' I said, looking around, 'it'd be very similar to this.'

Mami clucked her tongue. She started to walk faster. When she resumed speaking, the haughty edge to her voice was gone. 'Yes, but I mean, with nothing written down.'

'What difference does that make?'

'What difference?' she parroted. But she did not answer.

I was left with a vague unease following this conversation. I had never really broken the law. I had hardly broken a rule. This was not due to a concerted effort on my part, but more a result of my fearful nature. I disliked risk. The night we first met, it was mostly drink that gave me the courage to follow Mami home. But if, as Mami was suggesting, she had rarely observed a rule, how was I to proceed?

We passed a theatre, or what might have been a theatre. The Japanese characters above the door looked a little like *eigakan*, but were not—not exactly. I looked for the two basic alphabets I knew, for *hiragana* or *katakana*, but there was mostly only *kanji*—thousands of complex little stick houses stolen from the Chinese. I could extract no sounds from which to puzzle out meanings. Far more telling was a queue trailing out front. People flapped tickets in gloved hands, their breath white. I noticed the snow was starting to abate, that the flakes were smaller and no one was looking up anymore. A mother tried to pull scarves over children's faces, but every time she got one up it was pulled back down while she fished for the next. I counted seven children in all, swirling around.

Mami dragged me into a smaller street, talking quickly and loudly. 'My argument didn't make sense before, I know. I've never tried to explain what I do, not even to myself. It's difficult.'

'Why?'

'I don't steal to thumb my nose at the government or anything, if that's what you're thinking. I'm not a communist. I just steal sometimes. Like that ticket. I saw that fat, lazy stationmaster sitting there and knew somehow I could travel for free. Like there was a little sign in front of him that said: "Mami can travel for free. Everyone else, please refer to the set prices".' Mami ran her hand down the columns of this imaginary sign, the rubber band from the train still wrapped around her fingers. While presumably she saw vertical Japanese characters, she spoke in her fluent but oddly accented English, the sort of accent you could never place.

'This might be off the topic,' I said, 'but are you truly bilingual? I mean, are both languages the same for you— equally easy?'

'No. English is what I use for thinking. Isn't that strange? I'm Japanese and I think in English. It's not that I don't like Japan or speaking Japanese. I like both. But all through my schooling I liked English more. It was the language spoken in the classroom and I think it was just easier after a while.'

'So you went to an international school?'

'My father insisted on it. He hated memorising English from books and tapes.'

'Have you ever been overseas?'

'Never.'

'Are you planning to go?'

Mami shrugged. 'I could live in Korea but I don't want to. I know Tokyo. I see those little signs. Private messages just for me: "Mami Kaketa Can Have This". And Mami Kaketa takes, believe me. That wouldn't happen overseas. Overseas I'd have to be normal.' This last word fell from her mouth like spoilt sea urchin.

'How awful,' I said sarcastically.

'I'm glad I've told you about my little signs though. Once I told this Japanese boy and he went crazy. Pure madness. He said, "You can't do that! That's no way to live. Where's the honour in that sort of selfish approach?" Too many samurai movies. Honour? Please! What a joke.'

'Maybe.'

We walked on in silence until I asked, 'Why Korea?'

'Why Korea what?'

'How can you live there?'

'Because my mother's Korean.'

'Really?'

'No. She was born in Korea but doesn't speak much Korean, so she's not really Korean at all. She's only Korean because her parents were. Maybe I couldn't live there. I don't know.'

I did not understand this but had the distinct feeling Mami wanted me to drop the topic. We entered a larger street and soon passed the futuristic Fuji TV building. Mami explained that people could walk through its centre-piece—a 1200-tonne sphere—for a fee.

'This whole area's known for dating,' she said. 'All my female Japanese friends have been dragged to Odaiba by at least one unoriginal boyfriend. Some of them, the ones that have been unlucky in love, have been here fifteen or twenty times. Personally, I could never do that.'

'Come here fifteen times?'

'No, I've been here thirty times or more. I mean I could never be brought here—not even once. It's okay when a girl chooses to come to Odaiba, but to be dragged here—ugh. There'll be nervous, lifeless couples everywhere tonight, the boys all hoping to get laid just because they brought a girl to Odaiba.'

'So why do you come?'

'The ferris wheel.'

Mami must have noticed how little this excited me, but she perhaps mistook my apprehension for a manly lack of enthusiasm.

'It's over 115 metres high,' she said, 'with excellent city views, but we have to save it for tonight. It's no good during the day.'

'What will we do until then?'

'Walk. I like walking here. They reclaimed land from the bay, made a little extra space. You can walk without your hands getting caught up in other people's. You're not always brushing past everyone or slamming into them, having to say sorry when you're not.'

We wandered around Odaiba aimlessly, waiting for the sun to set. Mami was correct. There was no shortage of space. The footpaths were wide and attractive. Occasionally a monorail zoomed overhead past tall, glimmering buildings. Tourists said hello solely on the basis of my appearance. And the young Japanese couples Mami had warned me about, many clearly working hard at first dates, kept popping up everywhere, hand in hand.

At one point I wondered why Mami had not asked me more questions. How was it she was so at ease knowing so little?

'I should tell you more about myself.'

'Should you?'

'Shouldn't I?'

'Okay, tell me who you are,' Mami said.

'Like how? What would interest you?'

We paused near a toilet block in a park. Mami thought for a moment. 'Give me all the details you'd normally try and hide,' she said.

Thinking myself in possession of an attentive audience, I bent down to take a sip of water from a small silver drinking fountain, but when I stood, wiping at my mouth and flapping the cold out of my fingers, Mami had walked on. I had to jog to catch up.

'You don't want to hear?' I asked. 'It's not important. I just thought—'

'Get on with it.'

'Okay. Well, my father was a priest, then a teacher— now retired. My mother's a housewife, though she's worked on and off as a secretary. I'm an only child and—'

'Secrets,' Mami said.

'I'm coming to one. My family's quite poor.'

'How poor?'

'We rent.'

'That's your best secret?'

'It's one secret—one I normally work to keep when home. The area we live in doesn't really know what to do with poor people. It's easier to let them think we're rich. Or well-off, anyway.'

'What else?'

'I don't have a degree. I had a uni offer after school, a pretty good one, but came here instead. A guy told me where to buy a fake diploma, how to get a Japanese visa with it.'

'You look scared they'll still catch you.'

'I am.'

'You've never done anything like that before?'

'No.'

She smiled. 'See how easy it is. It's an illusion, all these rules. We can do whatever we want. We just have to dare.'

'I had no choice. I had to get over here, get away.'

Mami appeared not to hear this, or not to want to. She said nothing until we reached the water's edge and, since I did not want to babble, I too remained silent. It was a relief to see her open her mouth.

'Once, they were setting up cannons here to shoot at your type, at Admiral Perry and his "black ships". Now there's a rule against taking pot shots at whites in the bay, and they've taken the cannons away. Whenever our views change, our rules change too, but we forget that bit; we forget we changed the rules and go on believing they're intrinsic, that they're unquestionable.'

'You want to shoot cannons into the bay?' I asked jokingly.

'Of course not. That's not my point. Listen, if you need a piece of paper, find it, steal it, have it made, but live your life and forget rules, because in fifty years there'll be a new rule—Subsection L or something—saying it's all right to come to Japan without that piece of paper, but you'll be too old.'

'So I did the right thing,' I said, not asking but surmising.

'You're here. That's what you wanted.'

The sun set slowly. A vivid pink appeared out on the horizon and lights clicked on, first aboard the boats in the bay, then on both shores. As it grew dark whole ships were reduced to pinpricks of light bobbing amidst a vast, empty blackness. Only the Rainbow Bridge gave any sense of distance, long and bright in the watery void lying between our pier and inner city Tokyo. We stood staring. I had earlier given Mami my denim jacket and was now beginning to feel the cold. I wanted to move on. I wrapped my arms around my chest and thought about the girl beside me—her delicate, feathery neck and perfect chin. But the cold still bit through.

'You get cold so easily,' Mami said, noticing me shiver and adding, almost proudly, 'not like me.'

'Then can I have my denim jacket back?'

'No.'

Queuing for the ferris wheel, I resorted to jumping on the spot—partly to keep warm, partly to hide my nerves.

'Why do people do this?' I asked. 'Queue to go up like this?'

Mami shot me a look. 'Because it's fun.'

The line moved another two steps forward. I wanted to turn and let couples pass so that we could keep our distance from the thing. But Mami had me by the wrist.

'How's it fun?' I asked.

'It just is.'

When I looked at the wheel, I had to look straight through it and on towards the sky. Focusing on the enclosed cabins swaying softly in the night only made me want to bend double. There was a relentlessness in the way they climbed, neither fast nor slow. The apex terrified me.

'Can we not go on it?' I asked.

'It's fun.'

'Can we not, please?'

'You're just scared.'

From this point the queue took fifty-four minutes. I timed it to take my mind off the so-called ride. We followed the patrons in front of us—a young anxious boy and a bored, beautiful girl—through makeshift lanes, up stairs and into the mechanical bowels of the machine. Attendants waved us forward, all perfectly relaxed. We waited for our cabin to be vacated by a trendy couple still absorbed in conversation. Then I let Mami climb in, and the instant she was seated she started talking.

'I love this thing. Sometimes when I'm sad I get in alone. They never try to force anyone in with me. I get the whole cabin to myself and spend the loop thinking about reasons not to jump. You're not the only one who thinks about falling, about dying.'

'Not now, please.'

'But there are always reasons not to jump, so I end up back on the ground, feeling better.'

'Can you not talk, please?' I ducked my head to enter the box. The attendant locked us in, walking alongside our cabin on a long boarding platform. He checked to make sure the door was secure.

'Enjoy your ride,' he said in polite, emotionless Japanese, before turning to the cabin behind.

We were seated on opposite bench seats, knees up high. While I inspected the lock on the door, Mami played aimlessly with her rubber band. It was a miserable lock. Aside from the fact it could not be opened from within, thus preventing an easy suicide, it was wholly inadequate—the sort of catch commonly found on flyscreen doors. But there was no time to complain. In a matter of seconds it was just the two of us trapped in a cabin smaller than a golf cart. Below, the queue swung out and away. People's features became indistinguishable and the cabin swayed in the night breeze. I tried to sit as still as possible. Mami, however, stretched out on her bench seat, unfazed by the interminable increase in altitude. She seemed to be staring out over the bay. I dared not follow her gaze.

'Beautiful, isn't it?' she said, her voice loud in the enclosure. 'I only ever look out like this if I'm happy.'

'And if you're not?'

'Then I look out and down,' she said. 'But don't worry, I'm happy.'

My throat felt tight. There was no air in my chest.

I wished Mami would shut up, but she kept on talking about previous trips up and around the wheel.

'Once,' she said (just as I felt we must be nearing the full 115 metres), 'once, I rocked a cabin like this the whole way round.'

'Oh-don't-say-that-now.'

'Like this.' Mami grinned. First she made only small movements, shifting on her seat. Then she stood up and started to swing the booth backwards and forwards, throwing her weight into it.

'Jesus-fucking-hell-sit. Sit!'

'Relax, will you?'

'Sit!'

Laughing loudly, Mami increased the momentum of the cabin's swing until I could anticipate each rise and fall—up, down, levelling out, up again and down, like a ship in heavy seas. She was unrelenting, throwing herself into it. I wanted to vomit.

'The floor's strong,' she said. 'Look!' She began jumping as if on a trampoline, open palms striking the low roof. Every time she jumped, pulling up her knees, I felt sure she would simply vanish—fall noiselessly to her death.

'And this little lock here—'

'No!'

'—on this door.'

I was too horrified to stop her. All I could do was watch as she lined up the flimsy door and, still smiling, dropped a shoulder. Without the slightest hesitation she let herself fall, holding her shoulder firmly forward so that it slammed into the top of the door. The cabin shuddered and I screamed. Bile filled the back of my mouth.

Somehow, miraculously, the thing held. Mami was knocked down onto the floor, laughing hysterically and slapping at her leg. I retched again, the taste of vomit strong.

'Fuck you,' I managed to say.

After this excitement the cabin quickly resumed its regular sway, but I spent the journey down worrying it had sustained damage, that it would drop from the wheel. Whenever Mami tried to speak I ordered her to shut up. If she moved, I threatened to punch her.

Later, finding our way home, I felt a surge of anger I could not articulate. It welled in my chest. Sitting in the Yurikamome train, Mami said nothing. It had finally occurred to her how upset I was. I vaguely regretted having threatened to punch her but she showed no sign of anger. Instead she seemed to have forgotten everything, giving the impression I was being a bore, even a disappointment. Eventually we reached Shinbashi Station, where Mami had to change trains. We walked to her platform. Her train was preparing to depart, doors open. Expressionless commuters stood packed inside like cattle awaiting slaughter, occasionally exchanging positions but mostly moving on the spot. More and more pushed their way in, making space where there was none and opening phones in preparation for the trip.

'Can we buy ice-cream?' Mami asked. 'Normally I buy ice-cream after Odaiba. We can both get out of the station again without losing our tickets. I'll talk to the station-master.'

'I need to go home.'

'Suit yourself.' Mami backed into the carriage, the train doors sounding their usual piercing warning. Men found a way to accommodate her, happy to have her body pressed against theirs, and glanced at me as if looking for envy.

'Goodbye,' I said.

Mami, pulling the feathers from behind her neck and keeping her eyes fixed on mine, seemed sad for the first time. 'But I'm taking your jacket,' she said as the doors hissed shut.

How to Kill
a Cockroach

I met my first girlfriend, Tilly, while killing (or trying to kill) a cockroach. Hardly romantic, but with us little was. We were best friends from the outset.

This took place well over a year after I moved to Japan, towards the end of my second month in Nakamura's. My room was overrun with cockroaches and I was holding fort with nothing more sophisticated than an old *Time* magazine. Tilly found me trying to upturn a wardrobe Nakamura-san had prudently nailed to the floor.

'What the hell are you doing?' she asked, leaning in my open doorway, arms crossed. She was a tallish, pale, bony girl with freckles and vaguely curled red hair which she kept under control with a few strategically placed hairpins. Her green eyes kept me staring at her face long after I had intended to look away.

'What am I doing with what?' I asked.

'With that wardrobe?'

'There's a cockroach under it.'

'And you're going to kill it?'

'With this magazine,' I said, 'if I can get a clean swipe at it.' I pointed beneath my wardrobe and shrugged.

'You're Australian?' she asked.

'Yeah. You?'

She nodded. 'Tilly.'

'Noah.'

'Nice to meet you, Noah.'

I stood and dusted off, but she did not offer to shake hands.

'You're new?' I asked.

'No, I live near this room. Can I tell you something about cockroaches? I don't know if it's true or not, but it might help.'

'Help would be good.' I sat heavily on my bed.

'Well,' Tilly continued, 'from what I've heard, when a cockroach gets scared—which I think we can pretty safely say this one is—it lays eggs. So even if you do find it and kill it, its children'll soon be running all over the place.'

'What would you have me do?'

'You need chemicals ...' Tilly's voice tapered off and her eyes wandered across the room, taking it in, the starkness of it. They lingered on the wardrobe.

'What?' I asked defensively.

'Last night I thought I was going to die. I was lying there and I thought, I'm going to die. Your wardrobe just reminded me.'

'The earthquake?' I had forgotten this quake. It had

been strong enough to rouse me and I had dozed through the aftershocks, dimly aware of my window rattling in its frame.

Tilly nodded. 'I have a wardrobe exactly like yours but no bed. So I was lying on the floor on my futon, too scared to move, looking at this wardrobe and trying to decide what it would hit first—me or the opposite wall. It was nailed down. I checked afterwards. But at the time I didn't know that. So I was wondering all sorts of crazy stuff. Who'll find me? What will they find? What facial expression will I have?' She grinned lopsidedly. Her teeth were crooked but beautifully white. I loved this smile right away, just as much later I would love other imperfections in her: the hundreds of brown, almost black moles that coated her thin, milk-white body, or the way she took up new hobbies like great handfuls of sweets, stuffing them into her schedule and spitting them back out half chewed.

'I can't afford chemicals,' I said, returning to the original topic, which had never quite left my mind.

'Well, you might as well give up now. I read somewhere that if all the governments of the world pooled their funds they could never hope to eradicate cockroaches. You, with only your magazine, don't stand a chance.'

'You seem to know a lot about cockroaches.'

'Not really.'

'Do you own spray?'

'Of course.'

'Can I use it?'

'Now?'

'I want to hit this wardrobe with it.'

So we went to Tilly's room, collected her spray, returned

and draped a misty chemical plume over my wardrobe. Tilly waved her hand in the air, pleading for me to stop, but I kept my finger down. I did great sweeps of the room like a crop-duster. Swooping, banking, then coming in again.

'C'mon,' she said. 'Let's find something to do until the smell clears.'

'Like what?'

She dragged me out of the room and into the corridor, which also smelt strongly of bug spray.

'I don't know,' she said. 'Let's get lunch. Find a nice—'

'I can't afford nice.'

'Well, from a convenience store then. Surely you can afford that?'

'I guess.'

We walked to the nearest 7-Eleven, outside of which a young, pretty girl in uniform was emptying the recycling bins. She tried with both hands to hoist a plastic bag full of empty bottles from the biggest bin, her elbows out, then dropped it and let out a soft, displeased grunt. We entered without helping her.

The store was devoid of customers. The elderly man behind the counter was busy stacking cigarettes. He looked oddly satisfied with his job, as if it suited him perfectly, and greeted us with genuine warmth. We ambled to the section selling box lunches and, while debating what to eat, heard an ambulance arrive. The sirens caught our attention. We stood in front of the porn magazine section staring out the window, watching an ambulance pull up in front of a generic brown building across the road. Two abnormally stocky Japanese men climbed out, each with 'Fire Brigade' written on their uniform.

'What are they doing in an ambulance?' Tilly asked, confused.

'I have no idea.'

For a moment she was quiet. 'I don't like ambulances,' she said finally.

I waited but there was no story. We continued to watch, absorbed by the unfolding scene. The two firemen approached a rotund elderly lady. She wrenched up the sleeve of her tracksuit and pointed into the brown building. Words were exchanged. The two men nodded gravely, then unfolded a stretcher and wheeled it inside. The elderly woman remained by the ambulance.

'So,' Tilly asked, while we waited for something more to happen, 'why are you so poor?'

'That's a long story.'

'We have time,' she said.

'True.'

'Unless it's private.'

'Not really. My last company hired me in Australia to work here. They helped me get a visa and apartment and all that, but decided not to renew my contract after a year. That was about three months ago. In other words, I was fired.'

Finally settling on *onigiri* rice triangles, we moved towards the counter to pay.

'What were you doing?'

'Teaching English.' We handed over the correct change and I followed Tilly outside. The elderly woman was still waiting by the ambulance for the firemen to return.

'So why didn't they renew your contract?'

I leant against a warm brick wall. Winter had seemingly let up overnight; a day earlier it had been possible to determine the point at which my breath began to curl upwards, but now it was invisible. Around us people were wearing T-shirts.

'Who can say? Performance, maybe. I thought the school was a scam.'

'Why?'

'I don't know. Most of the students I only taught once. It was always one on one. A student would arrive, take a seat in my little green booth, perform a rote-learnt self-introduction, then show me what page they were up to in the company text. I never saw them again after that. The company discouraged it. They liked to be able to drop students in on whichever teachers were free. It was like a sweatshop that way, only they made a selling point of it. "Learn from the entire English world." They charged extra for variety but there was no continuity.'

'How many lessons a day?'

'Me? Twelve, with five minutes off between each.'

'Ouch.'

We both stared into a clear, blue sky. Despite my initial reluctance I kept talking. 'Leaving my subsidised apartment wasn't much fun. I'd become pretty attached to that whole area, even though it was way out in Chiba. I knew where everything was: the supermarket, the convenience store, the chemist, the dry cleaners. I'd memorised them—not the Japanese characters, but cartoons painted on a window or a certain type of door handle. You know how that works. Now I'm lost again.'

'Do you have a new job?'

'Not yet. I've launched a sort of employment campaign.'

The two firemen exited the brown building. They were at either end of the stretcher, which now had an old man lying on it. The section of stretcher beneath his head had been tilted upwards and he stared into the ambulance. He was wearing a transparent ventilation mask and looked sleepy. The elderly woman took his hand, then released it, standing back to let the firemen load him in. She looked calm, like maybe this happened a lot.

'Heart attack?' I asked.

Tilly shrugged. 'They'll have to say goodbye soon, though. He should just get on and die.'

'Why?'

'Because long goodbyes are awful.'

We walked back towards the hostel but decided to keep on going; something about the place felt uninviting. Tilly walked fast with her long, white, freckled arms swinging ahead of her.

'You walk with one foot sticking out, you know,' she said, turning back to watch me.

'I know.'

'It looks funny but I like it.'

I tried to straighten the offending foot but it felt odd. Tilly copied my walk and acquired such a stupidly exaggerated gait I had to laugh. She would not stop mimicking me.

'So,' she said, shunting herself along, 'the old hostel must be a change from your apartment?'

'Quit it.'

'Quit what?' she asked, affecting a look of ignorance.

'You know what.'

'Fine. I can't do it right anyway.'

She pulled her foot in, grinning.

'And since you're interested,' I said, 'it's not that bad.'

'What?'

'The hostel.'

'Oh.' She pointed at my foot. 'I thought you meant having feet that go different ways.'

'Except for the stray cats—the way they hang round.'

Tilly frowned. 'I happen to like the cats.'

'Why?'

'I just like cats, I guess. Any sort. I tried breeding them for a while.'

'Here in Japan?'

'No, back on the farm.'

'You come from a farm?'

Tilly nodded in a lazy, circular sort of a fashion. I was intending to ask more about this farm, but another question bullied its way in.

'What about the hairless ones?'

'Do I like them? I like them especially. They're the toughest of all.'

'You're definitely the first tenant I've heard say that.'

'I've been here a while,' Tilly said. 'Three years teaching English. A lot of people have come and gone, but the cats, hairless or not, have stayed put. Japan can be lonely—the way people just up and vanish. But I'm sure you know that. Were you alone in your last place?'

'Living alone? Yeah.'

'How was that?'

'Good—at first.'

'At first?'

'Yeah, at first there was nobody to tell me what to do. No one to clean up for. Nothing to remember. The place was mine. I could let it rot or clean it every fifteen minutes. Whatever I wanted.'

'And then?'

'Then … I don't know. I just sort of lost my confidence, I guess.'

'How?'

'Too much alone time. It was always just me in this one small room. I found it impossible to meet people. All my neighbours were Japanese and they came and went from jobs. Most said hello but that was as far as it went. If I said anything else they looked at me like I was crazy or going to mug them. They were all shy, afraid. And after a while the outside world began to feel …' I caught myself, finishing dismissively with, 'I guess I became the same.'

'The outside world began to feel …?'

I tilted my head as if in protest, then gave the answer. 'Menacing.'

'Menacing?'

'You really want to hear this?'

'Of course.'

'Late in the year I started to have nightmares—well, one recurring nightmare. I dreamt that my skin came out in red boils and there'd be yellow pustules in my armpits. I kept waking up, picking at them, scared. I'd think I was ill. I'd wonder where to go for help, what to say, but then they'd vanish. I changed sleeping pills but it didn't make any difference.'

'What do you take sleeping pills for?'

'Sleeping.'

'You don't sleep?'

'About four hours a night, but never in a single block. Always an hour here, an hour there.'

'What happened to this dream?' Tilly asked.

'Shortly before I moved here I decided it was because I was spending all my free time locked inside my apartment. Aside from the odd supermarket run, I never went out. Not for anything. In my defence, there was nothing much to go out for.'

'You didn't make friends at work?'

'There was never time. People came in, taught and left—just like me. I tried to make friends with a few different Japanese people, but it wasn't easy. I never got far beyond simple pleasantries. It felt like an invisible screen dropped down, like I was being watched or studied or something.'

Tilly nodded. 'And the dream?'

I realised then what a change the hostel had made. It had dropped me back into society. There was no longer any way to escape people. I squeezed past them in narrow corridors, heard them laughing, shouting, crying—peeing even. I cooked with them, waited for them to finish with the phone, removed their sodden laundry from the unbalanced washing machine and hurried my meals down beside them. 'The dream vanished the moment I came here.'

We had walked a small loop and were now coming up on the hostel again. Stray, lazy, hungry cats of all shapes, sizes and colours milled about the entrance hoping to get inside. One—a proud, white thing with a brown face and tail—put its nose to a car bumper. When someone shut the car door it jolted, ran a few metres, then quickly recovered its composure. It looked around threateningly, as if to make sure none of the other cats had noticed its panic, before sauntering off.

There was a sliver of momentary silence, then came a truck slowing for lights and an advertisement broadcast from a passing ramen noodle cart. It occurred to me that Tilly had said little about herself. It was the first hint I would have of her inherent secrecy, her tendency to hide behind a battery of questions.

'So, what about you?' I asked. 'How did you come to be here?'

Tilly smiled and pointed to a kitten, a tiny ginger thing. 'That one's my favourite,' she said, 'the skinny quiet one with the sad but shiny eyes.'

Vertigo

*N*oah, *You must be loving having the room to yourself for a while. I'm enjoying home more than expected, though Dad is ill. I don't know what it is exactly, but he's quite frail so I'm going to stay here another month. The farm's looking good. It's summer here, of course, so it's dry (which means we'll probably have to harvest soon). When I first got back two weeks ago, Tokyo seemed close. Now the details come slowly. All I can picture with any real clarity is you in our ratty little room. I hope you know how much I enjoy sharing that room with you, even if we fight.*
Love,
Tilly
P.S. Don't repeat the mistakes of last year—there's insect spray on top of the wardrobe.

I folded up the printout and turned to Phillip. He sat on the edge of my desk, tall, lean and bored.

'So?' he asked, rubbing at the long, heavily matted hair he had again let turn dirt-brown between photoshoots. He gently set down a large, balsa-wood glider. He had been painting this while I read the e-mail. Everything smelt of chemicals.

'So ...' I started, sliding the printout into my pocket. 'Don't you see?'

Phillip stood, stretched lazily, then flopped back down onto my bed. For a moment he appeared frozen. The ceiling light in my room had blown and we were both making do with the limited blue light of a small second-hand TV.

'I can't paint in this fucking light,' he said, sitting up again and nodding at the glider.

'Do you see?'

'See what, Tuttle?' he asked, irritated and unable to stay still. He dropped his paintbrush into a clear sandwich bag and sealed it with a sigh. Then from a pocket he plucked a can of beer.

'For me?' I asked.

'You don't drink.'

'I do sometimes.'

'And it gets you in trouble or makes you sick,' he said. 'What's this all about, anyway? Talk.'

'She's serious,' I said, feeling foolish.

'That's why you said no to ice-cream with Mami? Because of Tilly?' Phillip shook his head and affected an expression of dismay. 'Scared of heights *and* girls, huh? I still can't believe you did that, Tuttle.'

'Did what?'

'Said goodbye to this Mami girl.'

'Things are serious with Tilly, I guess.'

'You guess? Things are what you decide they are.'

'Meaning?'

'Meaning just that.' Phillip opened his beer. The can hissed white, froth rolling down the back of one hand. He licked it up carelessly. A year earlier, when I first met him, this clumsy clean-up might have surprised me. Phillip's looks and sinewy, sculpted body advertised a certain dexterity, intellect and panache which did not tally at all with reality. He was a complete klutz, a man with only rudimentary control of his body. And he was a nerd, too. The glider on the floor was testament to this. Given wood, glue and a desk he could go days without eating, manically cutting and pasting. The problem was Phillip hated all this about himself. He preferred to live up to people's first impressions wherever possible and masked what he lacked in co-ordination and intellect behind a confident, often callous air.

'You look like shit,' he said.

'I'm tired. The boys in my primary school are trying to stick their grubby pointer fingers up my arse again. They do it whenever I turn around.'

'Why the …?'

'I have no idea.'

Phillip took a long slurp of beer. For a moment, nothing more was said until anxiety forced my hand.

'So what should I do?'

He shrugged. 'All I know is,' he said, 'it should've been me this Mami girl came to, not you. She's obviously just looking for a ride. But you're no good for that. You're too damn serious. That's your problem. You didn't even bed her.'

'Definitely not.'

'Jesus.'

'There was the other, though.' I gestured as if shaking dice in my half-open hand.

Phillip forced a superior laugh. 'A little hand job? Tuttle, Tuttle, Tuttle. Anyone'd think you have two families the way you're going on—one in Tokyo and one up in the hills. Sure, that's a nice enough e-mail from Tilly, but you've got to make up your own mind.'

I felt anger surge in my upper chest. I was a year his senior but nineteen-year-old Phillip had fallen into his comfortable routine: condescension carried in brusque, brutal advice.

'First of all, I don't know when it became serious with Tilly. I always thought the two of you were lonely and screwed each other to keep out the cold. But forget her for a minute. What's up with this Mami bird? You must like her. If you didn't, you wouldn't be so twitchy.'

'I've told you the whole story, more or less. She hit on me in a bar.'

Phillip raised a single, dubious eyebrow. 'So you're sticking to that?'

'I was drunk and—'

'—she took you to her place.'

'Yeah. We talked about furniture and fashion and … I don't know … stuff. It was good—relaxed.'

'You've told me all that.'

'Then she started undressing. Not seductively, but like we'd been living together for years. She didn't hide a thing. I didn't want to look. Well, I did. But I didn't feel I could. I thought that would be … I don't know, perverted. I just kept on talking about furniture.'

'I thought you said she lived in a hotel. What was so exciting about her furniture?'

'She does, but it's nothing like a hotel room. It's more like a private apartment near the top of a hotel.'

'Which part of Tokyo?'

'Near Tokyo Station.'

Phillip whistled. 'Money.'

'Money. The hotel's five star. Anyway, she must have been frustrated with me talking because she looked across and said, "I want to help you get off".'

'And you said?'

'I said no. It felt wrong.'

Phillip stood and paced my room. He seemed weary, as though he had been explaining quantum physics to a child. When he flopped back down on the bed, all the air in his chest rushed from his mouth in a single, un-controlled exodus. 'Keep going,' he said, without forcing any real strength into his voice.

'When I didn't do anything, she asked if I was gay.'

'Why didn't you just say yes? The perfect out.'

'It didn't occur to me.'

'You didn't think to tell her about Tilly? That would have done it.'

'That seemed wrong too. Here I was saying all this drunken stuff: "Yeah, I'll come up. You're beautiful." I couldn't suddenly say, "Actually no, now you've got me in your hand, I just remembered, there's someone else". And anyway, I don't think she cares about Tilly.'

'Tuttle, you really are a curious fuck, you know. I can't get a fix on you. I've never seen you do a thing since moving in here. You're the most bone lazy, antisocial, aimless guy I know. You never go out, you never plan anything. Then just once you do go out, and suddenly you're with this girl who's amazing and you want to ditch her? The poor girl. You know what I think—you were fine until you thought about Tilly. You can't ever fucking think for yourself.' Saying this, Phillip's voice lost its amused tone. He became almost aggressive.

'Can we drop it?' I asked.

'Have some fun. Go visit this Mami girl.'

'No.'

'Does she know where you live?'

'Yeah.'

He beamed. 'Perfect.'

'That's why I went out with her the second time. She came here. And now she has my denim jacket.'

'She'll come again.' Phillip tapped the brown of his painfully handsome head. 'I know women. They're different to us—or to me anyway.'

I was suddenly tired of his arrogance. 'You know how to bed women,' I said. 'Beyond that you know fuck all.'

Phillip stiffened and stretched out on my bed.

I rubbed my face and eyes.

'Sorry,' I said, 'that came out wrong.'

'You're probably right.' He stared straight up at the ceiling, jaw tensing. It was a wonderfully strong, stubbly jaw, the sort of jaw that propped up whole lines of cologne; I wanted to take back my apology.

I sat listening to a strange banging through the wall and began to wonder just how many women Phillip had brought back to the hostel. Countless. So many I doubted even he knew. Most of them he did not share a language with. And, while I might have envied him the sex, I liked to think I pitied Phillip, this boy who lived in a dive so he could knob it with the crème de la crème of Tokyo. He spent whole pay packets on single evenings and no one could argue his life was dull. At least not until he came crashing back down to earth, to trashy Nakamura's, to spend weeks making model planes. The model who made model planes.

Also, I had seen Phillip fall madly in love twice before, and it was these two frenzied, unexpected eruptions—first of passion, then of fragility—that cemented my pity and enabled me to see past his fierce, all eclipsing arrogance.

The first girl had been a Russian hostess, the second a flight attendant. Although the first worked in a bar, letting men hit on her for a fee, and the second served food and drinks on domestic JAL flights, they were in essence the same girl. They were sharp-witted, domineering types, and neither was in the least awed by Phillip's arresting beauty. He had gobbled up both greedily like a long-starved trout going for a lure, only to be cast back into the murky depths of bachelorhood. After each unhooking he moped at my doorway, doleful and lonely.

Now, he appeared to be brooding, his brilliant blue eyes unblinking. Even his breathing was subdued as I pressed on in vain, trying to salvage our conversation.

'I don't know how she found me here, but somehow she did. I must have mentioned the place in the bar that first night, before I knew she was interested.'

Phillip sat up and winced. Six abdominal muscles flexed beneath his T-shirt and I realised he had been doing one of his controlled holds—engaging in what he liked to call 'incidental exercise'.

'That one hurt,' he said.

'You want to know why I went out with her the second time? Because she turned up—there it is.'

'There it is. Nothing to do with being in love.'

'Nothing at all.'

'Well, I find that very convenient, Tuttle.'

'Why?'

'Because you won't mind if I go after her.'

I shook my head. 'I'm not introducing you.'

He drained the last of his beer and crushed the can on the carpet, giving out a cocksure laugh. 'You should. I'll solve all your problems.'

Two days after our conversation he brought the glider to my room for a final inspection. It was a beautiful enough plane. The wings were at least two metres wide and curved at the ends. The paint had been applied with care, being both uniform and striking. And there was a cockpit with two pilots inside.

'Let's take it out then,' he said.

'It'll be dark in an hour.'

'I know. I've been working to get it ready.'

We walked for fifteen minutes, the glider in hand, occasionally throwing it out ahead of us. Soon it was dusk. The sky above remained relatively bright but the roads were increasingly dim. We talked only in short bursts and never about anything more controversial than the glider's tendency to drift left or right. Eventually we came to a towering freeway. It must have had eight lanes, though we could only see the rain-stained, shuddering concrete underbelly. We made our way to the nearest pair of pylons, standing in the void they created.

'Here's okay,' Phillip said, pulling out his lighter.

'How much did you put in it?'

'Enough to do the job.' He sparked flame and held it to the wick in the plane's tail. I wondered why Phillip had given it wheels. We were launching it by hand and it would never land, but I said nothing and stood quietly, admiring the glider and listening to the cars and trucks overhead.

'The fireworks were easy to pull apart,' Phillip said.

The wick caught. I stepped back. 'Just throw it, will you, in case you're not quite the munitions expert you think.'

Phillip hoisted the plane above his head and pointed it between the sets of pylons. He flung the glider, aiming it to the left. At first it looked like it would shoot out from under the freeway towards a parallel sunken road.

'Shit,' I said.

'Wait.'

Then, sure enough, the glider altered its path mid-flight, curving back towards the right.

'One of my best,' Phillip said, a second before the craft disintegrated. A sharp retort reached us, more a ping than a bang, the sound bouncing off concrete. Balsa and other debris rained lightly from a cloud of smoke, spiralling down onto drab, weed-littered concrete.

'Now,' said Phillip, dusting off his hands, 'are you going to introduce me to this girl or not?'

'I've been thinking about that.'

Phillip sat beside me at a bar deep in the foreigner-infested Roppongi. He smelt faintly of glue and was oblivious to the lusty looks coming from just about everyone, bar staff included. Despite fitting the stereotype of a boozing *gaijin*, I felt exposed and out of place. I wanted nothing more than to leave.

'Exactly what time did she say she'd be here?' he asked.

'Eight.'

'Eight? She's late.'

Phillip called to a barmaid. Already staring at him she fumbled and almost dropped a wineglass.

'Two more beers,' he said.

I thought again about leaving. Matchmaking had been a stupid idea from the outset. I would probably get my denim jacket back, but I was beginning to think I deserved to lose it. My only motivation to stay was preventing Mami from appearing at my door whenever the urge so struck her.

Six people were working the bar, an impressive set-up. There had to be at least a hundred different bottles of spirits on three long glass shelves. Each was a different colour. Some were blood-red, some fluorescent-green, one a swirling, smoky-grey like the outer edges of Mami's irises. The music was jazz and, jiggling my knee, I swivelled. There were fifteen tables in the place, all well spaced. I counted them, then counted them again to pass time. A small area had been kept clear, possibly for dancing, though no-one was making use of it. Instead, the mood was intimate.

People's conversations were hushed, the dim lighting suggestive of sex and sophistication.

'She really is late,' said Phillip, a little amazed.

Two beautiful women arrived at the bar for drinks. They both glanced at Phillip.

'Got a light?' the taller of the two asked him.

'No.' He focused on me. 'Where is she, Tuttle?'

'I don't know.'

'Waiting for someone?' asked the shorter of the two women, who was still all of six foot. She had a slight Slavic accent and, like her friend, a model's sharp, sensual features.

'Yeah,' answered Phillip distractedly. He tapped a finger on the bar. The girls waited for him to say more but he had no interest in either. I tried to match his indifference but could not. I kept glancing furtively at both. They must have been in their early twenties, though one was slightly older than the other. Each possessed a unique, abstract beauty which provoked in me, if I let it, a surge of fear—fear that flowed into despair. I wanted to initiate conversation but the words felt heavy and ominous, like a plane before that first skyward lift.

'I've never known girls to be late,' Phillip said, taking a cigarette from the shorter girl's packet without asking. He gave only the slightest hint of a nod, as if certain she would not object. 'Normally they're so punctual.'

'Need a light?' asked the taller girl without sarcasm.

'Thanks.'

'Punctual … That's not quite my experience,' I said. 'But then, I expect we date different women.'

'Hope not.' Phillip again checked the main door. I realised then that something about Mami Kaketa, some-

thing in my portrayal of her, had excited him. I had in-
advertently set off another of his peculiar infatuations, sent
him thrashing after another lure.

In uncustomary retreat, the models slunk away. Trying
to stay calm I bummed a cigarette from the youngest of the
Japanese bar staff, a handsome boy with dyed hair. He
reluctantly handed over a bent-looking thing which I puffed
until a nauseating giddiness set in. I stubbed the cigarette in
a perfectly clean ashtray, vaguely sorry to fill it with such
filth, then shut my eyes. Phillip nudged me.

'That her?'

It was.

Mami located me and started to walk towards the bar.
She looked irritated when I stood to let her sit beside
Phillip, only mumbling a greeting. She remained distant
and quiet and twice threw me glances, like private insults.

'Mami Kaketa, this is Phillip Philpott. Phillip, this is
Mami.' The two stared at one another in silence. Mami
looked for all the world as though she could have spat in his
face.

I pressed on with my strained introduction. 'Phillip's a
model. He's done ads you've probably seen. Men's underpants, that sort of thing.'

'Nice to meet you,' said Phillip.

Mami kicked me in the shin with a pointed high heel,
never taking her eyes off Phillip. He returned the gaze
unsteadily, then let it drop to her outfit. Mami was wearing
a strapless white dress which revealed the slightest cleavage
and ended halfway down her shapely thighs. To this she
had added gold earrings, a gold necklace and gold
bracelets. Even her high heels were gold.

'I just have to go to the bathroom,' I said. 'I'll be right back.'

This announcement earned me an especially vicious scowl from both parties, and I scurried away.

The toilets were drab, in stark contrast to the bar. I avoided the short urinal and stepped into a flimsy cubical. I urinated in uncharacteristic circles, around and around the bowl, agitatedly plotting escape. But it was hopeless and when I returned to the bar everything was exactly as before. Mami shot me frequent looks, although her now black eyes gave away nothing beyond distaste. She looked to be on the verge of leaving, which concerned me. She refused a lemon sour and only sipped at her glass of cold tea while Phillip—for reasons beyond my comprehension—droned on about fishing.

'Marlin can really swim,' he said. 'One got caught off the coast of Australia, then was hooked again four years later near Costa Rica.'

The bar drew me away from his talk, as it did Mami. I found myself following her gaze, first towards the bar staff, all glancing at Phillip, then towards the jukebox (an anachronistic, vintage piece everyone seemed to want to rub). Mami's eyes eventually came to rest on a small, silent TV off in a corner. This TV was a concession by the interior designer to good business sense. A number of North American types huddled around it as if it were a fireplace. They were all professionals and drank premium beers in big gulps. With drunken eyes they stared at the screen intently, absorbed in an ice hockey match.

'I love ice hockey,' Mami said. 'It's a unique sport.'

I confessed to understanding nothing of it.

'Do you know,' she said, seeming to cheer up a little, 'that in ice hockey it's okay to bash each other up? You see it all the time. It's great. They stop chasing that puck around, drop their gloves and go at it, punching each other. The referee just stands back and watches. How many sports do you know like that?'

'Boxing,' said Phillip.

Mami glanced at him, and answered with a steadfast silence.

Phillip swapped to tequila, buying rounds and drinking Mami's when she palmed them aside. Soon his balance began to betray him and a small swag of female admirers, far from losing interest, redoubled their efforts to seduce him. Coming to understand that Mami was not the least bit interested in anything he had to say, and unable to tolerate the humiliation, he eventually allowed himself to be dragged to a table full of young available women.

Mami immediately asked, 'Why did you bring him?'

'He wanted to come.'

'So?'

'Sorry,' I said, not bothering to argue.

Thirty-odd minutes later the bar closed. Phillip—now carried by three impossibly young girls—gestured up the frosty street.

'We're going this way for ramen noodles,' he called. Drunk people bumped my shoulders as they passed from behind, a few muttering apologies.

'You go ahead,' Mami called back. If her words gave

the impression we intended to catch up, her voice told Phillip that she wanted nothing more to do with him, not then or ever. He stared back, puzzled, hurt even, then shrugged and let the young women pull him away. When Mami turned back I expected the same treatment, but her face was conspiratorial.

'Let's get noodles,' she whispered, turning me in the opposite direction. 'I know a place that's open all night.'

She led me into a maze of small dark streets. I was excited and confused. Why did she choose me over Phillip? I could not say, not exactly. I focused on the touch of her fingers, the smell of her perfume, the clack of her gold heels. I was, despite myself, proud to be in the company of such a beautiful girl.

The restaurant had only three tables, evidently certain it would never be struck with an influx of business. We were the only patrons. The chef spent most of his time standing in front of an old TV mounted to the ceiling. He could well afford to spend long nights doing this because he had an apprentice who did all the work—cooking, serving and cleaning. This young man looked fed up as he placed two bowls of soy sauce noodles in front of us.

'Enjoy your meal,' he said flatly, eyes bloodshot.

Occasionally the chef would laugh and point at the TV for our benefit. We drank nothing stronger than green tea, eating and talking quietly about whatever popped into our heads. Outside the alley was empty, motionless.

After the assistant cleared our bowls, Mami dropped her chin onto the base of both palms, fingertips beside her eyes.

'You should come and get your denim jacket.'

'I'm not sure that's a good idea.'

'But you want to?'

'I suppose,' I said, trying to hide a welling desire.

'Good. We'll go then.'

The chef gave us a discount and held open the door.

'I told you it was great food,' Mami said, phoning for a cab in the deserted alley.

'Best Chinese ever.'

I tried to locate the moon but the sky was featureless. Nearby a window was edged open and there came the ticking and soft whoosh of a heater being lit. I smelt kerosene.

The cab driver wanted to speak English. I could not see him. His bucket seat had swallowed him whole. But I could hear him. He owned a set of 'World English' cassettes which he played for us, rewinding the sentences he knew best and repeating them aloud. I offered what little advice I could but he did not understand a word. Mami was far more help. She gave him an explanation of grammar in Japanese, which he ignored.

'I'm female,' she said to me at last with a sigh. 'I look Japanese and I speak Japanese. What the hell do I know about English?'

Outside her hotel, Mami greeted the doorman. He bowed deeply, asking me if I had luggage.

'No, just visiting.'

'Enjoy,' he said, leaving me to wonder if I had seen the hint of a smirk on his puffy, small-featured face.

Inside the lobby—a study in opulence—my every whisper echoed uncomfortably. It took an eternity to cross the marble floor and I was relieved when we finally entered the elevator. Mami pressed a button for the twentieth floor and, as the doors closed, reflecting the two of us, my relief turned to dejection. Staring at myself beside such a stunning girl I had the feeling life would defeat me; that whatever I did or did not do in the ensuing hours I would inevitably be drawn back to them, either by regret or nostalgia. Or by both. As if listening to me, the doors reopened for two businessmen who decided, after much debate, not to enter. I suspected I was being given a last chance to flee. The front desk staff all stood stoically with their hands behind their backs, and a bellhop—a trainee—bowed.

'Home at last,' Mami said, as the elevator doors finally shut.

Mami's hotel room was exactly as I remembered. The front room went on without end and served a hundred different purposes. Mami washed her face in the bathroom, then padded across to the stereo, tossing CDs left and right.

'CDs,' she said with a groan. 'Either the disc turns to shit or the music does. All my best ones have cracks. Look. Look at this.' I looked at a CD well beyond repair.

'That was a good CD,' she said, before glumly adding, 'I should get an iPod, but there's something unsettling about those things. They're so generic, so insipid, so ... *white*. Like little dishwashers.'

I moved around the room turning on identical lamps. There seemed to be hundreds of them, all with bland, beige covers. Eventually I sat down on her enormous bed.

'What's with all these lamps?' I asked. 'All your other furniture's unique. But these lamps are—'

'There you go talking about the furniture again.' She smiled. 'Those lamps? They're the originals. They were here when I took this place. Everything else I've added.' She pressed play on a remote and moved away from the stereo. I heard a CD spin, then the opening verse of a song—possibly Lennon's 'Instant Karma'—until it began to skip and Mami clicked it off with a huff.

'Lamps are what make hotel rooms into hotel rooms,' she said. 'Most people think it's the minibar, the beds or the chunky phone. Even the Bible, if you're that way inclined. But it's none of those. I tossed all of that out because it's the lamps. There can only be one "hotel thing" when you move into a place like this. After that you have to make it your own or you feel like you're living in a display home.'

'It's not something I've ever had to think about.'

I lay back on the bed, tired. Mami lay beside me, curling in. I realised she was now wearing a navy-blue slip but had not noticed her changing. The silk was slippery and cool beneath my palm, like melting ice.

'You turned on a lot of lamps,' she said softly, half biting, half sucking at her bottom lip.

'They're good lamps. You were right to keep them.'

'Thank you.'

She looked beautiful close up. Her nose was small but at this distance somewhat wide and her mouth was long. She was incredibly thin—too thin. But it all fitted. Everything matched up. Looking at Mami, her various shapes, I felt a small but pleasant ache inside me, as if fighting off orgasm.

Soon she was asleep. I stared at her for as long as I dared, then looked away. I was worried she might wake to find me interested in regions I had no claim to. I scanned the room. The bar was untouched, which struck me as odd. All the bottles were full. I wondered if the hotel staff topped them up, if they cleaned the place whenever Mami drifted out to do whatever it was she did.

But what puzzled me most was the cluttered nature of the room. There was a large flat-screen TV with a DVD player (though only one DVD, *Roman Holiday*), the bar, seven or eight couches, a desk, a walk-in closet, an en suite and an antique dining table. In addition to this, scattered across the floor were countless *Vogue* magazines. Not just American *Vogue*, but the British, French and Spanish editions too, some open, others upside down, pages splayed.

I wriggled free and rolled off the bed. I entered the en suite—which was about twice the size of my hostel room—and urinated as quietly as possible. Then I sat down inside the deep, dry spa and extended my arms without touching either side. When I tired of this I climbed back out and crossed to the sink, where large mirrors on opposing walls placed me at the head of an army of clones. Since I did not have a toothbrush I squeezed toothpaste onto my finger, wiped my teeth as best I could, cupped water in my hands, slurped, rinsed and spat.

With this done I returned to the room in which Mami was sleeping. I crept close to her, eyes near her lips. She showed no sign of waking so I decided to explore further. I entered a hallway, conscious of the sound of my socks over the carpet.

One door led into a dining room, another a conference room, neither of which appeared to have been altered by Mami. I opened the third and last door at the end of the hallway and entered a Japanese-style room. This room had tatami matting and was divided at its middle by open, paper-thin sliding doors. I had a vague sense of stepping back in time until I noticed a collection of photographs. They were all in identical black frames and were of naked Japanese women. Many of the women were bound with coarse, heavily knotted rope and one was suspended from a barren tree. I circled the room a few times, taking in each photograph. Then I lay in front of the window and stared over the city below.

All of Tokyo was strikingly uniform. It had replicated itself the way cells do: identically save for minimal error, the genesis of evolution. The buildings were square and squat, and atop the very tallest large red bulbs pulsed silently, warning off aircraft. I thought of the view from Mami's front room by day. Saturated with morning sun, Tokyo had looked like a demolition site. The sharp, square buildings—all white, grey or brown—had taken on the look of scattered bricks. The only exception had been the Imperial Palace, a napkin of green at the centre. From such a height it had been easy to identify the grey roofs shrouded in green, the beautiful white walls beneath and the various glinting moats. It had intrigued me to think the Royal Family lived there still, sheltered from the city by water alone.

I stood and stretched.

Now, by night, the palace grounds formed a black void with only a minimum of lights scattered throughout. The street directly below me was hidden from view. I had to press myself to the glass and peer straight down to glimpse it. Vertigo turned in my stomach, but despite it I felt safe. The world was comfortably cut off from me. I could look down on it with the cosy objectivity of a scientist peering through a microscope.

As I turned away, however, Tilly came to mind, focusing a growing sense of my own treachery. I tried to determine how it was she spanned the height, how it was she leapt up, intruding. I realised with surprise that I wanted to share my exploration of the hotel room, relate it back to her like an excited child.

I decided not to stay the whole night, and to forget about my jacket. This seemed the only sensible course of action. In return for walking away I struck a deal with myself. I would say nothing to Tilly about my two hotel visits so long as I never contacted Mami again. At four a.m., before the commuter trains started up, I wrote Mami a brief note and used a magnet to attach it to the small fridge where she kept milk for morning coffee.

Dear Mami,
You fell asleep. I let myself out. You can keep the jacket.
Cheers, N.

'Cheers' seemed a poor choice of word but nothing else fit.

I found my way to Tokyo Station and onto an early train, sleeping throughout most of the journey home. At one point I worried that Mami was sitting beside me, talking. Then I realised I was sliding from my seat and, coming to, banged the back of my head on the window.

Commuters stared, but Mami was not one of them. She had not followed me, and my relief was laced with disappointment.

A Loan

I was at this time still working half days in a large public primary school, teaching English on rotation and moving from one class to the next. It was not normally a difficult job, so long as I had no interest in doing it well. Mostly I led the students in song (always the same song, since teachers tended to select 'Ten Little Indians') and was paraded around like any other atypical attraction—say a fireman, or a large, shaggy white dog. I liked my students. They tagged along beside me, reaching up for my hand, and asked about my hobbies, exact eating habits and blood type, as if my difference could be pinned to one of these three key variables. I liked the less dogmatic teachers, too. But I was not at all sorry to take two days off after visiting Mami's hotel. I cited non-specific illness and the principal —either kindly or thinking it some virile foreign bug— told me to recuperate fully before returning to amuse.

It was during this hiatus that I first met Harry.

He found me draped over a TV room chair watching a talk show in which a panel of women detailed their stand against dependence on men, listing exactly which gifts they would and would not accept from a suitor. At least, this was my best guess at the topic. It could just as easily have been an erudite discussion of the impressionists, with an emphasis on Sisley.

'You understand Japanese?' Harry asked from the doorway, impressed.

'Sometimes.'

'I'm Harry.'

'Noah.'

I stood and offered my hand, and thirty-something Harry, who came up to my neck, shook it firmly (as if his handshake was a point of pride). His curly light-brown hair was thinning on top and he had a bulbous nose. He was in no way handsome, with small, calculating eyes and a coin-slot mouth, but there was something oddly amiable about him.

'You like sport?' he asked.

Not having expected this question, I hesitated. 'Mostly.'

'Great. I'm looking for someone to watch sport with around here, to share a beer with. I just arrived. How about hockey? Watch it?'

'From time to time.'

Harry fell casually against the doorframe. 'Great sport, hockey,' he said. 'Just like that Australian Rules football of yours. Mean but fair.'

'What room are you in?' I asked, wondering how he had picked my accent.

'Two-ten. Just off the boat from Hawaii.'

'Two-ten? You're my new next-door neighbour. I thought that Subramani was still in there, but—'

'Subramani? He the hockey fan?'

'I don't think so. Why?'

'There's a hockey poster in there. That's what got me thinking about hockey.'

'Oh that. That's been there forever. Gretski, right? Subramani tried pulling it down, but it rips the paint. No one wants to pay Nakamura-san.'

'Nakamura?'

'The fat old Japanese woman over the road—the one who runs this dive.'

'Oh her,' Harry said, head lolling in what I took to be a nod. 'She didn't say a word, just wrote a price and how long I could stay.'

'You're unlucky you're not black. She likes the black guests. They're taken care of.'

'You're kidding?' Harry massaged his ample belly.

'No. She loves black foreigners—male or female. They get the best the place has to offer. The rest of us are an economic necessity.'

'You're serious. How about that.'

At that moment, appearing from nowhere, Lin Huang slunk past in one of her moods. As always, she appeared not to have a rumple of fat on her emaciated frame. Bones jutted out beneath her skin as they do from drought-stricken cattle, scarcely hidden by her nightgown. Her hollow face spoke of a deep mistrust and both her feet dragged beneath her dolefully, like runty animals beaten in their infancy.

Harry gave her a warm smile. 'Hello,' he said. But she dropped her head and hurried on upstairs, arms clasping tightly at her torso.

'You'll get used to her,' I said. 'She's in the room opposite us. I don't know why you've been put up there with me. It's sort of the International Floor. Nakamura-san normally puts the Americans downstairs.'

'Perhaps she doesn't consider Hawaii part of America.'

'Perhaps.'

'You know,' he said without warning, 'I'm thinking about working my way into international trade.' Harry began examining random objects with the fierce but fleeting interest of a child—a Japanese magazine, a power point, an empty Asahi 'Aqua Blue' beer can. 'I just need to find things I can—' he broke off mid-sentence and peered behind the TV, but seemed not to discover anything especially novel.

'Find?'

'Ideas. I've got plenty of capital,' he said, 'presuming the damn banks get on and make my transfer. What is it with the banks here?'

'They're not easy.'

'Well,' he said, 'soon I'm going to export those toilet seats, the ones at the airport—the heated ones. They're perfect. I have a friend who's a builder. He'll include them in his projects as a sort of extra.' He paused. 'What about this place? Any hidden gems?'

'I doubt it.'

'Mind showing me around anyway?'

'What, now? Okay.'

I started the tour by leading him down to the basement—dark and dank. Ground water had seeped through thin walls and stale air hung thickly. I pointed out splotches of black, tumour-like moss on the roof and other discolourations smattered across the plaster. Harry nodded at each, then pulled at a tattered cord hanging from the ceiling. He stared expectantly at the room's one bare bulb as if, being Japanese, it might prove saleable. It remained dead and he shrugged.

'Smells musty,' he said.

'This is the kitchen section.' I pointed out a rectangular gas stove atop a rickety card table. Harry examined it carefully. He turned all the buttons, one at a time, then picked at blackened noodles scorched to the metal and made unintelligible observations. Inside the griller he found only flakes of aluminium, melted cheese and rubbery chunks of meat.

'What about that?' he asked, pointing to the basement's only other feature—a ping-pong table. It stood unevenly in a far corner of the room. Missing a leg, this table looked set to collapse at any moment, though in truth it was still quite stable. Moisture had curled the corners of the playing surface, giving it the look of a bizarre Asian antique. The net had been stolen, and both poles had been snapped off and tossed to one side like discarded butter knives.

'That's for ping-pong, but there aren't any bats.'

We made our way back up the creaky staircase to the American Floor. The rapper 50 Cent roared inside one room but there were no gangstas when we passed, only a weedy, pale boy shooting monsters on a PC. Further up the corridor a fat, black woman and middle-aged man with a basketball were attempting to compile a list of actors with the initials D.Z.

'Notes of interest on the American Floor,' I said softly.

'They have the TV room, obviously. They also have sinks in their rooms. And one or two of them have balconies. We have nothing like that.'

We climbed another set of stairs to the International Floor. These stairs were in worse repair than those coming from the basement. I pointed out that one or two of the steps were broken, leaving gaping holes which were difficult to remember when drunk. Harry climbed the last step and came to a halt beside me, panting. We stared along the stark grey corridor.

'Welcome to the International Floor,' I said, just as Moaning Man stepped from his room.

'Who's this?' Harry asked.

'We call him Moaning Man. We suspect he's related to Nakamura-san. Otherwise it's hard to see why she'd put up with him. Normally he just sits and smokes or walks round the block.'

Moaning Man set off in his usual strolling gait. He only ever broke this stroll to slap a wall, normally with the sole of his shoe.

'Is he dangerous?'

'Moaning Man? No,' I said without conviction. 'He's harmless. He lives in his own little world, although walls irritate him.'

Moaning Man passed us, mumbling to himself and lighting a cigarette. His name—which was used by the entire hostel—was a misnomer. His moans contained words. He was perpetually engaged in conversation with himself and now seemed displeased with everything he had to say. His face was set in the deep frown of a man waiting anxiously to counter sustained reproof.

'Don't ever stand between Moaning Man and a nasty wall,' I said, with a small smile.

'How am I meant to know which walls are nasty?'

'There's no way to tell. Assume all walls are nasty.'

Behind us Moaning Man booted a wall and shouted at it.

We hurried on, stopping when we reached the bathroom.

'This is the only bathroom in the place,' I said. 'There's a urinal on the American Floor, tucked inside a sort of broom closet. But for everything else, you have to come up here.'

The taps interested Harry. He examined each in turn, then tried to straighten a crooked wall mirror.

'It's filthy,' he said.

Having been in the hostel a year, I had grown used to what Harry now recoiled at: permanent stains inside the pit toilet, black hair-like grit around the plugholes and mould between every tile. None of it overly perturbed me, except perhaps for toe-prints gouged from the layer of grey slime in the shower recess.

'Get shower shoes,' I said. 'And now, if you'll follow me down this corridor to the grand finale ...'

My grand finale was nothing more impressive than a bulky vending machine. It sat at the end of the International Floor corridor. Leading Harry to it, I explained the unit had a right to feel cheated. There were over six million vendors in Japan, which meant six million possible locales. Yet this old machine had been placed in a sort of vending machine purgatory. No one used it, but no one wanted to scrap it, either.

'Left to rot, it's become somewhat confused,' I said. 'It rejects 1000 yen notes and can't recognise the newer

500 yen coin. Often it gives out Diet Coke instead of CC Lemon, or Pokari Sweat instead of Aquarius. And that's if it does anything at all, which normally it doesn't. I should add, though, it's been known to give out large amounts of loose change. So if you like to gamble, it beats those yakuza casinos in Shinjuku.'

'That's it?' he asked, laughing. 'That's your grand finale? There's no temple or anything?'

'Welcome to Nakamura's.'

Harry suggested we celebrate my tour with a drink. I tried to include Phillip but he was absorbed in lacquering a new model—a small biplane—and wanted nothing to do with me. Probably he was still upset. He seemed to have taken my eating noodles with Mami as a slight, and I regretted sharing the detail.

It was already dark out. Harry and I walked quickly to keep warm, arms folded. Since we had no idea where we wanted to go we quickly ended up in side streets which offered little hope of a salubrious bar. Most bars around here, I suspected, would include feminine company in the drink bill. I explained this to Harry and he listened with interest as a woman on an unadorned, single-gear bicycle, wearing a pleated skirt and conservative high heels, overtook us in the half-light. An intelligent-looking child wrapped in a red coat sat in the booster seat behind her. This child, eyes blank but seeing all, reminded me of a palace guard.

'And these bars are really everywhere?' Harry asked.

'Snack bars? Yeah.'

'Are they brothels?'

'I don't think so. I've told you pretty much all I know, sorry.'

Harry looked frustrated by my haziness. He lined up a lidless plastic bottle, but when he tried to kick it his small foot and stumpy leg sailed harmlessly over top. He stumbled forward and the bottle rolled once, mockingly. Above us an old man taking in his washing paused to watch, so I took a short run and booted the bottle up the empty street, listening to the hollow rattle.

'That's how you kick it!' I yelled.

'Thanks,' Harry called, running after it, then changing his mind and turning. 'Hey,' he called back, 'since we can't find a normal bar, let's just go to one of those bars with women.'

I shook my head. 'No. They're not my scene. Anyway, I can't afford *ichi man en* for a bottle of cheap whisky.'

Harry was confused by the number. 'How much is that in US dollars?'

'About a hundred.'

He shrugged as if this was no expense, and walked on ahead.

A moment later, somewhere in a room high above me, a woman cried out, not in fear but happily, as if play-fighting or lovemaking. It stopped me dead. I wondered if I had even heard it—it was that kind of fleeting, otherworldly sound. At home people's lives had been tucked away inside two-storey forts, but here they hung out over me, carried by coughs or small children crying, by silhouettes passing behind closed curtains—even by blaring TV sets. There were literally thousands of people surrounding me and I wanted to linger, to peer into one lit room after another. But the idea of skulking on the edge of other people's happiness only exacerbated my loneliness. I thought of Mami's hotel room, how appealing it was to look in on a life and how different to step inside.

Irritated by the thought, I jogged to catch up to Harry.

To my surprise Harry attached himself to me. I became his letter of introduction to far more than just the hostel. Three days after meeting him I watched him pull a saucer from the conveyor belt, position both chopsticks in his left hand with his right and, like a man arranging a puppet, try to find a hold on a portion of tuna.

'We've kind of become good friends, haven't we?' he said.

I nodded, thinking how little I knew him.

'Then I want to make you an offer.' His voice was businesslike. 'The fact is, I need a small loan and I'm in a position to offer an excellent rate of return. Normally I'd go through a financial institution. This is not how I operate. But I'm eating with chopsticks and nothing is normal.'

We were in a small sushi restaurant. The tall wooden stool upon which I sat, feet off the ground, was rickety. I felt as if it might collapse at any moment. The boy preparing rice behind the U-shaped conveyor belt—moulding it into rectangles with practiced, wet hands—threw me frequent, nervous glances.

'This loan would be short term,' Harry continued. 'Three days tops.' He sipped at his steaming green tea and his eyes hardened.

'How much do you need?' It was my intention to plead poverty after hearing a figure—any figure.

'No more than 20,000 yen. This morning I learnt the transfer from America will take three days. I should have brought more cash. I'll repay you 25,000 for the favour of a three-day loan.'

'That wouldn't be necessary,' I said cautiously.

'I insist. I don't want to hassle with a foreign bank, and even if I do they'll ask for something like that. Why not give it to you?'

I nodded, unconvinced, and tried to think of a way to let him down.

'Then we have an agreement?' he asked.

'Well …'

'Only if you're comfortable with it.'

I ran some rudimentary figures in my head. I had saved almost 350,000 yen living in Nakamura's. What Harry wanted was only a small portion of this total, but instinct told me to decline. The problem was I felt somewhat awkward turning him down over lunch. I would be trapped with him afterwards and it seemed easier to buy a speedy end to the matter.

'It'd be a pleasure,' I said at last. 'I'll give you the money tonight.'

'Thanks. I appreciate that. I can't believe the banking over here. I have a card, but I can't get it to work in a single Japanese ATM. How about that.'

'I've had the same problems moving money,' I said. 'It's common when you first arrive. Like I said, I'm happy to help.'

I was not at all happy to help, but could see no way out

of it. Harry nodded. He seemed to be planning what he would say next—selecting his words in advance and running them through his head silently.

'I'm moving a smaller portion first—to live on—then a larger portion later in the month. The latter will take a hell of a lot of organising, but it's a better rate. It is worth the fuss since I'm bringing over my life savings.'

To this I said nothing. Harry struggled to get a slab of tuna to his mouth. Having raised it halfway he dropped it, and a portion of rice fell to the floor, breaking into pieces as it went, like a tiny snowball. Neither of us moved to clean it up. I focused on a pile of empty, stacked plates, counting and recounting them. The sum total seemed to be different each time.

Now that my gesture was made I felt I had been cheated. I looked around as if for witnesses. There were only three other customers in the restaurant: a salaryman, his ugly middle-aged wife and their thin but voracious teenage son. All three were seated on the opposite side of the conveyor belt. They shovelled sushi into their mouths and chewed like cattle, eyes inert, jaws moving in methodical circles.

'There's definitely money in sushi,' Harry said.

Suddenly I wanted to be left alone. There was something unsettling about his constant talk of money. I thought about retracting the impulsive offer, but could not. I stood up. 'Let me get the bill,' I said, trying to soften the effect of such an unexpected departure.

'You're going?'

'I have to, sorry. I forgot something.'

'Well, I might stay on a while,' he said, remaining seated. 'I'll get the bill.'

'You're sure?' I asked.

'Absolutely.'

We shook hands.

I wandered back towards the hostel, stopping at a stand to buy skewered chicken so I would not have to venture out a second time for food. The enormous, grinning man inside thought he knew me, presumably having mistaken me for some other, significantly more social foreigner. Waving off smoke from the grill he asked after my daughter in broken but confident English.

'She's well,' I said, as it began to rain.

He gave me a free skewer, fresh off the grill.

'For the daughter,' he said.

Walking on, the pavement steadily darkening, sauce spilt from the skewer onto my shirt and I swore, trying to wipe it off before it seeped through the material. All the way back, people crossed the street at the sight of my enraged face, and my mood was in no way improved by the arrival of a letter from home.

My father never embraced the internet or e-mail. His neat, handwritten letters always arrived in the same bland envelopes with a pretentious wax seal that read 'Charles and Diane Tuttle'. My father believed in those wax seals almost as firmly as he believed in God. He could not post even a card without first putting it in an envelope, stamping it with the seal and protecting it against all evil.

Every letter was more or less the same. Penned in his firm but cursive hand, they opened with a sort of stilted disclaimer. Something like: 'Please do not take the following as indication I have rejected your perspective outright. I have not. However—'

After this opening he was invariably limited to a single page. One A4 sheet onto which he crammed lectures on God, the church, marriage, family and the exact state of my beleaguered soul. Souls fascinated my father. Somehow—and it really did puzzle me how—he melded them into his assessment of all things. Shortly after I fled to Japan, he wrote:

Japan is a well-developed nation boasting an admirable standard of living, but its origins cannot be ignored. Save for its small Christian (non-Catholic) population, it is, at heart, a heathen country. It will do little to steel your soul and much to coax it awry.

Needless to say I never replied to such musings. And since he had little space for day-to-day news, we had fallen out of touch.

I read the letter lying on my bed listening to the tick of my plastic wall-clock. I always opened my father's letters beneath this clock. That way, afterwards, I could follow its steady tick until my fury abated (sometimes I even managed to put my worries so far out of mind I fell asleep to the sound). Around me the hostel room was neat and smelt clean. In one corner there was a broom and dustpan, into which I had swept a large pile of hair, dust and grit. The wax seal crumbled.

Dear Noah,
Your mother is presently missing. This is the only way I have to contact you. Please ring. Please come home immediately.
Sincerely,
Your father

I sat up. I considered for a moment, distractedly, the likelihood of my mother having been abducted. Stranger things had happened in the world. Of this much I was certain. But I could not believe anyone would want to abduct my mother. The letter made no sense. I kicked over the dustpan, outraged at the thought of returning home. Then, worried and wanting news, I rang my father. His voice, when the call finally connected, sounded familiar, despite my not having heard it in two years.

'Hello?' I said, swapping the receiver to my opposite ear. 'Hello?'

'Noah?'

'Dad. Hi.' I did not want to ask how he was. It seemed an asinine question considering the letter. But without this familiar starting point I could not think where to begin. My jaw kept opening suddenly, only to close, like a fish in the final throes of death.

'Where's Mum?' I asked eventually. There was a long silence.

'Tell me,' my father said, 'has your mother ever spoken to you about a women named Celeste?'

'No,' I lied.

'Well, it seems she's safe.'

'Who? Mum?'

'Yes.'

'How do you know?'

'It seems, Noah. I didn't say I know.'

'Can you tell me what you do know?'

'Not on the phone, no. Come home.'

I nudged at a piece of chewing gum with the tip of my sneaker, trying to conjure a prudent reply. The hostel phone

booth was no larger than a refrigerator. To its dull walls
tenants had affixed all manner of ads, some for phone cards,
others for sex. I ran my eyes over each, one after the other,
as if for inspiration.

'Okay,' I said, relenting. 'I'll get a flight home.' I could
see no alternative.

'For good?'

'No, just to visit.'

'Ring me when you've booked it.'

'Okay. Bye.'

'Goodbye.'

After hanging up I could not stand to be in the hostel.
My room felt like a dank cave. I walked to the train station
and sat inside its rumbling frame. Japanese people passed
me by. Most wore suits and looked to be in a hurry. They
left a cold impression.

I had set myself down opposite a payphone where an
elderly woman now dropped a handful of coins. They
clattered loudly. When she stooped to pick them up, talking
into the receiver as she did so, she could not reach even one.
A few metres away a six- or seven-year-old boy broke free of
his mother's grip and stood staring at the scattered change.
His hands were at his sides, fingertips twitching as if about
to draw unseen pistols. His eyes never left the money. He
took one step towards the closest coin. The woman on the
phone peered at him. Then his mother called his name and
he shot up the stairs like a startled lizard.

The elderly woman finished her call, unconsciously
bowing as she said goodbye to the person on the other end.
She collected the money and methodically climbed a wide
staircase to the train platform, leaving me staring at the

payphone. I envied her—envied her having someone to call. Before Tilly returned to Australia we had agreed not to waste money on international calls and not to e-mail more than once a week. Tilly had initiated this and I had agreed, unaware how lonely Japan would become without her.

I needed to speak to her. I could not hold off until I was back in Australia. Strings of thought had clogged my mind like dental floss in a drain, forming a solid, putrid blockage. I could untangle nothing. Everywhere I looked I saw only strangers. Even my parents were strangers. There was no one but Tilly. I decided to call, to tell her about Phillip's moodiness, about Harry, the loan, my father's letter and my mother's disappearance. I would tell her about my trip home and ask if I could visit her, perhaps even suggest we drive north.

The call connected without delay.

'Hello,' she said softly.

But I remembered Mami's blue slip, her sleepy breath on my neck and, afraid to lie, hung up.

Dinner with
the Livingstons

A week later my flight touched down in Melbourne.
The jolt was like being rear-ended in traffic. One of
the compartments fell open and a woman's purse dropped
to the floor. I stared out the window, watching the flaps
lower and slide out stages on the back edge of the wing.
There was a sustained shudder and the plane lurched
slightly towards the terminal. I found the forces involved
dwarfing, and to take my mind off them I thought about
the 25,000 yen Harry had given me three days after our
lunch. It was the easiest 5000 yen I had ever earned. I had
put it towards securing my hostel room for four more
weeks. Nakamura-san, if I understood her Japanese
correctly, had guaranteed to leave everything as it was.

My father met me in the Arrivals area. At first glance
he was as I remembered: tall, scrawny and a little
ungainly—like a rope. He had not seen me exit through

the automatic doors and was busy inspecting other passengers, eyes sifting through them. One young woman carrying a screaming child caused him to frown.

He spotted me before I could reach him and in that instant I saw he had in fact changed. He was now almost completely bald and his face showed weakness, frailty and fear, emotions foreign to its stern English cast. Instead of waving he brushed down his suit jacket and pulled it taut. He stood as rigid as a post. I dropped my bags in front of him. Blood thumped in my ears and my face flushed an uncomfortable, searing red.

'Welcome home,' he said.

'Thank you. It's hot.' I tried to smile but it felt fake, like smiling for a photo. My father's hand was dry and chalky when at last he offered it. The shake had no real strength and I was relieved to let go.

'The car's in the car park,' he said. 'I see you've collected your bags already.'

'Yeah.'

'Shall we?'

'Sure.'

All sorts of people, many overweight and sweating, hemmed us in as they waited for loved ones to emerge from the doors. It was bright in the terminal. The walls seemed to reflect the sun. Two children, oblivious to the world around them and shouting abuse at one another, swung around my legs, treading on my feet. A stooped woman, pursuing both doggedly, almost clipped me and thrust up one hand in apology.

I threw my backpack over my shoulder, grabbed the suitcase handle and tried to follow my father.

'I think it's this way,' he said, not offering to take a bag.

Outside the sun bore down unmercifully. A layer of sweat itched its way up and out of my forehead. It rallied into drops then rolled down into my eyes. I kept within a metre or two of my father, inspecting his suit. It was a brown thing from the seventies, like every other suit he owned. My father wore suits year round, regardless of the temperature, and always with a collared shirt.

He pointed out the car. 'There it is.'

It was no surprise to see the old Datsun. It was as much a part of the man as his suit. But it was nevertheless a disappointment to find it cowering there between two Mitsubishi sedans. I dumped both my bags, circled it, then pulled my finger through a layer of dust on the rear window. It had only two doors, one grey, the other primer-pink. The rest was an awful flecked blue. The rusty hubcaps on the back wheels were a different pattern to those on the front, and both rear indicators were smashed out. Little globes hung on long red wires, bouncing gently in the morning breeze.

We climbed in and belted up. I wriggled in the lumpy, unaccommodating passenger seat, its vinyl scorching hot, while my father battled to get the engine started.

'It's been playing up,' he said, as though it had not been temperamental all its life. 'It's the heat. Summer sometimes gets to it.'

'I see.'

The engine spluttered to life, then roared fiercely, like a dragon waking to a sword. People stared but my father did not mind the attention. Unlike me, he associated poverty with honesty.

He talked to me as if I knew nothing of my home city.

'This freeway system Melbourne's got is a curse. I don't have an e-tag thing, so we have to call up to pay. Now they're saying something about using it too much.'

'Really.'

We waited for a blue light—deep behind the dusty, plastic screen that defined the dash—to fade away.

'What did you do about your job?' my father asked.

'I told them there was a death in the family.'

He grumbled. 'You shouldn't ever lie like that.'

We drove to the car park exit wordlessly and paid to be let out. It felt anticlimactic to be back in Australia. I kept expecting something to happen, but without knowing what. Then it occurred to me it was as though I had never left, as though in all the time I had been away I had really just been at home, living as I always had. My memory of Australia and its memory of me ended at the same point. Neither of us could do anything but pick up from where we had left off. Japan was unrecognised here, just as any changes which might have taken place in Australia, within my father, were unrecognisable to me. Certainly from the outside everything looked similar enough to assume nothing had changed. Driving along back roads (to avoid paying the toll), the factories we passed, all with their roller doors down and cheap brickwork graffitied, looked as they had travelling to the airport two years earlier. Only the cityscape had changed. When it fell into view it looked small and timid.

Home was exactly as I remembered. It was the same diminutive apartment with its wood-veneer kitchen, drab but cluttered living room and two boxy bedrooms. No wonder my mother had left, I thought. Personally, I had not dwelled on the place once since packing my bags.

Every breath since leaving had been fuller, as if my life began the moment I slid my keys back under the locked door. The TV sat atop the same Akai cardboard box. And above this, Jesus, perfectly white and with ragged, rock-star hair, still looked upon me with a fixed, condescending calm. He held out both his arms as though delivering some inarguable point, and I remembered that, as a child, I had often sat wondering what it might be.

Something, however, was different. It took me a moment to determine that most of my mother's possessions were missing. There was no bookshelf holding her complete set of classics. Her reading light was gone. And in the kitchen, where the lino was now peeling up from corners of the floor, her prized knife set had vanished. This, above all else, knocked the air from me—robbed me of the confidence I had been so careful to affect. If there was one thing my mother fussed over it was her cooking knives. She found a certain perfection in them, in their craftsmanship. And without them the kitchen was not the kitchen at all, but a foreign space. It was difficult for me to picture my mother standing in it, turning a knife over, maybe deciding to sharpen it. Or to picture the different dishes she had experimented with on those nights when my father, usually insistent on sausages and sweet potato, did not care what was served.

'You can put your things back in your bedroom,' said my father.

'Thank you.'

I walked past my parents' room, facing the sun and stained an off-brown by canary-yellow curtains, towards my own room, stark and bare. Here the same humourless sun streamed through, untroubled by curtains. The room had been gutted, save for the bed. Even the little desk I had sat at to study for my school exams was gone. I had expected to feel awful entering this room without my mother in tow, peeking over my shoulder to make sure everything was in order and ready. But it was such a prison, and so reflective of my father's personality generally, that a part of me secretly rejoiced at her escape—a happiness barely tinged with grief.

My father appeared at the door, looking forlorn. 'You must be tired,' he said. 'What was it, a nine-hour flight?'

'Eleven.'

'The Livingstons are coming for dinner. Do you remember them?'

'Vaguely.'

'They heard about your mother. I haven't seen them for years, but they rang. I felt I should invite them.'

'What will we eat?'

'I'll get takeaway later on.'

'Okay. I might have a nap.'

He only nodded. The apartment's oppressive silence rolled over the two of us like a wave in a calm ocean, perceptible, but only as a surge in that which prevailed. My father tapped a fingernail against the wooden doorframe. Clearly he had something he wanted to convey to me, some onerous, slippery lump of information, much like vomit, that he wanted up and out before the guests arrived. But no matter how he cleared his throat, he was unable to find a way to bring it up. He walked back through the apartment to the kitchen with it still rumbling inside his stomach.

I slept for hours, tired from the overnight flight. When I finally woke it was already dark. I thought I was still in Japan, in the hostel. People were talking and it took me a moment to realise one of them was my father. The flight, the touchdown and the airport all came back in a rush of soundless images.

'Shit,' I said.

I listened to what I could of the conversation while I showered, flossed, brushed my teeth and put on deodorant. They were talking about the Australian Football League, a topic for which my father had no shortage of anecdotes. In the time it took to ready myself for an entry he told five long-winded tales, all of which I had heard him tell a hundred times before. Perhaps our guests had too, because their laughter was scant and forced. I checked my face in the medicine cabinet mirror and saw I had forgotten to shave. There was a distinct line where my pale skin ended and red stubble began, but I could not bring myself to hunt for a razor and cream.

I entered the living room with all the warmth I could muster. I was dressed down in cargo shorts and a tatty Japanese T-shirt, on which was written 'Forever until the death ripped us apart!' My hair felt dirty beneath my palm and my shoes were full of holes. I could tell that my father was disappointed. He tossed our guests an embarrassed smile before waving me towards him. Beneath the single living room light, his bald head, gratuitously buffed with a lotion, shone like vegetable oil.

'Noah,' he said, 'you remember the Livingstons.'

'Of course.'

The Livingstons were three in number: an obese, bearded man with a toupee, his thin, haggard, bleach-blonde wife and a beautiful, surly young girl of perhaps seventeen or eighteen. This girl seemed to me to be an amazing accomplishment for any two people, let alone the pair claiming to be her parents. My father reminded me of their names in an obvious fashion he clearly felt to be subtle.

'This is Steven, his wife Alison, and their daughter Anna. You went to kindergarten with Anna. That's how we first met the Livingstons. Sort of a PTA thing, wasn't it?'

Mrs Livingston nodded sharply.

'Nice of you to come,' I said, before taking my seat at the dining table, surprised to learn Anna was twenty, like me. My father had done his best to clean the apartment. He had lined up motley cushions on the 1980s Ikea couch, straightened the magazines on the coffee table and put some sort of a cloth over the cardboard box supporting the TV. But there was still no escaping the clutter which defined the room. There were thousands of *things*, all acquired over time and kept for no reason. They were artefacts mostly, made from pine cones and whatnot, and all picked up on family driving holidays. There were also countless plastic folders, two filing cabinets, five or six vases, assorted pens, a model car and a hundred or more keys. The latter, clumped on wall hooks like fruit, must have been baffling to our guests, even if they knew my father liked to hoard things. Whenever he stumbled upon a key he invariably pocketed it, then took great satisfaction in hanging it on a hook. Locks, by contrast, hardly interested him.

I realised I was still embarrassed to have people see the place. Especially a pretty girl. She looked bored and was ignoring the story her father was trying to tell. Probably she had heard it before, although a second and third retelling could not have hurt. I was having a good deal of trouble understanding its thread.

'The native deer in …' he said, before pausing to think. A bottle of wine had been opened, which was unusual. Though my father had poured himself a glass, it was untouched. The only other person drinking was Mr Livingston and he appeared to have consumed two beers and most of the bottle of red wine on his own. He had a flushed excitement about him, cheeks splotched red.

'The native deer in Finland,' he resumed, 'took a real battering in the war, what with Russia traipsing through and then the Germans. Although the Germans were welcomed, I suppose. Though not by the deer. Did you know that Finland has the highest number of sport shooters per capita in the entire world? I didn't, but they're all out there, looking for these deer. Not to mention problems with crossbreeding, by which I mean farm deer … interfering with the wild population. Of course, the ones we have now at our place near Berwick aren't from Finland. But I find deer fascinating.'

Mrs Livingston looked mortified by this proclamation. 'You're slurring your words, dear,' she snapped coldly. 'Don't pour yourself the last of that beer.'

But Mr Livingston went ahead and poured the dregs into his glass anyway. He kept on about deer, their daily routines, until it occurred to him no one cared, that he was being a bore. He quickly and conspicuously changed the topic. 'Have you heard Anna's news?' he asked.

'No,' said my father.

'Well, let me tell you. She—' Mrs Livingston poked her husband between the ribs and hissed. He twisted away from her sharply, like a carp from an electric shock. To my amazement he kept on talking. 'Yes, Anna's becoming a model.'

'Really?' asked my father, looking at Anna. 'I don't think we've ever had a model visit this house.' There was very little humour left in my father's words; he was a man with no interest in drinkers or the media. He kept his focus on Anna, who appeared to be perfectly relaxed. She raised a single, plucked eyebrow.

'Yes,' said Mr Livingston, 'she was discovered in a train of all places. The man who scouted her says she can do catalogues, things like that. From there, who knows? Perhaps she could join a soapie.'

Anna fell back in her chair. She wore a tight top and her small breasts jutted out at my father like a rebuke. She toyed with her navel ring. 'I want to be an actress,' she said. 'Or a TV host. Or anything in the media, really.'

'A news anchor, perhaps,' suggested my father.

'Except that.' Anna flashed a simple, sharp smile across the table. There was no question of my father understanding its meaning.

I kept staring at Anna's face. As a matter of course, this soon led me to stare at her body. From where I sat I could make out the exact shape of her upper torso: wide shoulders running down through an impossibly slender middle, then back out to her hips. I knew better than to stare but it was such a beautiful shape. There was nothing else remotely interesting in the room and Anna could have held my attention in a storm. She brushed a long strand of blonde hair from her face, refusing to acknowledge my existence.

'A country girl in modelling,' her father said. 'Who would have thought? Though I think the country is good for the skin. Certainly, the animals appear to be healthier and ... well, it's the air, not to compare anyone to an animal.' He fell quiet.

'Berwick's hardly the country,' Anna said tersely. 'And anyway, I was born in the city.'

'Of course you were. I was just talking about the air.'

'Do shut up, Steven,' said Mrs Livingston. There was now malice in her tone. I had the impression the pair behaved like this at every dinner party, that it was a sort of dance. It was obvious in the way they moved and spoke to one another. Certainly Anna hated them both with an equal vehemence. She sat waiting to leave, hardly touching her food.

The heat of the Australian dusk, the trace of a nipple through Anna's top, her midriff, the shape of her tanned calves and her slender jaw all made me want to have sex. Entirely too late it occurred to me I was getting an erection. I squirmed in my seat, trying to accommodate the development. I knew I should stop looking at Anna, but I kept stealing glimpses all the same, kept trying to lock the image of her away inside my head. Anna must have been aware of my discomfort. Lust surrounded me, I felt, like a fart, evoking a strong sense of perversion—even guilt. But she offered no acknowledgement of my hankering. Instead she maintained her disinterest.

My father spoke. 'Noah, get Mr Livingston a beer from the kitchen, will you? It seems he wants another.'

'What ah ... What type?' I asked, arm over my lap, not daring to stand.

'I only brought one type,' said Mr Livingston.

'I'll get it then.' But I did not stand. Everyone stared.

'Well?' asked my father.

'Sorry, but I was wondering … elk. I was wondering about Finnish elk.'

My pants strained.

'Elk?' asked Mr Livingston.

'Finnish elk,' I repeated.

Saying the word 'elk' out loud, I tried to shut Anna from my mind, tried to picture elk fighting or doing their business behind thin, Finn pines. But Anna was firmly set in my head. She was all I could see, naked and nuzzling into my neck.

'What about elk specifically?' asked Mr Livingston.

'I think,' said my father, 'we've moved on from that topic, Noah.'

Mr Livingston leant in to refill his wineglass. Like a snake striking at a marsupial, his wife tried to pull the bottle back upright. But his hand evaded her with practised dexterity.

'I don't mind,' he said. 'If I can answer, I will.'

'The beer,' said my father, a little grimly.

But Mrs Livingston shook her head and pointed to her husband's freshly filled wineglass. 'Beer's not necessary. He's perfectly well catered for.'

Mr Livingston ignored her. He scratched his toupee. 'I don't even know if an elk is different to a deer. The business about deer in Finland I heard from the man who sold us our ducks. Or was it an SBS documentary? I'm getting mixed up in my old age.'

'In your drink more like it,' said his wife bitterly.

At this Anna shook her head. She reminded her parents they had to be home for a phone call. The entire family then made excuses, stood and quickly left, as if the words 'phone call' held some special significance for them.

My father, pouring his untouched wine down the kitchen sink, watched the Livingstons reverse their sedan from the front driveway. 'That wasn't a very civilised meal,' he said, face illuminated by the headlights, then falling into a soft gloom.

'What do you mean?'

'Fancy a girl like Anna aspiring to become a model. She seemed quite bright. And Mr Livingston, all proud. It's not an industry I'd ever like to see a daughter go into. The eating disorders, the superficiality, not to mention the amoral pornography that's par for the course. She looked like a nice young lady.'

'I guess,' I said, recognising my father's tendency to express his worries vicariously and feeling certain my mother would not be raised. But he surprised me.

'Mr Livingston's changed since I knew him. Not that I ever knew him well. The Livingstons were more your mother's friends.' My father paused at this mention of my mother. I thought he might continue to talk about her but having spoken badly of Mr Livingston he retreated instead into explaining himself. 'I mean, it would be a shame for people to view Anna as an object, would it not? Or am I just an old out-of-touch ex-priest?'

I wanted to ask what Anna had offered the table all evening. As far as I could tell my erection was the only evidence she had visited. Most of all, though, I wanted to be back in Japan beneath my clock, listening to its steady tick. 'She was beautiful,' I said with a calculated shrug.

'Yes, she was.' My father matched my shrug and again

paused, this time with the shadow of a smile. 'She reminded me of your mother, actually. It was her age mostly.'

I did not want to listen. My eyes pulled away, moving over the room as if in search of permission to ignore him: the kitchen corners I had been backed into as child, flinching at his impromptu sermons; the table where we said grace and ate in silence; the peeling ceiling, the church newsletters, the bills, the radio he scoffed at. I had told myself (after my father first mentioned Celeste) that I was returning to talk with both parents, to broker a reunion. But taking my father's reading glasses from on top of the fridge and turning them over in my hands, I realised I was home to visit my mother.

I wondered if I had understood all along what was happening. I had felt next to no shock at the news my mother was missing, only fear. Perhaps some of my confusion was a show—a show put on by me for my own benefit, so I would not have to face the announcement beneath the mystery. I knew I had to see my mother as soon as possible. I wanted to know she was happy with her choice. As for my father, I could forget to pity him simply by handling his glasses.

I had never once put these glasses on. He had often sent me in search of them, but I had never squinted through the blur or affected an academic look in front of a mirror for fear of being caught. Now I noticed his eyes following my fingers, following the lenses. He wanted to tell me off, to tell me to put them back, but could not, not without abandoning the topic of my mother.

'She was about Anna's age when I first met her,' he said, turning away and running the hot water. 'She joined the church fundraising committee. That's how we met. I'd

seen her before, here and there, but ...' He paused, shut off
the tap, aimed a squirt of washing liquid into the sink, then
dunked and scrubbed a saucer. I put the glasses back on the
fridge, uncertain what to do. When he handed me the
saucer, wet and soapy, it slipped straight from my fingers
and smashed on the lino. Shards shot out. Midway up my
left shin, pale and withered from lack of exercise, a small
bubble of blood swelled and quietly burst.

'I'll get the first-aid box,' my father said, irritated.

'Thank you.'

Love and Lust

Once, when I was about nine, I was taken to Celeste's front gate. It had not been my mother's plan to take me but my grandparents, who normally babysat, were attending a funeral.

This was how I knew her name.

We had boarded a tram and played 'I Spy' until I asked where we were going.

'Celeste's,' my mother had said. 'She's a friend of mine, but your father wouldn't like her. If he asks, tell him we went shopping.'

'We didn't go shopping.'

'We will after I see Celeste. So you won't be lying. You're just not telling everything.'

'Why not?'

'Why not? They're different, Celeste and your father. They'd fight about very, very silly things and I'd have to say goodbye to Celeste, which I don't want to do.'

Eleven years later, I remembered this conversation perfectly, but I was in no way certain I could retrace the journey. It was not that it was an overly difficult or long trip. It was not. The problem was identifying Celeste's gate. All I knew was, it was odd. Beyond that, nothing. Not how it was odd, or its shape or colour.

Having set an alarm after the Livingstons left I woke at six the following morning, dressed without showering and quietly let myself out the front door. The deadlock clicked resolutely, like a firing pin, but my father's bedroom window remained dark. Outside, the moon was obscured by solid cloud, the air comfortable on my skin. The houses I passed were all quiet.

I walked with my head down from Hawthorn to somewhere near Kew. Brick walls formed a solid boundary between the footpath and the houses they guarded. I began checking the gates but found nothing odd. A little after six-thirty an old-style tram clanked past, metal wheels grinding in dry tracks. The driver clanged his bell at a turning motorist and behind him a student woke from a tentative sleep. This student was probably a rower, facing morning training. He pulled his head groggily from the window pane. I knew his sports uniform well, knew the exact school to which it belonged because I had worn it myself. I thought of the stained-glass windows he would be staring up at in just a few hours, the gloom their brilliance costs a room. I thought of wet wool and heard lofty voices crackle, asking everyone to stand.

All this was inside my head but roused no nostalgia. I had never felt I belonged to the school or suburb in question. And I did not miss either. On the contrary,

I shied from both. It was common knowledge that the Tuttles were poor, that my scholarship was awarded not on the basis of merit but honourable poverty. While I did not feel at home in Japan, I was no more at home here.

I gave up looking for Celeste's house, sat down beneath an elm tree, pulled off my right shoe and peeled the top layer of skin from a blister. Two middle-aged women in sports attire approached, headphones blaring. They looked ahead unswervingly. The taller had a wind-out lead in one hand extending to a labrador, a fat rumbling old dog which ran a few steps only to stomp its feet down and let them slide over the concrete footpath. Every time it did this, it took a yank on the cord to get the obdurate animal moving again. The women passed on by, tossing me last-minute frowns. I had the impression my bare foot was like faeces to them: something which spoilt their stuffy suburban vista and should never have been outed in public.

I stood, replaced my shoe and again tried to picture Celeste's gate. I had been left standing outside the gate while my mother went in to see Celeste and must have stared at it for fifteen minutes. What did it look like?

My search was just beginning to take on a slightly farcical feel when I finally saw it—a perfectly odd gate. While most gates in the area were made of metal or wood, this one was constructed from cutlery. Knives, forks and spoons, now a lustreless silver, had been welded together so that each flowed into the next naturally, as if these utensils had been produced with a gate in mind.

'Cutlery,' I said, letting out a laugh. 'How in the hell did I forget that?' The gate was set deep in a tall, white brick wall. Farther along I located and pressed a red button on an intercom.

'Who?' asked a sharply accented voice.

'Noah Tuttle. I think my mother's here.'

'Aha! Yes. This is Celeste.'

The gate clicked open automatically, popping an inch out of its frame. I stepped into a small yard covered in brilliant green grapevines. The leaves of these vines, each the size of a saucer, accorded the yard an almost magical feel. I half expected elves to appear with platters of food on their shoulders. The fact it was a small yard added to this appeal. It felt wonderfully private, as though only a select few ever crossed into it from the outside world.

'Hello?' I called. I was standing on a path bordered with empty Coke bottles and overflowing with metal bottle caps. They sounded like seashells beneath my sneakers.

'Hello?' I called again. 'Anyone here?'

The bottle-top path led to a narrow three-storey house. The upper levels had balconies while the lowest appeared to be constructed entirely from glass. This level was empty and I could see directly through it to the brick wall at the back of the block. There was not one foundation, column or other item of framework supporting the two floors above. Nor was there furniture or a single fitting inside. I hesitated. Part of me, reluctant to be deceived, wanted to press on, investigate. I felt like a child presented with a sleight of hand—there was an urge to puzzle it out. But I remained still, staring at this house, narrow within the garden walls like a portion of cake in a box. Birds chattered aimlessly on a circular cast-iron table to my right, and when I turned my attention to them several flapped up into a nearby persimmon tree, where they sat squawking. This tree was the only plant—aside from the vines—on the block.

'Anyone here?'

I started towards the house. I was halfway up the path when, looking behind me, I noticed a green aluminium shed shrouded in vines. This shed was tucked in a front corner of the yard, opposite the gate. Somehow, probably because of the vines, I had failed to notice it. But now a door flung open and without warning a plump, pyjama-clad Asian woman stepped out, looking me up and down without embarrassment. The door behind her was heavily padded and, with it now open, loud classical music sent the birds in the persimmon tree flapping for the sky.

The woman, clearly in her fifties, twirled a metal can-opener by its handle, one hand resting on a voluptuous hip. Then, grinning like a child, she stood straight.

'Quick quick,' she called out.

'I'm here to see my mother.'

'Quick quick!'

I had assumed this woman would accompany me into the house. But, with an upside-down hand, she gestured for me to step inside the shed. When I did, my eyes hardly able to see in the gloom, she pulled the door shut, bolted it and dropped the opener onto a pile of identical openers. This pile came to my knees, spilling across the floor.

'What is this place? Why have we come in here?' I shouted over the music. But I could hardly hear my voice; I had to imagine the words. The woman, silhouetted in the light of a battered desk lamp, put on a welding mask. She shrugged, turned her attention to a workbench with a small vice, dropped the mask's visor and tapped the welding rod to get a light. For a moment I felt as though I was staring into the sun. Then came blackness.

'What are you doing?' I shouted.

'Wait wait.'

White splotches danced inside my eyes, maliciously centring themselves in front of anything I attempted to look at. I tried to blink them away. She again welded together two perfectly good openers, ruining both. How she did this without burning holes in either her flannel pyjamas or abdomen I could not say. New splotches joined the dance.

'Are you Celeste?' I yelled. 'Can you show me where my mother is?' But the woman waved me off, beginning to sway in time to the music, a big smile on her podgy face. Her lips, as if instruments themselves, moved in time with the melody.

'Like?' I think she shouted.

'What?'

She cupped a hand behind her left ear, already lodged at a right angle to her temple, and demanded, 'What you say? Say again!'

'I said, "What?"'

She frowned, finding a remote control amidst the openers. The music cut dead and, just as there had been an absence of light following the welding, there was now an absence of sound. In the furious silence I had the sensation we had detonated something. I could not hear a thing—birds, traffic or any of the noises which had filled the enchanted yard on the other side of the padded door.

'What you say?' she asked again, voice expanding like a pressurised gas to fill the room.

'Is Mum here?'

'Dips, *ne*,' she said nodding.

'What?'

'Okay, I am Celeste. Dips is here now.'

I had no idea what she was talking about. 'You're Japanese?'

'Sort of, sort of no,' she said. 'C'mon. All done. We go see Dips now, shall we?'

Celeste exited the shed, crossed the front yard with me in tow and slid back an almost invisible glass door. She gestured for me to enter.

'Dips?' she called, following me in. 'Dips? Where are you?'

The floor had tatami matting. Four walls, all made of glass and meeting each other squarely, formed a long rectangular void. We did not linger to appreciate it though. Celeste led the way, her face turned towards me as she talked of welders, up glass stairs to the second floor. At a glance this level looked like any normal apartment. It had solid walls, carpet, doors, power points and a digital television. We passed through a beautifully appointed kitchen and down a long hallway filled with ghoulish paintings, finally stopping in front of a closed door.

'Dips?' Celeste called out, rapping this door with one knuckle.

'Yes?'

My mother's voice.

A moment later the door opened wide, revealing a bath-room. Steam billowed out, running along the low ceiling. My mother, her hair longer than I remembered, wrapped a towel around her head and smiled. She wore loose-fitting jeans and a singlet.

'Well,' she said, 'it's fantastic to be able to *see* you!' Without the slightest hesitation she stepped forward, scooped me up in her arms and gave me a hug, tightening her grip in degrees until I finally protested. I felt a smile burst forward, become a laugh, then censor itself. I hardly knew my mother in these surrounds. I could not recall ever having seen her so animated.

'It's been a while since I've done that,' she said. 'I'm thrilled you've come, but I have to ask, did you tell your father about this place? The address?'

'No. He was asleep when I left.'

My mother rubbed the back of my neck with an outstretched hand, examining me as a tourist might a statue.

'Dips?' I asked.

'A school name,' she said dismissively. 'I can't believe you found your own way here. I was going to have Celeste call. Thankfully, though, that won't be necessary.'

At the mention of her name, I turned to ask Celeste about the front gate. But she had vanished.

'Interesting house,' I said to the empty hallway.

'It is.'

'Is it Celeste's? I don't see much evidence of a husband.'

'Yes, all hers.'

'And who is Celeste exactly?'

'Celeste? Celeste is Celeste. A school friend. An old school friend.'

I followed my mother as far as her bedroom, lingering at the door while she removed the towel from her head and used it to dry her hair in a careless fashion. The room, spacious and with vertical blinds, was dimly lit. In one corner golf clubs and a tennis racquet were propped against the wall. The unprepossessing single bed was perfectly made. And the bedside table, the only other furniture in the room, was devoid of books or a lamp. I wondered at the new interest in sport, and what had become of my mother's classics.

Content to leave her hair somewhat damp, she led me back through the apartment towards the kitchen. Celeste certainly had money. The basics—the carpet, furniture and fittings—were all modern and expensive-looking. Yet on both floors, over all this, or rather, built into it, was a curious addition: art. Bizarre works of art caught my eye at every turn. Celeste was an artist who chose as her palette the most mundane, everyday items available to her. In one room there was a vacuum cleaner with a thick skin of condoms, all in fluorescent, transparent wrappings; in another, a lamp made of tightly woven twigs. In the kitchen the fridge had been turned into a skyscraper, complete with lit windows and tiny business people working at cluttered desks. Even Celeste's dog, a Great Dane which carried itself around the apartment like a stallion, often breaking into a canter, wore her art, its thick collar studded with old bike pump valves.

'I like it,' I said uncertainly.

'Do you really?'

'I don't know.'

'Then you shouldn't say you do. That's a bad habit. It's hard enough working out what you do and don't like in this world without lying.'

'That's a very serious thing to say. You sound like Dad.'

'Well, in many ways your father's a smart man.'

We brewed coffee and, blowing steam from the tops of our mugs, stepped onto the second-floor balcony. A view of the front yard greeted us, the shed's aluminium roof barely visible through thick leaves.

'She'll be deaf soon,' my mother observed, nodding towards the shed. 'Already I have to shout at her. But she only enjoys music when it's loud. It's been that way as long as I've known her.'

'Why isn't there any art in the front yard?' I asked. 'Compared to inside, there's nothing. Only that path and the crazy old gate.'

'It's what Celeste calls her "Pretty Much Normal Zone". If she has to entertain people who can't appreciate what she does with her life—and there are more than a few—she does it in the front yard. She rarely invites people inside the house. Not unless she's opening it up to the public for an exhibition, and I can't remember the last time she did that. All her shows have been failures. Newspaper people get in and they find it too easy to mock. If you ask me they're scared, but—'

'Scared?'

'Scared to like it. Or maybe it's just no good. I really don't know.' My mother withdrew a pack of menthol cigarettes from her jeans, unwrapped it, checked under the lid for a number, then selected the corresponding cigarette, counting her way from the front left filter. She had always been superstitious about which cigarette to smoke first, fearing cancer, and it pleased me to see this superstition remained. I looked her over as she lit up.

My mother might have been a little heavier, but not overly so. Her greying hair had the same severe style it had had all my life, administered with a hand mirror and sewing scissors, and her jeans were still faded and frayed from overuse. In fact, the only real difference was her skin. Previously dry, pale and often besmirched by acne, it was now clear and moist. There were three sharp sunburn lines —one just above the collar of her singlet and two halfway up her arms. The long forearms, toned and coated with fine, almost white hair, were deeply tanned. I pictured the golf clubs and racquet in her room, so alien to my understanding of her.

'Must be nice not to have to sneak out for a cigarette,' I said. My mother smiled and nodded.

'It is, though I'm smoking too much now.'

And here the conversation stalled. From our vantage point we could make out the tops of trucks passing on the opposite side of the wall. One or two belched smoke and I followed a burst up into nothingness. Somewhere off in a side street schoolgirls were laughing.

'Are you angry with me?' my mother asked finally.

'Angry? No, I don't think so.'

She rubbed the back of my head with her free hand, roughing up my hair. She had a beautiful face. Most of it was her smile, but there was something more. She was one of those lucky women who aged gracefully no matter how little sleep she had, or how stressful her daily routine. Though not without wrinkles, my mother's face still held a certain youthfulness from every angle, impossible to define because it had no substance beyond an impression. Even her hair, the colour of cold ash, did nothing to age her.

My mother smoked calmly. Whereas my father had been eager to speak, she did not appear to need to. I could not be sure, however, as I found her difficult to read. She had become impossibly complex in the space of a few years: more like me, with hopes, miseries, strengths, weaknesses, convictions and doubts all suddenly on display. Before, she had been my mother—nothing more, nothing less. Now she was human and flawed, confusedly looking for happiness. I felt scared for her, and the realisation was as unwelcome as it was unsettling. I had never worried for a parent.

'What's Celeste doing with those can-openers?' I asked.

'No idea. You never know until she's finished.'

'Was she always like this?'

'No, I don't think so. To be honest, I didn't know her well at school. She only attended for a while. The middle years. We were awful to her. And people were probably awful to her family, too, because they went back to Japan and she finished high school and university over there. She only came back here when she was in her forties, after a messy divorce. That's when we met up again, realised we'd been in the same year. She has three grown sons I've never met.'

'How long will you be staying with her?'

'As long as she'll have me. I'm her chef. It's a live-in position.'

I felt, hearing this, an obligation to ask, 'Did something happen?'

'With your father? No.' My mother butted out her cigarette forcefully, squashing it into her coffee cup. 'Nothing ever happened.'

That night at dinner Celeste took a long time to settle. She kept pulling her shirt out from between the three neat rolls of fat circling her stomach.

'Thinking,' she kept saying to me. 'Still thinking about openers. Thinking, thinking. Sorry. Must not, I know. But what to do, what? So many fucking openers.' She asked for ideas (which we gave and were rebuked for), and only began to let go of the topic after a third glass of wine. 'Aha!' she shouted at one point, banging the table. 'That's it! I'll take them apart, then put them together, but all mix up.' Her face dropped. 'No, no good.'

'Celeste, Noah is living in Japan, remember?'

'I remember. Of course I remember.' She turned on me and spoke in rapid, flowing Japanese. Sentences leapt from her, all tumbling over one another. The speed of them marked such a change from her halting English that they sounded beautiful—free. I tried to understand, to pluck words like tadpoles from this stream but they slipped past, hiding among one another. Embarrassed, I had to ask for a translation.

'I don't know,' Celeste said with a smile. 'In English, I don't know. Fucking very difficult.'

'Have you made many new friends over there?' my mother asked somewhat optimistically. I nodded, then followed this nod with a shrug. My mother knew of my tendency to avoid people, to remain on the periphery, watching. But clearly she hoped Japan had cast a social spell. I thought about explaining the truth: that Japan had only removed the guilt of isolation, not solved it. Whereas once I had felt awkward and alone amidst my family, my school and hundreds of others with my skin tone, my accent, my exact eye shape and colour, in Japan I was an outsider by default. It was automatic. Japan expected nothing from me. No laborious introductions, no ritualised meet and greet, no chitchat, nothing with subtle layers of judgement leading to exclusion, since there was no club in Japan I could ever plausibly possess the requirements—blood, language or profession—to join. Which meant there was no need to feel rejected. It had taken a year in my cocoon of an apartment to learn to pass through Tokyo like a stray animal, interested only in myself, to realise all communication with non-fluent English-speaking Japanese people was (despite occasional pangs of guilt at my lack of effort) perfunctory—more an exchange of sounds than words—and to see foreigner friends as a simple convenience. Outside our homelands, none of us cared who we surrounded ourselves with. I would never have befriended Phillip in Australia, nor he me. But I feared any attempt to explain that my isolation no longer wounded as it once had, that I was at ease with it, would sound callow—or worse, callous. I dared not—even to this new mother—say I had emerged caring only for myself.

To my relief, my mother let the topic drop and went to collect plates. It had not been my intention to stay for this meal, or to stay the night, and I felt trapped, but Celeste had talked me into it. 'Tomorrow,' she had said, 'maybe your mother is dead. Cold as pebbles, and you say, "No! Not my mother? How? I did not stay with her!"'

So now I sat feeling out of place and uncomfortable— like Australia was the foreign land, like I had left home rather than returned to it. My mother put down the dinner plates one at a time, playing both chef and waitress.

'For you, sir,' she said, before circling the table to Celeste. 'And you, madam. We can't forget you.'

'No,' said Celeste. 'Or I stomp.'

My mother had prepared a rather conservative dish; it seemed there was only room for one artist in Celeste's house. Nevertheless it was cooked to perfection. We ate in near total silence, savouring each mouthful, until Celeste asked me, 'So ... you have girlfriend, Little Dips, no?' She was chewing with her mouth wide open. I could see yellow capsicum and bean mush churning inside, like clothes in an industrial dryer.

'I do,' I said.

My mother put down her knife and fork, the latter still laden with food. Their soft clank against the plate sounded ominous, but her voice was happy, surprised.

'Really?' she asked.

'Yes.'

'Love or lust?' Celeste wanted to know, causing me to laugh nervously.

'What?'

My mother groaned. She glared at Celeste, who eagerly topped up my wine, eyes alight. She made sure to get every last drop from the bottle, our second for the evening. In the centre of the table, three stout candles flickered and blurred.

'Love or lust?' Celeste asked again.

'I'm not really sure I can answer.' This sidestep, articulated carefully for fear of slurring, sounded cold. I glanced towards my mother and added, 'Or maybe love, I guess.'

'So no lust, *ne*,' said Celeste, shovelling more food into her cavernous mouth.

'What?'

'It's not a bad thing, Noah,' said my mother, 'assuming the two are mutually exclusive, which is what Celeste believes.'

'It's not a good thing, also,' said Celeste, stabbing sky-ward with her fork.

I had the impression I had been nudged into an ongoing, private debate. Celeste, never taking her eyes off my mother, shrugged.

'Maybe I am wrong,' she said. 'Do you feel lust, Little Dips? Tell me.'

'I'd rather not say.'

'More wine!' Celeste stood and walked to the kitchen, still chewing. Moments later I heard a cork pop from its bottle. My mother and I waited in silence.

'So?' asked Celeste, returning, a third bottle of wine held high as if maybe she intended to put out a fire with it. She had removed her jumper in the kitchen and her T-shirt revealed ample, fatty bosoms, bouncing with every step and sagging, udder-like, as she moved to sit down.

'I feel lust, yes,' I said, voice level.

'You do?' asked Celeste.

'Yes.'

'Good,' she said. 'You are a man in this case, and honest.' She poured out wine for herself, urged me to drink, then offered the bottle to my mother in a casual, sweeping fashion. It was a token gesture because she set the bottle down before my mother could decline.

'But now,' Celeste said, hardly able to stay in her seat, 'be sure, Little Dips. Lust. Do you feel this for the girlfriend? What's her name?'

'Matilda.'

'Like the song?'

'Like the song.'

'Okay. So, do you feel lust?'

'I said I did.'

'Just yes or no, *ne*.'

'Yes.' I reached for my wine and took two gulps, disguising them as one. Celeste, glass to her lips, sipped steadily. Finally she said, 'Then there is no love for Matilda, no?'

'What?'

'No love. Lust equals no love. Love equals no lust—for men. Sometimes women too, I think, but that's different.'

When I looked to my mother she only shrugged.

'What if I feel love *and* lust?' I asked.

'Not possible.'

'Why? How do you define love?'

'Love? When lust goes away, when it drops dead but you stay together, because apart is too difficult. Simple, *ne*.'

'And lust?' I asked, a little awkwardly.

'Always want to fucking. Always. Morning, noon, afternoon, dusk, night, dawn. One, three, six, eighteen times a day. Never leave the hotel. Sex, sex, sex, sex, sex, and then more sex. If you are in lust this is your life. The life you have before this you think is death. You never want to be out of lust again. But you must.'

'And what then? What comes after lust?'

'After lust? There is love or nothing. And you are still in lust, so no love yet. Or maybe ever.'

Before I could retort (if I could have retorted) my mother cut in. 'Celeste's definitions are black and white. She has a low opinion of certain people and matters. She's inclined to voice this dissatisfaction in the guise of healthy debate. So if I were you, Noah, I'd either tell her to mind her own business or find some way to change the topic.'

'Actually,' I said, struck by my mother's unruffled calm, 'I'm tired and a little out of it.'

Celeste's face had turned nasty and her eyes hung on my mother's nose. The two might well have been cheating at cards.

'I really need some sleep,' I added, 'because tomorrow I'm going to visit this girlfriend.' The declaration came as a surprise even to me. But now that it was a plan and not just an idea, now that I had set a date, it felt right. Celeste's house was no more relaxing than my father's; everyone was wrapped up in the one event, like tangled wool. I worried, far from unravelling anything, that I would only make matters worse. At least I could talk to Tilly. 'She's in Australia and ...' My drink-sodden head spun and my voice trailed off. I stood, picked up my plate, then put it down again. 'Thanks for dinner, both of you. It's been nice meeting you, Celeste. Where should I sleep?'

Celeste waved an arm off behind her, eyes still on my mother's nose. She took a sip from her wineglass, then toyed with a napkin, twisting it and letting it spin back out. Both the glass and the napkin blurred and multiplied.

My mother, having watched all this, now rose. 'I'll show you the way to the guest room, Noah,' she said. 'You look a little sick.'

At ten the following morning, having spent most of the night vomiting, I dragged myself into the kitchen. My mother offered to drive me to the station and five minutes later we took Celeste's Saab. It had that distinctive new car smell which, like everything else this particular day, made me nauseous. My mother never once searched for gears or needed to fiddle with the radio to find music. It was as if she had owned the car all her life.

'By the way, I think this is great news,' she said.

'What?'

'About Matilda. Ignore Celeste.'

'I liked Celeste.'

'I'm glad, but she has her moments. Does Matilda know you're visiting?'

'No.'

'No?'

'She doesn't know I'm in Australia. I never told her.'

My mother ran water up onto the windshield—the pump humming somewhere beneath the bonnet—then flicked the wipers. Bug intestines streaked and faded as the song 'Karma Police' rolled into ads on a commercial radio station. I watched the stereo's digital columns jump and fall in time to a man shouting about furniture. Mami's matching hotel lamps came to mind.

'You look worried she'll tell you not to visit,' my mother said.

'What?'

'Matilda.'

'I don't know that I've thought that far ahead. Maybe. But she's still sharing a room with me in Japan.'

'Is she? So you're aiming to surprise her?' My mother shot me a sideways glance. She reached into the glove compartment for a cigarette, depressed the dashboard lighter, and lit up. Acrid smoke filled the cabin, killing the new car smell.

'That's about the size of it,' I said.

'Where does she live?'

'Down in Gippsland somewhere. In the country. I've got the station name in my wallet.'

'Then I might as well take you to Flinders Street Station. That's where you'll go from.' Without warning my mother checked her rear view, then yanked sharply on the steering wheel. Like a cat being stroked the car could not have been happier to have some real attention. Four small bumps—tram tracks probably—caused my head to loll. The city, visible off in the distance, entered an unregulated spin. And when we pulled out, facing entirely in the opposite direction, I threw up.

Somewhere behind us a car tooted.

'Sorry,' I said, watching a puddle of watery vomit sink into my lap, as if through a sieve.

'Nerves?'

'Very funny.'

My train journey to rural Gippsland was not pleasant. For some reason the seats faced one another, so that I had to sit staring at a toothless old man with a can of beer wrapped in a plastic bag. When my station finally came the payphone swallowed every coin I had.

'Fucking thing,' I swore, before noticing an obese woman in a cherry-red American pick-up. She had stopped to stare.

'Can I help you?' I asked rudely.

'Can you help me?' The woman laughed. She raised up the heavy arm hanging over the pick-up door, revealing a great slab of pasty, bone-white flesh. It wobbled like jelly in a bag.

'No good putting coins in there,' she said, nodding towards the payphone. 'Lost are you?'

The back of the pick-up was filled with fencing materials. And on top of these sat an especially fat boy of eleven or twelve, like a dead weight. He stared at me expressionlessly.

'I'm fine,' I said, before looking down the desolate street and changing my mind. 'Actually, I was trying to call a taxi. Where's another phone?'

'Only one. Where you going?'

'The North property.'

'North of where?'

'North. Matilda North.'

'The Frog Man!' shouted the boy, startling me. He bounced a couple of times and the barbed wire and metal beneath him creaked and scraped. His mother leant as far out the window as her ample frame would allow, frowning.

'Jesus Christ, Gizzard, sit still.' She turned back to me. 'They're a fair way out as I recall.'

'Where's the local taxi service?'

'Forget that. Get in.'

'You'll take me there?'

'Well, I won't abduct you, if that's your worry.' She tossed her head towards the lump above the fencing materials. 'I've got three of them.'

'You sure it's not out of your way?'

'I'm sure it is a bit. But I'll take you. Unless of course you'd rather pay for a taxi, in which case me and Gizzard here will get on.' Gizzard, peering down at his left breast, looked up vaguely like a dog hearing its name in conversation. With a sigh he climbed down from the corrugated iron and wire, and opened the passenger door for me, following me in.

Walled by flesh, I looked for a seatbelt.

'Forget that,' said the woman. 'Doesn't have one. Never did.'

'How far is it?'

'Fifteen k or so.'

'Well, this is kind of you.'

'Gizzard, sit still!'

I stared through the enormous front windscreen out over countless brown paddocks. The midday sun stabbed between roadside gums, flicking on and off like a ceiling light. It pleased me to see gums. Magpies, moving in flocks, swooped from treetop to treetop, their squawks muted by the sound of air over the unyielding pick-up. We slowed for roadworks, passed a bored-looking man with a sign, then sped up. Here and there a tractor trawled by.

After twenty minutes of talkback radio—how dare the banks!—I was dropped beside a purple paddock. There was a gate with a sign: 'Willoughby'. Nothing ornate. The words had been burnt into the wood with something thin—a soldering iron, perhaps.

I opened the gate, careful to close it behind me, and started up the lengthy gravel driveway. There was an obvious beauty to the endless purple lavender, and something sweet but grassy in its smell. The bushes were planted in gently sloping rows a metre or so apart, and between each was a narrow dirt laneway. There appeared to be nothing but lavender in the paddocks, save for a far-off house and a lone twisted gum.

I set off for the house. The summer day had turned unexpectedly cool; there was an icy breeze which persuaded me to stop, drop my backpack and grope through my possessions for a jumper. Cloud—white and fast-moving above the driveway and dark and stationary on the horizon —drove vast, menacing shadows over the flowers. Normally a brilliant light purple, the plants seemed to bow beneath the weight. Each shadow came rippling in at speed, and as I turned to watch one silently depart I noticed there were in fact two houses, the second a deserted-looking shack.

Something about the air, agitated as it was, led me to think it might rain, and I pressed on. I approached the larger of the two houses, a weatherboard, like an enormous stump in the featureless fields. A man was hunched outside sharpening a thin, hooked sickle. When he stood, hearing my feet on the gravel, I felt I was looking at an academic. He had a small potbelly, close-shaven grey hair, tired eyes and an unmistakeable air of intelligence. He wiped at his forehead with the back of one hand and nodded tentatively, perhaps trying to decide if he knew me.

'I'm looking for Mr North,' I said.

'No one here by that name. Who are you?'

I glanced over at the smaller shack, but there were no signs of life.

'Noah Tuttle. I'm a friend of Tilly's.' The man nodded. Now that he was upright I saw that he did not stand straight. His back retained a hunch near the neck, accentuated by teepee-shaped shoulders. Behind him the weatherboard house—paint peeling from its walls, creating a curious white, pink and blue map—groaned in the breeze. The man glanced back at it, then at me. His face conveyed distrust.

'My name's not North,' he said. 'But I suspect I'm the man you're after.'

'Oh?'

'Matilda's father. North was her mother's name. Mine's Willoughby. Jim Willoughby.' He took my hand and shook it, not as a farmer would but as though the two of us were meeting in a café to discuss Keynes.

'Is Matilda here?'

'She drove into town to get some things. Should have been back an hour ago, actually.'

'Mind if I wait?'

'Nope. Coffee?' His eyes ran over my backpack. 'You look tired.'

'I am, yeah.'

Mr Willoughby led me through a sprawling front yard without a fence or flowers. The grass was all dead and brown except for one lush patch with a dribbling, upturned sprinkler at its heart. When he pulled the flyscreen door back its rusted hinges chirped like a dolphin.

'Needs oil,' he said, holding it back for me. 'We're about to start harvesting in earnest though, so it'll have to wait.'

'Thank you,' I said, slipping past.

The house, like most farm weatherboards, appeared to have had rooms added as the family within it grew. Some were well put together, obviously by carpenters. Others were not. The front alcove belonged to the latter category. Large and airy, the windows were filled with flyscreen instead of glass. A yellow sofa, red stuffing partially eaten out by vermin, sat at one end, reminiscent of a rotting corpse. And beneath my feet oil-stained floorboards, most tacked over with plywood, creaked with every shift of weight.

Mr Willoughby opened a second, heavier door and gestured for me to follow him in. There was nothing ornate about the living room or kitchen. Both were rustic and yet well maintained, making use of a variety of finished timbers. Most of the household appliances looked to be from the seventies and one wall was coated with posters detailing frog breeds. The ceiling lights all had attractive stained-glass shades, and down a dark, carpeted hallway I could make out a sunlit bathroom and lime-green bathtub with silver legs.

'Come through to the kitchen,' said Mr Willoughby. 'How do you have your coffee?'

Before I could answer a four-wheel drive ute pulled up outside, its tyres skidding on the gravel. I heard the dolphin cry of the screen door, then Tilly was in front of me, blinking. She was thin—terribly thin. She had cut her hair short like a boy and seemed to stand with less certainty.

'You've come here,' she said.

'Hi.'

The kettle clicked off. Though Tilly's first expression had been one of distress, she quickly recovered her composure and dropped the two shopping bags she was holding to give me a perfunctory hug.

'You startled me,' she whispered in my ear.

'Maybe it was a bad idea.'

'No, it's not.'

It was strange not getting lost in her hair. Normally it swallowed me up, but now it was so short it spiked my forehead.

'Dad,' she said, 'before I forget, can you check the water on the ute? It's running hot again.'

'Falling to bits like everything else round here.'

'I'll make coffee,' I said.

'Fine. Matilda, come with me, show me what it's been doing.'

They stepped outside. Unable to hear what was being said I watched Mr Willoughby through the kitchen window. He pulled up the Landcruiser's bonnet and, bending from the waist, fiddled with a few coloured plugs. Like most things on the property the ute looked to be an old model, well preserved from the outset in anticipation of hardship. Mr Willoughby nodded to his daughter a few times. She put her hand on his back and he stood straight, or as straight as he could. He slammed the bonnet down with a little more force than was necessary and turned for the house. He found me searching through the fridge for milk and looked to be furious.

'So I imagine you'll be needing somewhere to stay?' he said curtly.

'For a night or two, if that's okay?'

Mr Willoughby only nodded.

'Is there anything I can do?' I asked. 'To help out while I'm staying?'

'Yeah. The firewood. I haven't had a moment to look at it. I'll show you later on. But for now, grab that backpack and take it through.'

Tilly took me to a large but stark room. She gestured for me to sit on the bed.

'Your dad didn't seem very happy with me staying,' I said.

'It's not you. He's always up and down, especially around harvest. We have to cut 32,000 plants in the next fifteen days and three of the staff we had lined up have pulled out.'

'What do you do with it all?' The mattress, when I sat, felt like a stack of wood slats. A Tom Roberts print hung in one corner, letting me know I was in the guest room.

'We send it overseas mostly—send it fresh. That's why we have so many plants. We don't even dry it. We'd be into tourism, into oils, soaps and moisturisers, even lavender lollies, if Dad was a social creature. We'd run a smaller, prettier place. Other farms round here do it and do it well. But Dad likes one burst and then nothing for the rest of the year—a little planting, some rabbit-shooting and weeding, but nothing hard. He's got a few reliable buyers, so we normally just scrape through.'

'How did he get the buyers?'

'No idea. Letters, I think, years ago. So …' Tilly said, hanging on the word and inhaling in such a way as to suggest we had adequately canvassed the farm, 'give me all the news.'

'What news?'

'Your news. Tell me about the hostel. No, better yet, tell me how you ended up here.'

'Here? Sightseeing.'

'Very funny. Is Phillip with you?'

'Why would Phillip be with me?'

'Oh, I don't know. I just can't picture you deciding to fly to Australia on a whim. I thought maybe this was his idea.'

Through a window I watched Mr Willoughby enter the yard and call for a dog. No dog appeared. He swore, scanning the horizon, then dropped a can of sloppy food onto the ground. Picking up a sickle, he set off for the closest lavender field.

'Home's strange,' I said.

'What do you mean?'

'Something happened. I don't know what—don't want to. Mum's moved out.'

Tilly sat down beside me, dropping a hand onto my thigh. 'Since when?'

'I'm not sure. It's weird but not bad—not yet. It should be bad but it doesn't feel that way. If anything it's weird because it makes sense. Like I've known forever. There's nothing to ask even if I wanted to.' After this admission, we dropped back onto the bed and lay in silence a while. I heard the dog gulping its food outside.

'You've lost a lot of weight,' I said eventually.

'Farm food. It'll come back.' Tilly paused. 'Do you want to talk more about home?'

'Not right now. Maybe later.'

'Tell me about the hostel, then. Who's still there? Who's gone?'

'There's a new guy, Harry.'

'What's he like?'

'He's okay.'

'New people already …' Tilly smiled but I could see she was thinking about something else, something which caused her brow to flicker with concern.

We lay on the bed for hours, until the room's details— the painting, the knots in the pine, the edges of the sheepskin rug—were lost to a sluggish summer dusk. Only the white lace curtains billowing beautifully across the window were still visible. They looked like a pair of vain ghosts circling in front of a mirror.

I almost told Tilly about Mami then, but there seemed little point. Nothing had developed and the girl was history. I tried to convince myself it was Tilly who mattered now. It pleased me to have her lying to my left, breath soft. She had a concern for me matched only by my parents, but without the desire to steer. By sleeping together we could close ourselves off. She was like a warm room from which to listen to storms.

I lay thinking. When my mother asked if I had made new friends in Japan I had wanted to say no with smug satisfaction, to show how alone I was in the world, how straight I stood without the slightest support. It was an illusion I had painted around myself, an understanding of my life and the worlds I inhabited which paid little heed to Tilly's influence. If I was to be honest, it was Tilly who protected me from any sense of rejection and loneliness. And while I had no interest in moving forward with her—on into a life together, to marriage, to children—nor did I want to creep back from her. I wanted stagnation, a continuance of the same in every direction like the thin green moss atop a still pond, into which the Mami episode would only ever be a great, sharp-edged rock—the deep, *ba-boosh* heartbeat splash, the gaping brown wound and final, churning muck. Why bring all that up?

Before bed Tilly showed me her room—that of a younger girl, with pink walls, dolls, big fluffy bears and a Johnny Depp poster advertising *21 Jump Street*. It was odd to think of her as a child, and I could not help but wonder why it was a child's room, since she had lived at home until university. Off in one corner I saw pipes and a gas valve, leading me to suspect the room had once been a kitchen—the building showing its age. I guessed she must have moved rooms at twelve or thirteen. Presumably there was another room reflecting her final years of school.

We reminisced about Japan, about Phillip's model planes, about sushi and Moaning Man, then I went to bed, sleeping two hours at most. If Tilly did visit me in the middle of the night, it was during this time and I knew nothing of it.

True to his word Mr Willoughby put me to work the next morning. I had expected to cut lavender, having heard about the three absent staff, but apparently this was paid work and the positions had already been filled.

I had never split wood before and I found it difficult to say the least. Mr Willoughby would stack one chain-sawed block on top of another, grain up, then point to where the axe should land.

'There's always going to be a circle,' he said. 'You look for that circle, then you strike parallel with the grain. Never across. Across, and you'll get nowhere.'

The axe felt coarse in my hands. Its long, narrow head was roughly equivalent in weight to a brick. The handle was made out of a faded, pink plastic which I guessed to be fibreglass, and grey tape had been wrapped around one end. Whenever I swung the thing up over my head it mostly fell back down of its own accord. I always looked at the position Mr Willoughby singled out, but the axe thudded down wherever it pleased. Sometimes it sheeted off the block or missed outright, lodging itself in red dirt.

'There's a knack to it,' said Mr Willoughby, before ambling off to tend to the harvest.

It was a menacingly hot day to learn to split wood. Sweat dribbled from my hairline into my eyes. Mucus clogged my throat. I kept hauling the axe up into the air, feet braced, only to bring it down ineffectually. Tilly came to watch midway through the morning, dressed in jeans and an old Chicago Bulls T-shirt. She took the axe and gave me a demonstration, lopping blocks into two, then four.

'There's a knack to it,' she said, just as her father had.

At dusk Mr Willoughby brought me a beer. I sat, turned my empty palm up and stared at blisters full of grit. He dropped the dog food—still the shape of the can—into the dirt, then returned to the softly lit house without a word. Crickets harped as the dog cleared the side of the house at a run, pink tongue thrown back like a hanky from a car window.

The living room in which we sat contained three pianos. When I asked why, Mr Willoughby said, 'Family.'

'Family?'

'Big Catholic one,' he explained, rolling a cigarette. 'My father, for example, had seven siblings. Over time they all died and we ended up with their pianos. There are actually five in this house. For some reason we get the pianos.'

'It's a farm thing,' said Tilly.

Mr Willoughby nodded. 'As it is with clocks.'

I cocked my head. 'Clocks?'

'You haven't noticed?' Tilly laughed. 'Listen.'

I did. And sure enough I heard clocks. All sorts of clocks, tick-tocking. At a glance I counted one grandfather clock, three wall-clocks and a few antique silver alarms with bells on top. In addition to this there appeared to be a collection of wristwatches piled on the mantelpiece—all broken-in leather bands and lacklustre metal.

'You do have a lot of clocks,' I said.

Mr Willoughby finished rolling the cigarette but did not light it. Instead he chased bits of stir-fry around the plate with his fork. He had eaten less than half his meal but did not seem ready to give it up.

'Do either of you play the piano?' I asked, thinking I should have known if Tilly did.

'No,' said both firmly.

'How about you, Noah?' Mr Willoughby asked. 'Do you play an instrument?'

'The clarinet.'

'But he gave it up in Year 9,' Tilly added, standing to collect the dirty plates. 'His teacher told his parents they were wasting their money.'

'I see.' Mr Willoughby fumbled around inside his shirt pocket for a lighter, withdrew a hot-pink one, then lit his intricately rolled cigarette. Soon the smell reached me and I was struck with a sudden urge to smoke. I wanted something to do: I felt like a charlatan before this man.

Tilly left the room with a tall stack of dishes.

'Do you mind if I try and roll one?' I asked.

'Not at all.'

Mr Willoughby passed me the pouch of tobacco and packet of papers with curiosity.

'You smoke?' he asked.

'No.'

'Me either. I'm just taking it up, actually.' As if to prove this he blinked smoke from smarting, wrinkled eyes. I shuffled tobacco on the paper. When I licked it, most of the contents fell onto the table. A few strands stuck to my wet lips and fingertips like rusted wire shards to a magnet.

'How long have you been a farmer?' I asked.

'A while now.'

'What were you before that?'

'I was an academic—a biologist. That was before meeting Tilly's mother.'

'Where was she from?'

'Here. This was her family's place. It was a beef operation but her parents were too old to run it. I came in and planted *lavandula intermedia grosso* everywhere, then *intermedia super*. A little *angustifolia vera*.'

'Why lavender?'

'I thought I could do it all better. I had an abundance of theories and the sort of crude confidence that comes with never having farmed. Tilly's grandparents were horrified. They watched the place turn purple, shaking their heads.' At this recollection, Mr Willoughby smiled.

'So you moved here straight after getting married?'

'I slowly bought the place out, but we never married. Tilly's mother didn't believe in marriage.'

Tilly re-entered the room carrying three saucers.

'Marriage?' she asked, without waiting for an explanation. 'I'm afraid these aren't much better than the main course.' She set down the plates. On each was a soggy Anzac biscuit. She then returned to the kitchen for freshly brewed coffee while her father ate his biscuit, rolled another cigarette and slowly smoked it. I finished rolling my own, suppressing pride, and lit up. But, clamped shut at one end with saliva, it quickly went out.

As soon as the meal was finished Mr Willoughby excused himself from the dining table. Even at this early hour he seemed ready for bed.

That night, lying in the dark guest room on my wood-plank bed, still fully dressed, arms up behind my head, I thought about Tilly—tried to recreate her. Outside there was no traffic, only bugs and a lone, bellowing cow. I tried to recall the moles coating her body, their pattern.

Would she visit?

This question was answered by a soft knock and the sound of the metal knob turning in its wood socket. A shaft of light photocopied the carpet: Tilly opening and closing the door. Prior to her entering I had been able to make out a huntsman spider. Now it was gone. I could see nothing.

Tilly was quickly on top of the bed. I found myself aroused as she paused above, hands and knees either side of my body, soapy-smelling nightgown covering my face.

'Hello,' she whispered, breath warm.

Clumsily I tried to pull off my shirt, but it tangled around my head. She laughed.

'Shhh,' I said.

'Why?'

'Your dad.'

'His room's at the other end of the house.' She helped me pull off my tangled shirt, then lifted her nightgown over her body and threw it to one side.

'I'm not sure about this,' I said.

'About what?'

'This. What if your dad hears?'

'He won't.'

I could make out the shape of her freckled breasts in the dark. How many times had I seen and felt these breasts? I sometimes wondered that. How many times had I slept with Tilly? It was impossible to say but I tried to conjure a total. I guessed, in the preceding year, factoring in time spent apart, I had slept with her on average once every couple of days. This might have been a generous estimate but it provided me with a rough total—150 times.

'I'm going to go down on you,' she said, speaking like a doctor explaining an intrusive procedure. I said nothing and soon felt her tongue. But instead of thinking of Tilly I thought of Mami—the first night in her hotel room, her neck and hands. I pictured her kneeling before me, the pattern of her hair, the width and shine of each strand and the back of her neck. I felt her face with my fingers, could put it together as if there.

'God, sorry,' I said. 'That shouldn't have—that was—'

'I don't mind,' said Tilly, kissing my belly.

She licked and bit a nipple on her way back towards my mouth. And within a few minutes I was exhausted. My muscles ached from the day's work, a pleasant, full ache. The bed was trying to drag me down into thick, warm mud, trying to bury me in the bottom of a timeless swamp.

It was certainly Tilly above me. I could smell her skin, her sweat like a fingerprint.

'Excited,' I said, not sure how it tied into our conversation.

Tilly laughed. 'You're sleepy?'

I nodded, teetering on the brink of sleep. I wondered why Mami had joined in. I had often thought about other women while having sex with Tilly but never about a specific woman. Never a woman I knew. The women were all featureless. They had a shape, maybe even a nationality, but never a face. They could have been store mannequins.

I woke up. It was suddenly as though I had never been drowsy. I was wide awake and aware that, somehow, I had almost said 'Mami' aloud. Or had I said it? Feeling anxious and unable to make out Tilly's face, the curve of her mouth, I listened to her breathing. She sounded relaxed. She put her cold hands over my ears playfully.

'Can you hear me now?' she asked.

'Did I just say something?'

' "Excited" '

'Oh ...'

'Are you?' Tilly asked. 'Do you want to touch me?'

I did as requested. She felt thinner than I recalled—frailer. Placing her hand on mine she led me through a reciprocation of that which I had received, allowing for little autonomy. Despite being religious, Tilly had no qualms about breaking sex down into its essential components; deconstructing it so that, as an act, it facilitated maximum pleasure. Sexually, Tilly was a mystery. She would elect to have sex at odd times, then decline to make love when we were lying naked in bed, wrapped in one another's arms.

Or she would ask me to assume a position only to change her mind and place me in another, like a photographer preparing a nude model. So long as Tilly was in control she was happy to try just about anything.

She came—or pretended to. Then I set about trying to make love to her, set about proving to myself I could without reverting to fantasy. I kissed her face intently, her mouth and neck, and said whatever sweet things popped into my head. Tilly played along, but soon the sex was difficult—painful. Our bodies betrayed our lie. And with a frustrated sigh I gave up and rolled onto my back. My stomach churned and I went limp.

'Fuck this,' I said.

'Don't get angry.'

'Well it matters—before you say it doesn't.'

'I wasn't going to say that.'

'So it does matter?'

'Shut up.' Tilly stood and started to dress. The moment she let go of my hand, she was swallowed by darkness. Only her voice remained. 'It was me.'

'It's because of your dad being in the house.'

'I know.'

At this my anger turned to affection, then fear. Again I wanted to confess my secret to Tilly, but I was reluctant to confess until I could see her face. I thought about asking her to turn on the light, but she said goodnight and let herself out of the room before I could speak. I lay, stretched out on the bed, just as I had been before she visited. Only now I felt uncomfortable with everything that had taken place, the fact that I was naked, that I had entered her. I felt repulsed in fact. All lust had exited me in a single orgasm, leaving the sort of unease I usually only woke to after dreams. I got up to pee and, flushing, thought about Celeste, about love and lust. And nothing.

I climbed out of bed before sun-up, just in time to hear the back door bang shut. There was a gusting wind outside punching the house with hard-knuckled fists. The clocks rattled on the walls and the windows shuddered. Somewhere the cow was still bellowing. Pulling back the lace curtains I watched Mr Willoughby set out for the lavender fields. Around his neck he wore a camera, the sort a professional photographer might use. I saw the daybreak was going to be beautiful. The darkness was already receding. Posts and trees rose from an inky purple. I smiled. I rarely woke to such mornings and wanted to charge out into it like a child, leaving behind me forever the night that made it. But like all irrational surges of elation this one passed just as quickly as it had arrived and I began to get dressed. Finding my clothes in the dark room was difficult, mostly because of the way in which I had taken them off. Twice I stubbed my toe on the bed, hopping about like a fool before finally, blindly, groping my way through the gloomy house.

It was only in the alcove, warm, lavender-laden morning air on my skin, that I forgot the pain in my toe. I stared through the flyscreen windows searching for Mr Willoughby. The sun had taken its first tentative footing on the horizon and the fields, as if in greeting, were turning a lighter purple. A human shadow slid between the rows of flowers, moving at a fast but easily sustained pace, and without questioning the idea I set off after it. At the outer edges of the undulating lavender, it pressed on, down towards a gully.

This gully was easily the size of a football field and filled with fernery, a bed of green from which shot countless beautiful trees, mostly gums with their trunks pale and contorted. I looked them up and down, tan bark curled by the sun. From the soft green tops—thirty to forty metres up—came the echo of birds squawking as if in argument. I noticed the area was fenced off, presumably to protect it from cattle. One cow, down on its front knees, its wet nose on an angle beneath the live wire, trimmed the gully grass. Others—fat-bellied, older animals—stood squarely in the paddock and munched methodically on what little pick was left. Mr Willoughby reached the fence, paused and turned to face me.

'Morning,' he called. 'Be careful not to twist your ankle. When it's wet the cattle sink their feet in pacing the fenceline. Then it dries up and you're left with this crud.' I nodded, noticing yabbie homes amidst the potholes like nuclear chimneys.

'Sorry to follow. When I saw you leave, I felt like a walk. What's the camera for?'

'Growling Grass Frogs. In the swamp.'

We climbed through the fence and started on in. The foliage was thick and within a couple of metres we lost sight of both the fence and paddock behind. After a minute or two I stopped. Twigs had scratched my face and my sneakers were soaked. I peered up through fern leaves and vine to the tops of gums, bright and swaying in a gentle breeze unknown to me below. But Mr Willoughby did not dawdle.

He bashed his way around trunks and stopped at last in front of a wall of roots encased in thick black dirt. Vaguely circular, this wall—the fallen tree behind it invisible—stood guard like a parent over the swamp it had birthed.

'Listen carefully,' he said.

I did and soon heard it—a soft growling. Mr Willoughby pointed and I spotted a bright green frog lazily floating in the water, barely causing a ripple. It had a number of brown, wart-like spots on its back and alert hazelnut eyes with two black strips for pupils. The camera clicked and Mr Willoughby wound the film on. The frog dipped beneath the surface.

'That was the growling one?' I asked.

'Yeah. *Litoria raniformis*.'

'Why are you taking photos of it?'

'It's dying out. I've relocated a few to this swamp. The photos are for records.'

By turning over fallen branches sunken into dry mud we found a few more frogs of varying breeds, some large and pot-bellied, others small and fit-looking. I picked up each in turn. They struggled between my dirty fingers and kicked free. Mr Willoughby, if pressed, would tell me where they lived, what they ate and when they bred.

Only one was of real interest to me. 'What does that growling one eat?'

'Mice. Other frogs.'

'You're joking?'

'No.'

As we returned for breakfast the weatherboard house looked like a cardboard box set on a lavender bedsheet. The sun was well up in the sky. Mr Willoughby and I walked side by side in silence and, oddly, I almost expected him to ask my intentions regarding his daughter. At one point he stopped and tore up a flower, as if deciding how to posit such a question.

'Forty-five per cent open,' he said softly. 'That's good enough for me.'

'I beg your pardon?'

He spun. 'These flowers have been a little slow to open,' he said. 'Now we can cut them along with the rest.'

We walked in silence. When we stepped inside, having left our muddy boots at the front door, we could smell bacon and eggs. I crossed to the stove.

'Wash your hands,' said Tilly, trying to scrape a charred egg from the pan and not looking up.

She served a blackened breakfast and afterwards went to collect eggs from the chook yard. I found Mr Willoughby watching her through a living room window. Unaware he was being watched himself he looked miserable. He ran an index finger up and down one thigh. When he heard me he turned and cleared his throat. 'There's coffee in the kitchen, Noah.'

'Thanks, but I'm fine.'

This reply, and my walking towards the window, seemed to irritate him. Outside Tilly was playing with a pup. A larger dog bounded around her, ecstatically yelping and snapping at her heels whenever it found a chance.

Mr Willoughby drained the last of his coffee and turned to leave.

'She's a real farm girl,' I observed.

'I suppose.'

'Was she always like that?'

'Not really.'

'Why? What was she like as a kid?'

'Sick mostly.'

He walked away without another word. I heard him put his coffee mug in the metal sink, then the click of his study door.

For a while I watched Tilly tend to chores around the house. Depending on what she decided to do I changed windows, standing at each, hands deep in my pockets. She knew I was there. Occasionally she looked up to find me at a new window, quietly watching, and she would laugh mutedly on the other side of the glass—nervously, too. To distract me she had the salivating, delirious dogs perform tricks, but they either refused or muddled her commands.

Eventually, unable to tolerate my curiosity, she hid.

The following morning, well before sun-up, I wandered the house. One room led to another until I found myself conducting a tentative investigation of Mr Willoughby's study. It was cluttered, but not like my father's study. Whereas my father's belongings held no obvious purpose, everything Mr Willoughby owned appeared to be essential to his daily life. Documents of various colours were sorted into an array of cut-down cardboard wine casks. Pigeon-holes were filled with stationery and unused envelopes. And there were two bulky filing cabinets, keys in the locks. Everything was perfectly still in the pre-dawn. My breathing, loud to the point of seeming rude, stirred tepid, cooped-up air.

I went to the bathroom and slowly brushed my teeth. I brushed them far more conscientiously than usual, taking care with the chore until they felt slippery beneath my tongue. Then I went back to bed and, finding I could at last sleep, dreamt of a house devoid of things. There was absolutely nothing in this house. The floor stretched out endlessly. But when I climbed out a window, only just squeezing through, I fell into a world full of things—all the contents of all the rooms in all the world piled carelessly. Everyone went about their daily routine amidst prams, dish-washers, phones, cupboards, tapes, books, beds, condoms, keys, cutlery, medicine, computers, tables, bags, fridges, chopping boards, carpet, socks and dictionaries, without concern.

It was just after seven when I tripped on a desk lamp and awoke with a comical jerking of my legs.

I showered, dressed and ate another chargrilled breakfast. The toast was hard and cold, especially the crusts, and there was no margarine to have with the Vegemite. Feeling I had stayed long enough, I announced my intention to return to Melbourne that morning. Tilly, far from objecting, offered to drive me to the station. We left the farm hoping to catch the ten o'clock service.

'I never knew you were sick growing up. What was it?' I asked on the platform.

'Who said that?'

'Your dad.'

'It was nothing serious. Chronic fatigue. It came and went.'

'Do you still get it?'

Tilly shook her head, looking out along glimmering

train tracks. 'Listen,' she said, 'I'll need to stay a few more months and—'

'A few months? Why?'

She remained silent and watched as a toddler broke free from its mother and ran dangerously close to the sharp edge of the platform before being scooped up. Off in the distance the train appeared, rippling in the morning heat. It sounded its horn defiantly and we both watched it pull in, wheels squealing, the unnatural sound of weighty metal on metal. Tilly had to raise her voice to be heard over the engine.

'Take care,' she said.

'Take care?'

A loud whistle blew.

'You have to get in, Noah. Good luck in Melbourne and back in Tokyo.' Tilly kissed me on the lips, but only quickly, pulling back.

I stepped up into the train.

'Bye,' she said.

'That's it? You didn't answer my question. Why a few months?'

'The train's going.'

Angry, I shrugged, turned and without saying goodbye found a seat in the carriage. By the time I settled Tilly had gone. Up in the car park I could see the ute reversing, one tail-light flickering. The sight of the thing, small and miserable in the vast day, left me feeling desolate. A sudden burst of sun washed the scene of all colour.

I was oddly comforted by a desire to double back, and likewise by the impossibility of doing so. I sat and thought about Tokyo, about Mami, the hostel and the cats, until at last I was too tired to think. Gums began to roll by, faster and faster. Then came the edge of a town: a greasy garage, a milk bar, a school bus merging onto the highway and paddocks cut into hills. I let my head fall back and tried desperately to sleep.

A Tantrum

I returned to my father, as I was expected to do. But, having noted my absence, he spoke to me only when it was unavoidable and we kept to opposite ends of the apartment. In deference to his mood I did not visit my mother again. Instead, having made a note of Celeste's number, I phoned whenever he went out shopping or to church.

The day of my flight back to Japan I dropped my suitcase and backpack at the front door and sat at the table. My father said grace and we began slurping at tinned soup. There was no bread.

'Do you remember Miss Sinclair?' he asked.

'Yes.'

Noting my tone, he looked at me threateningly, then went on. 'I meant to tell you, she passed away the other day.'

I said nothing.

'I said she passed away, Noah.'

'Okay.'

'Well, she was your prep teacher. You could send a card before you scuttle back.'

'It's a bit late for that.'

He took an unhappy slurp of soup. 'I went to the funeral. People asked after you.'

'I'm not sending anything.'

Exasperated, my father threw his spoon down. Soup splashed onto his tie. I hoped that finally, after days of silence, he would raise the matter that was gnawing at him. But he persisted in circling it.

'What did the woman ever do to you, Noah?'

'What did she do? Aside from telling me God was listening to my thoughts and didn't like me? Aside from making me sit by myself at a desk because my letters were sometimes back to front? Aside from making me stand in a corner when she knew standing in a corner only made me wet myself? Nothing. She was a saint.'

'You hold on to all that?'

'It was my childhood.'

'Everyone's childhood is difficult.'

'I disagree.'

But he ignored me, saying only, 'It's how you view it that matters.'

There was more coming and I waited for it, welcomed it. He was riled, tired of dancing around my mother's departure, as was I. I felt a furious excitement. My body fluttered.

'You're not just immature, but selfish,' he finally blurted, eyes set fixedly on his paper napkin. I gently put my spoon down, afraid I might otherwise throw it; I had expected a less barbed outburst.

'Why?' I asked coldly.

But my father did not have a chance to answer. A bird flew head-on into the kitchen window with a thunk. I looked up, startled. Ordinarily I would have gone straight outside to capture it before it regained consciousness. I pictured the creature staggering and falling and hoped its stupidity would not rob me of my showdown.

'Why?' I asked again.

'I know you saw your mother. You came home to help but all you did was hold secret meetings—all the two of you did was plot against me. Is that my thanks, Noah? For supporting this family? For giving everything to it? Is this how you both intend to repay me?'

'Screw you.'

'Charming. I talk to you like an adult. I extend you respect and you talk to me like I'm muck under your shoe, like I'm not human.'

'You respect me?'

'I said I speak to you with respect and I expect the same in return.'

'Fine. I've seen Mum. That's because I'm her son. I've seen you for the same reason. And if you're expecting me to be involved in this—whatever this is—then forget it, because I'm not going to be dragged into it. It's between you and Mum and I hope you sort it out. I really do. But I can't be in the middle.'

'You are in the middle, Noah. This is your family. You leave now and there's no telling what might happen. You're needed.' His voice faltered and he averted glassy eyes. His reading glasses, wrapped in cloth, were off to one side and he ceremoniously put them on, as if to forecast the importance of his words. 'You have a responsibility to—'

'She left you, not me.'

My father leapt to his feet, pulled the glasses off and tossed them onto the table where they slid to a stop just before falling off.

'How dare you!'

'What? Talk to you like that?' I jumped to my own feet with an equal ferocity. 'Get off your high horse and listen for one—'

'You're a dropout, Noah. A loafer. Nothing more. Run back to your atheism, to your cosy hedonism.'

'No wonder Mum left you. You're a bully, like Sinclair.'

These words seemed to slug my father in the stomach. He crashed heavily back down onto his chair. Looking at his hunched shoulders, at his palms on his knees, I felt a stab of regret and even wonderment at the depth of my cruelty. He seemed to be crying. His upper back, the ribs clearly visible, shuddered slightly.

'Do as you please,' he said finally, waving me away.

'I will.'

I picked up my suitcase and backpack, walked out the front door and down the empty street, feet loud beneath me in the suburban quiet. I felt I was being watched but could not look back towards the house. Blood thudded in my ears as I listened for him, hoping he would call out, that we could somehow part on better terms. He must have followed as far as the garden because, after perhaps a hundred metres, I heard the front door bang shut. But there was nothing after that. No shout. Only the alarmed squawk of birds and the sound of a passing taxi, its tyres loud on the newly laid, stony bitumen.

I had no choice but to press on for the airport.

Mami Hangs
Herself

I resumed my job in the public school. It was as if I had never left. Every morning I woke at eight, queued to shower and dressed in tan slacks and a crinkled white shirt. To this semi-formal concoction I normally added a thin blue tie from my school days, the only tie I owned—a pathetic attempt at respectability.

After work I would lie in my room reading. Occasionally I did a workout or studied Japanese, though mostly I just read. Never good books, but soft-porn bestsellers which Harry slipped under my door as a sort of running joke (and, no doubt, as an attempt to have me join him on his outings to the city's seedier districts).

I spent a lot of time around Harry the first two weeks back. Phillip was working on the Japan Rail shoot, so it was Harry who accompanied me to the convenience store every evening for bento box meals and beer. I needed him. I was

missing Tilly, the idea of her as a partner. I would stumble
into the memory of her like a puddle and suffer an insidious
gloom, Tokyo having lost its cushion. Her possessions
surrounded me, filled the room with colour and clutter, but
I had no idea whether or not she would return, whether they
would ever be reclaimed. It seemed unlikely.

I thought about contacting Mami but lacked the nerve. I fell
deeper into an eddy, and soon the Tokyo weather was as it
had been when I first met Tilly. Occasional unseasonably
hot days took people by surprise. Girls, reluctant to cover
their legs even in the depths of winter, happily returned to
wearing impractically short skirts, modestly holding the
backs down with one hand whenever they encountered
stairs or escalators. Businessmen swapped their heavy black
suits for lighter, less black ones. And children showed a
predictable disregard for the slight chill that came only at the
very end of the day.

The weather and the sad meowing of a cat outside
my door sought to draw me back a year. I thought of
that first day I met Tilly, of standing outside the hostel
as the car door startled the proud cat, and of all that
followed.

I stood and paced my room. Tilly's running shoes sat in
the open cupboard, off-white and with the stitching starting
to come apart. They had been a new white when I met her,
a white that cut swathes in the dark room, inside the dark
bed when we both half stripped and made love in a giggling,
rough-and-tumble, come-what-may fashion. The shoes

then, the way they had been used to pin me down, had almost scared me. As had the sex. Afterwards I had often felt a certain panic at the intimacy inherent in the heady yet irrevocable act, as if I would forever be indebted to the girl, as if I had stolen from her.

Now, such a concern seemed absurd. Things had apparently run their course.

I went to the doorway to shoo the cat, but it led me to a discarded suitcase beside the vending machine, where I heard a softer meow. Lifting the lid, a large ginger kitten shot out, almost tumbling down the steep staircase before daring to glance back. Obviously it had stepped in, upset the lid and trapped itself, and I knew at once which kitten it was. It was bigger now, but unmistakably Tilly's favourite. I had saved the skinny quiet one with the sad but shiny eyes. Fed up, I kicked the suitcase after it.

Then came the official onset of the rainy season. Hemmed in by cloud and awaiting rain, I received a letter by courier from Mami. I opened it in Harry's room and read it aloud while Harry, pushing back the skin above each fingernail with a rusty butter knife, lay on his futon listening.

Well, it's clear you want nothing to do with me (or with your stupid jacket), but I'm going to go ahead and write to you anyway. This probably sounds melodramatic. But today, at exactly midday, I, Mami Kaketa, intend to hang myself in my hotel room. Perhaps you don't care. M.

'How about that,' Harry said, sitting up. 'Who's this girl again?'

'Someone I know.'

'A hoax, I'd say.'

'Maybe.' I tapped the eraser end of a pencil on my knee, thinking. 'What time is it?'

'About eleven.'

'Exactly, I mean.'

Harry rummaged through a cardboard box on the floor. His room had a transient feel to it, as if he planned to move out any day.

'Eleven-oh-three,' he said, plucking out a tacky digital watch with a green band and scratched face.

'You sure that's right? She was clear about the time.'

'I've had it since I was a kid.'

'Then we can get there.'

'We?' Harry smiled and shook his head. 'Not me. I've got a meeting—to transfer money.'

'I don't want to hear about some hotel hanging on the news. Not after this.'

'Then get moving.'

I stepped out into the corridor, only to glance at my wrist and duck back in for the watch. It had only one hole punched in the band and the LCD screen flickered, sections of numbers vanishing. I strapped it on as best I could and made a dash for Shinbashi Station, boarding a Yamanote Line train which ground through Yurakucho. Sweat dripped from my face onto the carriage floor, flashing sharply in the sunlight striking in between low-rise apartments and offices.

When the doors at last opened on Tokyo Station I ran

through its various tunnel-like wings, and then down a wide street towards Mami's hotel. The air was thick and soggy and at some point Harry's watch flew off my damp wrist without my noticing. I crossed the hotel lobby at a half-run and slipped into the open lift. I watched the numbers above the door. People got in and out at each floor and one woman holding a German novel smiled at me.

Wiping sweat from my face and trying to catch my breath, I located Mami's door and hammered on it. 'Mami?'

It was a heavy door and my hands bounced off. To lessen the pain I used the sides.

'Mami! Mami! Open up!'

I gave up hitting and placed an ear to the door but could hear nothing more than my own breathing.

'Open up, damn you!' There were no clocks in the corridor but I guessed the time to be around midday— a little after maybe.

'Mami!'

I kicked the door, stepping back and raising one leg with the aim of dislodging the lock from its frame and smashing the thing in. It shuddered and I hopped back-wards, swearing between gulps of air until I noticed I was not alone. A maid hung back a few metres, fearful.

'Keys,' I said first in English and then in Japanese. She shook her head and took a few steps towards her cleaning cart, piled high with individual shampoos, conditioners and soaps. Pretending to peruse these items, her hands shook.

'Emergency!' I shouted. '*Kiken!*'

At the word 'danger' she took another step back.

'No,' I corrected myself. '*Hijou! Kagi kudasai.*'

She said something in a mumble.

'What?' I screamed, infuriated. 'Just give me the key. *Hayakushite.*'

She suddenly changed her mind and nodded, tossing me the keycard from around her neck.

'Thank you.'

She started to walk away, broke into a run and sounded like a terrified waterfowl the moment she was out of sight. A green light flashed on the door, and after a click I flung it open.

Mami was not in her front room. Nor was she in the bathroom, the hallway, the dining room or the conference room. This fuelled my panic, legitimised it. I did not worry about the maid or police. I was set on saving the day. I paused outside the Japanese-style room, tried the handle and found it to be locked. When I put my ear to it I heard a definite click, like the cocking of a gun.

'Mami? It's Noah.'

'Stay away.'

Without the slightest hesitation I burst through the door.

Having never burst through a door before, and having been so coldly and effectively rebuffed by the front one, I expected significant resistance. When I hip-and-shouldered this particular door, however, taking a run up and striking it flush, it popped straight off its hinges as if made of plastic. For a moment I was confused, lunging. Then I crashed down on top of it and tumbled forward onto tatami, more sliding than rolling. I had banged my head. There was no pain but the sound of my skull striking wood lingered long after I came to a stop. One hand went to my hairline, groping blindly for blood.

I lifted my head to survey the room. Mami was standing on a chair, completely naked and with a noose around her neck. This was tied off to an aluminium bar of a type I knew well. I used an identical one to hang my laundry—an inch thick, but hollow with plastic caps at either end. Mami had set it on two right-angled windowframes in a corner of the room, forming a triangle; a crude but effective set-up. For a moment we stared at one another in silence.

'Take it off, will you? Please. This is stupid.' Speaking, I became aware of a swirling pain in my forehead.

Mami's lips curled into a smile. 'I told you I would.'

'I know, but take it off.' My voice hardened as I noticed further details. Mami had tied her feet up with the same kind of rope used for the noose—fluorescent yellow climbing rope. She held a short length of it and was trying to tie off her wrists without success. Her feet were purple and there was something small in her hands. Whatever this was, she seemed to be keeping it hidden from me.

'Are you scared?' she asked.

'Aren't you?'

'No.'

I moved to stand up but Mami rattled the chair beneath her.

'Don't come any closer.'

'Okay. But why send me the letter? If you're so damn bent on killing yourself, why warn me?'

'How can you be sure I'm bent on killing myself?'

'Don't play games.'

'You think I'm playing? Or you hope I am?'

'Take off the noose.'

'You know,' Mami said, 'it's a real noose. It's a good

thing my father keeps a laptop in the conference room. The internet's useful.' She paused, waggling the noose with a wry smile.

'Mami, please …'

'My father comes here once a month. Did you know that? My family's from Nagoya but he comes and inspects the hotels.'

'Really?'

'Mmm.'

'He didn't notice the porn on the walls or the noose, or anything like that?'

'I lock this room whenever he visits.'

'Get down and get dressed, will you? If you slip on that chair you'll die. Really die. It'll snap your neck and you'll be dead and none of this will seem funny.'

'That's the idea. Most people—well the ones who kill themselves like this—they strangle themselves. That's what happens. Death by suffocation. That didn't appeal to me so I learnt how to tie this knot and position it properly.'

Mami waggled the knot again, smiling.

'Just take it off.'

'Is that all you can say?' Her voice contained a trace of annoyance now. 'I might as well get on with it. Be on my way.' She widened her stance on the chair. 'Like you said, a split second and it'll snap my neck. Nothing to fear.'

She rattled the chair and I tried to stand. My headache was worsening by the second. Glancing back towards the door I wondered where the hotel staff were. Surely the maid had reached the lobby, alerted people.

'You've told them,' Mami said, noticing my interest in the doorway. 'You complete idiot.' She reached up for the rope. The chair abruptly went onto two legs and it seemed to me she was finding leverage to fling it from beneath her.

I leapt towards her just as the chair fell back onto four feet. For a split second Mami was still, her hands up, her eyes wide, her mouth ajar. She stared at me coming at her. No doubt she believed she was going to die. I hardly noticed the chair. I collided with her, clamped my arms around her hips, boosted her up and held her, my mouth puffed like a blowfish.

But in my haste to cover the distance I had moved too quickly, and my momentum caused us both to teeter. The chair, Mami's weight no longer on it, toppled, and I felt myself falling forward with no way to prevent it. I knew I had to let go of Mami, but could not.

Mami screamed. 'Get off me!'

I tripped on the upturned chair and fell awkwardly across it, losing my hold. Mami swung out and away. Above me, her bound legs jolted like a hooked fish. For a moment she appeared to be hanging by her neck, then I realised she had one hand beneath the noose, the other high up the rope. Whatever she had been holding was gone, flung out into the room.

As she began to swing back in I pulled myself to my knees and prepared to get a hold of her legs, but she swung in faster than expected and her knees crashed into and sheered off my shoulder. I was set to topple but, having reached a low apex, she came in on me again. This time she struck me from behind with her heel and pain-fully righted me.

I grabbed her waist as best I could.

'Get off!' she yelled. 'You'll kill—'

'Fucking stay still!'

Mami kneed me squarely in the face with both legs. I felt as though I had been struck by a shovel. My eyes smarted and watery blood wet my face and neck. Though I tried to keep a hold of her, my body gave out beneath me in segments like a building dynamited from the first floor up. I slumped, hands protecting my face.

Somewhere behind all this, in the recesses, someone knocked on a door. But my only concern was for Mami, swinging in her noose. Looking up through a film of tears I saw the aluminium bar bounce above her and dislodge. She seemed unable to break her fall. She fell silently and without emotion, like a crash-test dummy. Her body thudded and bounced on the tatami. The bar struck her left thigh and she let out nothing more than an irritated grunt. I tried to scramble to her, blood splashing onto my T-shirt, but she knocked the bar off her leg and, with increasing speed, loosened and removed the noose around her neck. Without looking at me she untied her feet, stood up shakily and crossed to a pile of clothes to dress.

'Coming,' she yelled in response to another sharp rap on the front door. She pulled on a pair of jeans and slipped into high heels, gripped her hair back, tied it off with a band and took a deep breath.

'Stay here,' she said.

I listened to her run towards the front door, her footsteps softening, then finally flopped onto my back. My face and chest were covered in blood, my nose felt hideously swollen, my head throbbed and I was thirsty. I heard three voices apologising profusely. Then came the sound of the front door closing and, though I kept on listening, nothing more. No one was left.

Mami returned to the apartment fifteen minutes later, by which time I had somewhat recovered. I had dabbed at my nose with toilet paper, gulped down a few glasses of apple juice and dropped my bloody T-shirt into a sink full of hot soapy water. As a replacement, I had found and put on a business shirt which I guessed to be her father's. She appeared out of nowhere.

'I had to see the manager of the hotel. I feel like a naughty schoolgirl.'

Wanting to convey my displeasure I stared at the floor.

Mami frowned. 'Okay, I'm sorry for kneeing—' she began, before shaking her head. 'You still haven't figured it out, have you?'

'What?'

'What I was doing.'

'I have.'

'What then?'

'Killing yourself.'

'Don't be stupid.'

'Then what?'

'Come with me,' she said.

I followed her back to the Japanese-style room. A section of the tatami was splattered red with blood.

'You see the photos on the walls in here?'

'Yeah.'

'Well, they're all by Araki Nobuyoshi.'

'So?'

'So stop being snooty and listen. Women go to him and he takes their photograph. At least, I think that's how it works. He sleeps with a lot of them, too, from what I gather. But afterwards he takes great photographs. I like the fact women go to him. That's my point. He doesn't tie up moaning models. Well, maybe he does. But he also ties up women who have decided to be tied up. The government arrests him for obscenity and the feminists get upset, call him a misogynist, but if women go to him, aren't they only doing as they please? Isn't there a perverse liberation in choosing to be 'obscene'? In choosing to be vulnerable? There's such beauty in some of these photos.'

'What does this have to do with you hanging yourself?'

Mami rolled her eyes and pointed to a large camera on a tripod tucked in a corner of the room. I had failed to notice it. Suddenly I understood.

'The thing in your hand,' I said. 'It was a remote?'

'I tried to keep hold of it. In fact, that's why I only got one hand up under the noose. But my body wouldn't allow it. It requisitioned the free hand, threw it up the rope. Were it not for that we'd have photos.'

'Maybe you could've mailed one to Nobu-what's-his-face,' I said nastily, sinking down against the wall.

'Maybe.'

'Assuming you lived.'

Mami crossed the room and picked up the remote control. She held it aloft as evidence, then tossed it to where I sat.

'You owe me one hell of an apology,' I said. But even requesting this I knew it was pointless.

'Pure madness!'

'Why?'

'You almost killed me.'

'I didn't string you up. You strung you up.'

'Yes, but the whole thing was safe so long as I didn't rattle that chair.'

'Which you did—the moment you thought someone was coming.'

'To get down.'

'You're telling me you never planned to kill yourself?'

'Of course not. I wanted to see the photo. To do that, I had to survive it. It was a private experiment.'

'Then you should have left me out of it.'

'I should have,' Mami said, surprising me. 'But it was too tempting to see if you'd come. Let's go for a walk. I want to show you something.'

'Not today.'

'Yes today.'

I collected painkillers for my headache and a few tissues for my nose. My health insurance had expired months earlier so there was little I could do but self-medicate. I followed Mami to the door where she spun unexpectedly.

'By the way, you can't come back here.'

'Why not?'

'The manager.'

'The hotel manager?'

Mami nodded. 'I promised him you'd never enter the building again and in return he promised not to tell my father about you.'

'What have I done?'

'Apparently you abused a maid. Something had her on strings. They're furious. I saved you. You don't under-stand how hard it is to get my father's employees to lie to him. Or even just omit sections of the truth. If my father found out about half the things I do, like the noose, he'd lock me up.'

'He should.'

Mami, oddly dressed down in jeans and a T-shirt, led me from the hotel to the Imperial Palace East Garden, a five-minute walk. We crossed a murky green moat, then passed beneath a tall wooden gate, inspecting a guard house which had once housed a hundred armed guards. From here the road into the garden was steep. Mami walked up each incline without difficulty, countering my belief she was unfit, and all the while refusing to tell me where we were going, what she wanted to show me. We crossed a number of open, perfectly manicured lawns to a large stone structure reminiscent of a wartime bunker.

'This is part of the castle tower from the 1630s,' she said. 'I'm pretty sure it was the tallest castle in Japan.'

'A history tour?'

Mami pointed back towards her hotel.

'No. I look out over the thing every day. Eventually I started asking questions, bought a book which I'm still reading, one chapter a year—*The Complete History of Japan*. Do you like history?'

'Not much, no.'

Mami laughed. 'There's that honesty again. Most people would have said yes to that question. It sounds better. But I'm like you. I find it hard to stick at history books. I only bought the one I have because I wanted to learn about this garden. That and because history books are good procrastination. I never feel like I'm wasting time reading *The Complete History of Japan*.'

'Just what exactly do you put off doing?'

'Study.'

'You're at university?'

'No.'

'Then what?'

'I'm between school and university.'

'Which means?'

'Which means I attend private classes.'

'For what?'

'Application tests.'

'To?'

'Universities. Well, one. Tokyo University.'

'And how long have you been doing this?'

'Two years. I could get in with a little help from my father but I don't want to, not just yet. Since there's no rush for me to get my degree or enter the workforce I can take my time with it, enjoy it. Quite a few people do that, take a year or more to get into university. I figure why not three? This is the rest of my life we're talking about and I'm quite happy to put it off. I do as little as possible most days. I'm not a bit like the Crown Princess Masako, depressed because she had to give up her diplomatic career and befuddled by the pointlessness of royal life. I don't understand her at all, her nostalgia for work. You'd hope at least royals could do nothing in this world without being made to feel inadequate.'

We walked on in silence, occasionally stopping to inspect plants or signboards, and when we came to the exit it appeared to be roughly opposite the entrance. A bored guard, resplendent in his palace uniform, asked for the tags issued upon entry. Mami handed them over with an automatic smile and we were waved through.

This exit led us onto a wide old bridge. It was a solid, sturdy mass of stone jutting from the perimeter wall and crossing the moat, dividing it cleanly in two. We moved to the left and peered down. In the water below heavy carp flapped along stone walls, churning the edges white. Some of these giant fish were a dull grey, others orange. Mami rested her arms on the railing. Unlike the tourists surrounding us she had no interest in the water. She looked diagonally across the moat towards a high wall on the Tokyo side.

'I jumped off that once,' she said. 'That's what I wanted to show you.'

'I don't believe you.'

'I did.'

I looked at her carefully, at her lips, searching for evidence of a smile. But there was not a trace of a curve there. She stared at the wall. Made of solid stone blocks, it ran from the city side of the bridge out into the distance.

'You're crazy, but not that crazy,' I said. 'That must be at least ten metres high.'

'I promise you, I did.'

'Why the—?'

'Because of a feeling.'

'A feeling? What sort of feeling could make you do that?'

Mami glanced across icily. 'What feeling? The same feeling that clogs my throat, makes my heart thud and sucks my lungs flat. That's what sort of feeling.'

'I've never had it.'

'When I get that feeling, I cry,' Mami said. 'I lock myself inside and I cry. Weeks pass with me just crying. I don't go to my classes and I hardly eat. And when crying does nothing to stop it, I do something crazy. The craziest thing I can think of.'

Though sincere, I had the sense Mami was delighting in all this, like a child picking at a scab to keep a prized wound. I tried to picture her running and leaping from the wall but could not see it. For starters, there were three guards at the far end of the bridge. Had the water been deep enough for her to survive, and had she been able to climb back up, they would surely have arrested her.

'Were you arrested?'

'I did it late at night. I chose a dark spot without guards, somewhere I could get a good run up, then I walked away and practised my jump.'

Mami found a rubber band in her pocket and wound it around two fingers. 'I was scared because I knew I was going to do it, that I had to do it. Once the idea was in my head as a way to feel better, it wasn't my choice anymore.' She flicked the rubber band. It shot from her hand and, losing momentum, fell to the water. Carp surfaced from the deep green, their ugly mouths gulping.

'After that I jumped,' she said. 'I was lucky. Overstep and I would've tumbled down. Jump too early and I wouldn't have made it. It's steep but nowhere near vertical.'

I dabbed at my nose with a tissue. 'Did you touch the bottom?'

Mami smiled. 'That's a secret.'

'How did you climb back up?'

'I'm not telling.'

'Because you don't know!'

'No. I know,' she said. 'I know because I did it. If you want to know, you do it.'

The Rainy Season

A week after Mami's make-believe suicide, Harry asked for another loan. His second request was far more substantial than his first—100,000 yen.

'I thought you had money,' I said, feeling yet more sweat leak onto my slippery face.

'I do. I still have most of the first transfer, but I haven't been able to finalise the second. The Japanese bank I'm dealing with keeps wanting to charge a fortune. It's a lot of money to move. I want to get it right.'

'I see.'

'My grandmother left it to me about five years ago,' Harry went on, as if to justify his worrying. 'I wasn't going to use it. But as soon as I landed here I knew.'

'Knew what?'

'Knew there was no point in slumming it. With a little capital, Japan's ripe. I'm only staying in Nakamura's as long as I have to.'

We crossed the road outside the convenience store and

sat on an old staircase. We had taken to using this staircase for eating. Harry peeled back the plastic wrapping on his bento box, then lifted the transparent lid.

'Shit,' he said, putting the meal aside. 'It's hot. They really microwaved it, huh?'

'You complained that it wasn't hot enough last time.'

'I didn't know they'd understand.'

I laughed, feeling a stabbing pain in my bandaged nose. 'When do you need this money by?'

'Today, if possible. I have the chance to buy toilet seats. They're fully heated and they're cheap, which is exactly what I want. Once I have them the pressure's off. I can get in touch with the guy I know in Ohio—the builder.'

'Ohio?'

'Ohio's dying not to feel the cold, unlike Hawaii. I'll need this money for a week. After that I'll repay you 125,000 yen plus a complete set of porn novels, since this is no small favour.'

At that moment it began to rain in earnest, first with a few heavy drops and then as a vertical torrent. The sky above Tokyo had been working itself up to this release. Depthless cloud, hanging thick and low, had blotted out all blue, and occasional hesitant drizzle had only driven the humidity higher, until the city felt set to burst.

Without giving it any further thought—as if this rain were a sign—I decided to take a risk. After all, how could it hurt? I had no reason to distrust Harry. He had repaid my first loan and was serious about money. If worst came to worst I would only lose $1000. People everywhere put far more on the line.

'It's yours for a week,' I said, water beginning to seep through my clothing.

'You don't mind lending it?'

'Not at all.'

'Great. I'll pay you back 125,000 yen in seven days.'

I shook Harry's hand distractedly. With the rain in my eyes and mouth as I looked up into the grey-white sky, my clothes sodden, I did not care about money. The weather had commandeered all reason. I grinned happily at the forces involved.

'How about that,' I heard Harry say beside me, voice a whisper.

'How about that,' I agreed.

My euphoria was short-lived. Humid Tokyo quickly irritated me. The liberal splashing of hot pink onto everything from computers to anti-constipation ads, the lack of consensus on which side of the footpath to walk, the drunken businessmen who fell asleep on crowded trains and let their bodyweight rest on those around them, the use of phones on pushbikes and the fearsome, iridescent lights which tumbled up and down wall-sized ads or burst from nowhere like silent explosions, all infuriated me. I wanted to switch the city off.

Harry went ahead and bought his toilet seats. The stack of cardboard boxes sat in his room, awaiting a next move. I was waiting, too. Rather than pay me back Harry had let the deadline slip, and I was beginning to get the uneasy sense there never would be any money.

'We have to celebrate,' he said, early one evening.

All I wanted was my 125,000 yen, but I thought it best to placate him. 'Celebrate what?'

'The toilet seats.'

We had wandered from the hostel down towards the fish markets where an older Japan—or traces of it—still lingered. Instead of immaculate department stores with well-groomed staff there were only stalls. Various fish—some packaged, some freshly sliced, others swimming—were on offer. Short, vaguely rural types with overalls and gumboots busied themselves inside and around the different shops, pulling in the bright canopies which extended into the narrow street or hefting up sloshing polystyrene crates. Children ran about waiting for their parents to finish up. At one table, a frowning old man speared eels through the head with a metal spike before slicing their writhing bodies into manageable slabs.

'Celebrate how?' I asked.

'A snack bar.'

I stared along the stark, small buildings above the stalls, all one room wide, many aluminium and rusted out like the hostel. A nearby two-stroke motor pained my ears. It would, I knew, be a blessing to leave the markets and exchange them for the curve of a female body, for the softness of a female face, even if this femininity came at a price and was a thinly veiled fraud.

'Fine,' I said.

'How about that.'

We walked on. It was almost dark, the sky lit by planes. I decided not to take Harry all the way into the city. It was too far. There was a place nearby—nothing special, but satisfactory. If he wanted more he was on his own.

'By the way,' Harry said, 'do you have my watch?'

'Shit, I completely forgot about that.'

'But you have it?'

'No, I lost it.'

'When?'

'It fell off when I was running to Mami's hotel. Sorry.' I contemplated offering to replace it but on account of the outstanding debt said nothing more.

I led Harry into a small building roughly the shape of a cigarette lighter. We waited for the lift to descend and stepped in. I pressed a pink button and we clunked up to a pink floor. There was hardly room to stand, so cramped was this atrium. Harry pulled open a door with 'Casanova's' written on it in a fancy, flowing script I found difficult to read.

'You been here before?' he asked.

'No.'

'How do you know about it?'

'Heard of it.'

The staff chimed a collective welcome and a middle-aged woman, Asian but with blonde hair, greeted us, bowing. I looked around. The drink bar was roughly the size of a chopping board. There were five tables: three out in the open, and two backed up against walls with couches, forming booths. Of these booths, the closest was occupied by a pair of dissimilar businessmen, one well into his sixties, the other in his twenties. The older man was inebriated. Drunkenness showed in his eyes, which—though he was looking at me—seemed to focus on a point somewhere behind my head. I nodded to him, annoyed by his gaze, and he looked away sluggishly.

The booth beside these two men was free and I made a point of staring at it.

'Everything's pink,' Harry said. 'Why pink?'

'Pink's girly.'

The woman with blonde hair gestured towards the empty booth. She was wearing a smooth, tight-fitting dress which thrust her small breasts forward and up.

'Table,' she said in English.

'Thank you.' I ordered a jug of beer and Harry sat down beside me.

'What happens now?' he asked.

'Someone—a girl—will come and sit with us. She'll tell us how wonderful we are and, if you're lucky, let you feel her breasts.'

'The blonde woman?'

'Someone a lot younger.'

'Good.'

'It doesn't worry you that we're being played?' I asked after a moment.

'No.'

Harry stood, crossed to a cigarette machine and purchased a packet of cigarettes. He unwrapped them and lit up. Taking a pretentious, contemplative drag as he returned to the table, he said, 'I don't have an objection to any of this, even to prostitution for that matter. If a woman wants to sell her body, as far as I can see that's her right. Just like if a man wants to sell *his* body that's his right. By extension, anyone who wants to pay for these services, well, that's their business. I'm not religious. I don't have God or anything like that muddling me up, so it's easy to see things in simple, shall we say … economic terms.'

'You've been to a brothel?'

'Many.'

'And you enjoy them?'

'You sound more interested than disgusted.'

'I am.'

'Okay. All but one,' Harry declared.

'Which one?'

'This girl in Thailand. She wasn't wearing anything but underpants, I remember. No top and great little tits. Anyway, halfway through this hand job she makes me put on a condom and straddles me. She hardly spoke English. I went along with it for a while, until sure.'

'Of?'

'A bad vibe. That may sound strange but I think of the world as waves—energy waves. Everything in life is made up of waves and waves always take the easiest path. It's all a lot more complicated than that and I won't get into it now, but that's the basic idea. The waves you're giving out, sitting here across the table, affect me; and the ones I'm giving out, in part a reaction to yours, affect you. If you jump up and tell me I'm a prick for screwing some Thai girl then I get bad vibes. I can either take the easy path, which is to get pissed off, or I can resist and keep on giving out good waves. Again, overly simplistic, but you get the idea.'

'Maybe.'

'The vibes I got from this girl were bad and I knew it had to do with me. I was upsetting her, even though she didn't show it. I don't believe in a god, like I said, but I do believe in karma. And my breed of karma dictates that those who dish out bad waves without due cause get the same back. Maybe not then and there, but sooner or later.

Why? Because waves always take the easiest path. So I told this girl no, paid and left. Even gave her a tip.'

'You felt bad?'

'Yeah. But let me be clear: prostitution—the idea of prostitution—wasn't the problem. The problem was bad karma. With another woman at another time I might've had a ball and gotten great vibes. Hell, I have on countless occasions. So there's your proof.'

I did not have time to question Harry about any of this. A young girl who I doubted was even twenty years old brought us our jug of beer. She laughed somewhat nervously at the sight of us, two foreigners sitting expectantly.

'I don't speak much English,' she said in Japanese.

Through her top I could discern the outline of her nipples, and her white denim pants appeared to have been made for a child. The way she laughed when I spoke, I might well have been the first man she had ever talked to. She sat and we all tried to communicate. But she did not stay long: with her youth and put-on naivety she was in high demand. The blonde woman quickly moved her to a table which had filled with five young Japanese men in exaggerated hip hop outfits, who welcomed her with open arms. They took a direct, hands-on approach, and though her eyes remained almost closed she remembered to giggle.

Fifteen minutes later, when we ordered a second jug of beer, an older girl came and sat with us. She proved to be sour-faced, although Harry got her to smile once or twice. She had narrow eyes which conveyed distrust and maybe contempt. Stuck for things to talk about we took to guessing each other's age. She guessed mine at twenty-five and—though I would have put her at thirty—I offered twenty-four in return. This set her small mouth in an unattractive pout. Apparently she wanted me to believe she was nineteen, which I was happy to do since it made no difference—I disliked her whatever age she was.

Harry eventually had me ask this second girl if he could squeeze her breasts. She shrugged, picked up Harry's lit cigarette and enjoyed a drag. Harry took this to be a yes. He went ahead and did as he pleased until the girl protested and the blonde-haired woman came over to move her to another table. Feeling genuinely awkward, I offered up the best apology I could, but no one was interested in hearing it. The girl Harry molested hated me for suggesting she was twenty-four far more than she did Harry for thrusting his hand towards her crotch, and the blonde woman wanted us to shut up and drink her exorbitantly priced beer.

'No bad vibes?' I asked Harry while we waited for a third girl.

'Yeah,' he said. 'But I took the easiest path—or my waves did.'

The last girl to sit with us stayed quite a while and Harry kept his hands largely to himself. He again appointed me translator, though this girl understood his questions well enough in English. So long as he talked about sex it seemed she had all the vocabulary and slang she needed. In halting English she told us she loved our eyes, our white skin and hair. She confessed to secretly wanting to sleep with foreigners and I believed her until she told Harry he looked like Brad Pitt.

'Really?' he asked, butting out his umpteenth cigarette and grinning. 'Brad Pitt. That's horseshit but don't stop there.'

When it came time to pay, Harry went to the toilet. I handed over about 10,000 yen for five jugs of beer. The establishment—like most snack bars—had taken the supermarket price and multiplied it by ten. I dropped the money on the counter with a sigh and took the lift back down.

'How did you like it?' I asked when Harry finally stepped into the steamy evening air.

'Great.'

I waited for more but he said nothing about the bill. He instead pulled his jacket collar up and, with his hands deep in his jean pockets like some balding, midget would-be James Dean, started off down the alley.

Two days later Phillip appeared at my door. 'Bored?' he asked.

'Yeah. You finished with JR?'

'A couple of weeks ago. Just got back from Guam.'

'Guam?'

'Guam.' But he did not explain. 'The posters are up. C'mon. You need to get out.'

We made our way into the city. Svelte women in miniskirts handed out plastic fans smeared with ads and Phillip made a point of conversing briefly with each. The air both inside and outside the station hung thick and still. People, most walking as if carrying an unseen boulder, dabbed attentively at their foreheads with handkerchiefs.

'How was Australia, anyway?' he asked as we made our way through a surging tide of bodies towards the Yamanote Line. 'How was Tilly? You didn't tell her about Mami?'

'No,' I said, searching for a way to avoid the topic. 'So how does this work? Are you the new face of JR?'

'Something like that. It's kind of a two-way deal. Here in Japan I'm advertising these Freedom Pass things. And overseas they'll use me to help sell discount packages to foreigners. They want the retiree market. You know—safe but exotic Japan, temple-hopping, a little drum-banging then home.'

'Good money?'

'Outstanding. Though for a moment I didn't think I'd see it. They sprung a medical.'

'A drug test?'

Phillip paused, letting a gaggle of loosely uniformed, self-absorbed high school students pass. One nudged him anyway.

'Can't have been—I passed. I think it was a medical to make sure I'd be around for a few more years. They're keen to have me do a string of these things.'

'So what was the problem? Why were you worried?'

Phillip shrugged. 'Truthfully,' he said, 'they couldn't find my heart.'

'You're joking.'

'I'm not.'

'Talk about incompetent.'

'Actually, it's not entirely their fault. It's on the wrong side. The tip of my heart's on the right side of my chest. Liver and spleen, too.'

'Backwards?'

Phillip nodded. 'It took them a while to track everything down.'

'Did you know about this?'

'Of course. I was born with it. DSI.'

'DSI?'

'Dextrocardia with Situs Inversus. Back-to-front guts. It sure baffled the Japanese doctor. There were lots of meetings. Eventually JR figured out it made no difference.'

At the ticket gates Phillip pressed his complimentary Freedom Pass to the flashing sensor. It beeped and opened compliantly. I had to buy a conventional ticket.

We boarded the train and Phillip's ad was everywhere. Dressed in a flashy suit he held up the new Freedom Pass. The message was clear even without being able to read the Japanese. Phillip was standing inside a busy metropolitan station while behind him stressed-out Japanese commuters battled to get through the ticket gates with regular, stamp-sized tickets.

'Like it?' he asked.

'I want one of those passes.'

'Good.'

Around us a few Japanese commuters made the connection between the blond standing beside me and the man in the glossy ads. They tapped friends and whispered.

Because we had no plans, we got off at Akihabara and followed the English signs 'To Electric Town'. When we stepped outside it was dusk. Buildings were lit but their lights were weak against the still-bright sky. Across the street the Sato Musen store's escalators ran diagonally up one wall, each atop the next and all encased in bubbled glass, people standing patiently on every level. In front of us, banners hung from streetlamps and flapped loudly in the evening breeze. And at a nearby white-striped crossing a grumpy-looking man unloaded a beeping delivery truck, wrestling boxes into the street like each was a troublesome drunk.

After wandering for a few minutes we entered a McDonald's for coffee.

'Have you met that new guy on our floor?' I asked, pouring in cream.

'Harry?'

'Yeah.'

'He introduced himself a while back,' Phillip said. 'A con artist.'

I sat up straight. 'Why do you say that?'

'He asked me for a loan.' Phillip shook his head. 'Don't give him the time of day.'

My stomach churned.

Three hours later I was pressing the phone to my ear so hard it hurt.

'I'm more just ringing to find out if you're coming back,' I said.

There was a soft groan at the other end of the line and I immediately regretted calling her.

'I don't know,' Tilly said. 'Probably.'

'When?'

'Sooner rather than later.'

'Tilly, what's going on?' I felt it was time to ask. 'I'm sorry to put you on the spot but I need to know. It was great seeing you, don't get me wrong, but things … they … they …'

'Felt different?'

'Right.'

'That's not your fault. It's nothing to do with you.'

'Meaning what?'

'There are things you don't know, Noah—about my family, about Dad.'

'Then tell me.'

'I will.'

'Not some day, Tilly. Today. You hardly ever contact me and you're always cagey when you do—what the hell am I meant to think?'

Tilly said nothing.

'Please, Tilly.'

I felt angry with her then, as if I was being made a fool of. I had placed the call from the train station and ran my eyes over the pairings that passed me, people sensible enough not to conduct their relationships from different ends of an ocean.

'You know he drinks.' The quiet voice at the other end of the line was hesitant.

'What?'

'Dad. You know he drinks, that he's an alcoholic. I've told you that.'

I had no clear recollection of ever having heard such a thing, but said yes.

'And you know,' Tilly continued, 'how Mum died.'

'Yes.' This particular secret I had been let in on—cancer.

Tilly again fell silent. I had the impression that if I said anything—even one word—she would discover a way to skip over everything and round up the call.

'You can't see it but Dad has bad burns. They're on his

body. When that happened all the drinking finally came to an end. Throughout my high school years he was sober, or close enough. But he's drinking again. Not all the time.'

'What caused the burns?'

'That's kind of a long story.'

'I don't mind.'

Another lengthy silence. My breathing was loud in my ear until she sighed and went on.

'Mum hated the hospital. All cancer patients do, I guess. After a while it just becomes a prison. There's hardly a draft of air, everyone's sick and dying, and it's difficult. When you have a terminal illness, befriending other terminally ill people only to watch them die isn't always the best idea. Well, I don't think it is. Mum did it though. At first it was a support but after it happened twice Mum wanted to come home, even if it meant dying on the way. That put pressure on Dad. The farm was doing badly and I was still really young—eleven years old. He was basically Mum's nurse. A woman visited sometimes but she could never stay. This farm's too cut off and she had a hundred others she had to help.'

I had never heard Tilly talk so candidly.

'Dad did amazingly well, you know, but no one can be perfect when things are messed up. They weren't married but basically he was losing his wife, his best friend. And at the same time he was trying to run the farm and get me to the bus for school and everything. He had nowhere to hide—nowhere that was his. So he drank. He'd always done it to relax, and it was natural to him to keep on doing it.'

A Japanese man in a bland-looking suit stopped a

metre in front of me. He put his briefcase down on the floodlit station floor, waiting for the phone.

'The problem was,' said Tilly's soft voice, 'drinking only stressed him. He'd get in these funks and growl at Mum, then regret it because who knew how long they had. By the time Mum was really sick he was drinking almost every day, trying to prop himself up.'

The businessman tapped his foot and checked his watch before glancing towards the train timetable. I shook my head.

'I was thirteen when Mum died. It's true what they say about thirteen, about it being unlucky. At first Dad did pretty well. The funeral and everything helped keep him sober. It gave him things to arrange and people to talk to. Then all that finished. There was nothing left to do. That was when we both finally knew Mum was dead.'

For a long while, as the businessman tapped one polished shoe, neither Tilly nor I said a word. I waited for more.

'Not long after Mum passed away I heard a noise in the front yard. It woke me. It was late at night. Dad had gone and piled up everything that belonged to Mum. I think he just needed another job, something more to do. But he was also drunk.'

'He was still drinking after she died?'

'Yeah, he started again after the funeral. I watched him splash lawnmower fuel all over this pile he'd made— furniture, photo albums, clothes, mugs, a guitar, a record collection … There was nothing of Mum's left inside the house.'

'And he lit it?'

'The pile just shot up. There was this whoosh and he covered his face with his hands, then it swallowed him for a moment. He fell, screaming, started rolling around like a madman.'

'What did you do?'

'Nothing. I couldn't move.'

'You didn't run outside?'

'Dad rolled on the ground till the flames were out then staggered into my room. He smelt of burnt hair. He told me to call triple-zero. Then I put him under the shower.'

The payphone beeped.

'I'm running out of money.'

'I'm finished anyway,' Tilly said. 'That's the whole story more or less. After that, he went to AA. For a long time he was great. He cheered up without booze, was a model father.'

Another loud beep.

'Listen, the payphone's going to cut out. I'm sorry, I should have—'

'Now do you understand?'

'Understand what?' I asked.

'I forgave him for the fire because I could see it marked an end to something bad, not just to good things. So it scared me coming home and seeing the bottles. He's back in the AA meetings. He doesn't like them but they help. I've got him back on Diet Coke and I don't want to see—'

The phone cut out without another warning beep.

'Shit.'

I hung up and the businessman stepped in, nudging me aside. By the time I bought a new card there was no answer at the farm.

Lexington Queen

Harry got laid.

Although this took place in the room next to mine it might as well have been a threesome. I heard everything —every grunt, every moan, every whispered request and every thank you. I lay on my back listening. The lucky girl, whoever she was, was not afraid to squeal and snort like some pained animal. She seemed unable to decide which sound best articulated her release. They would finish only to start up again minutes later, lasting a commendable half-hour each time.

Around dusk, quite exhausted, I went in search of a cheap meal. I found a largely deserted family restaurant, ordered a bowl of potato wedges and sat wondering what to do with the night ahead. After eating I paid the bill and began to walk without a destination in mind. A man with greying hair passed by on an old-fashioned bicycle. The type of bike was common in Tokyo; what caught my eye was the way he held a tray on the palm of one hand like a waiter.

I tried to see what was on this tray, but he whipped past me with a single sharp sounding of his bell and disappeared around a corner. I walked on, staring into apartments as I once had with Harry until, tired and with sore feet, I found my way back to the hostel.

Outside, a girl from the hostess bar—the young naive one—was smoking a cigarette. Though I saw a flicker of recognition in her eyes, she ignored me. I decided it likely this girl had come from Harry's room and guessed her to be his partner in the earlier activities. She wore stilettos, a skirt and tight-fitting top, just as she had while working. Her make-up was applied thickly, and with it she had accomplished a degree of prettiness without revealing too much of herself. I wondered if she was a prostitute, my interest purely fiscal. There was the question of my loan. By now I had little faith in the Ohio-bound toilets.

Stepping into my room I found Mami at my desk, writing a letter. She jumped up, alarmed, then suddenly angry. 'Don't creep up!'

My spirits leapt at the sight of her. Her eyes were puffy as though she had been crying. She picked up the pen she had been using and clicked it a number of times.

'I wanted to leave you a note and the door wasn't locked.'

'You can't keep coming here,' I said, without meaning it.

'You came to the hotel.'

'My girlfriend's coming back.'

'Listen to you ...' She laughed mockingly. 'Such a player.'

'I'm serious.'

'Just tell me when she comes back and I'll never visit again. But until then, can I sit? I'm tired.'

I gestured towards the bed and Mami sat down. Every item of clothing and every accessory she wore had been selected to convey something—an aloofness perhaps. Her hair was raked back and fastened in a ball behind her head. She had applied an almost white foundation to her face and used a blue lipstick and purple eyeliner. With such additions her skin appeared illusory, her features muted, leaving her with the cold, expressionless face of a porcelain doll. Yet it was not a generic face. Not like the girl outside. It spoke instead of flair, the sort of flair required to make oneself inhuman.

Her clothing completed this carefully sculpted statement. She wore ruby-red high-heeled shoes, purple stockings, a ruffle-edged slip, a silk dress and a thick, dark cashmere coat which fell to just below her shapely knees.

'You're all dressed up,' I said.

'With nowhere to go.'

'Why the make-up? Why so much of it?' I hesitated, then clumsily added, 'You're pretty without it.'

Mami laughed. 'You think that's why I wear it?'

'I don't know. Why do you wear it?'

'I saw something similar in a back issue of *Vogue* today and decided to put it together. I added and subtracted things though, so it's more an "inspired by". Not all mine and not all theirs, whoever they may be. In this case, Marc Jacobs, Miu Miu and Yoshi Yamamoto. Today's little project.'

'I like it.'

'Or you're glad I like it, right?' Mami smiled. 'That's what my father would say.'

'Really?'

'A practical man. When he sees me dressed up like this he always shakes his head, smiles and says, "I'm glad you like it". That—aside from the fact he pays for all of it without question—is his best attribute, I'd say.'

'He's quite conservative?'

'Conservative … no. He pretends to be in all his meetings, I think. He has to do that. But he despises conformity. That's why he became a businessman.'

'How does that work?'

'True freedom lies in money. If you don't have money, you conform to things. You have to.'

'What about his meetings and clients? Isn't that conforming?'

'In a way. But a little conformity at the office means he can fly to Europe in a private jet. That's freedom. Don't try and tell me you're free here in this glove compartment of a room, because you're not.'

'There are worse places than this room.'

'Maybe,' Mami said.

'You sound like you want to say "but".'

'Well, take a look around.'

'True. Your father has it all worked out by the sound of it.'

'Yes and no. Sometimes I think he has a little too much freedom. He's very pig-headed and he's always right even when he's wrong. For example, once he makes up his mind about someone he never changes it. If he doesn't like you right away he never will.' Mami paused, then added, 'Though I wouldn't mind being more like that. I come and go with people. One day I don't like them and the next I do. I can't tell you how I'll feel about you tomorrow. For a long while I was angry with you.'

'With me?'

She nodded, running the very tip of her tongue across light-blue lips. 'Not just you, but with everyone else, too.'

'But me especially?'

'In a way. You almost killed me. But in another way, no.'

Mami stood and took up her perch on my windowsill, half in, half out. For a while she stared at the one or two stars and scattered airliners visible in the Tokyo sky. Then without a word she climbed down and stretched. 'Things have been bad,' she said. 'I had that feeling I told you about, and I like that you left me alone. But now I need to shrug it off. If you help, I'll return that denim jacket. Do you have a cigarette?'

'No.'

'Very well,' she said, sounding almost English. 'We'll get some on the way.'

'On the way where? I'm actually quite tired.'

'You're always tired. You can't sleep, remember? Why not be tired somewhere other than here for a change? Don't you ever get sick of your ceiling?' Mami had not brought a bag but looked around for one all the same before leading me outside.

'I don't care where we go,' she said, calling a taxi from her mobile phone.

'You don't have anywhere in mind?'

'No.'

We waited for the taxi and, when it came, climbed into the back seat. The driver turned and asked Mami for a destination, but she informed him that she was Thai, that she could not speak a word of Japanese. She pointed to me and set about slipping on light-blue gloves which she had produced from nowhere, and which matched her lipstick perfectly. The driver looked at me dubiously. He raised plucked eyebrows.

'Roppongi,' I said, because it came to mind. He spun around and thrust the car into gear.

'Where are we going in Roppongi?' asked Mami.

'I don't know. You know the area better than me.'

'I doubt it. It's not the first suburb to roll off my tongue at night.'

'Then you should have directed the driver.'

I stared out the window. Office buildings scrolled past. They were tightly wedged together and well lit. There was a light rain blurring the convenience stores and traffic lights we passed. The driver, alternately steering and checking a global positioning system on the dash, tuned the radio into a Japanese talkback station.

Mami yawned and glanced across at me. 'Don't get all sleepy,' she said. 'Not yet.'

Arriving in Roppongi, we made our way through a number of bars, ending up at Lexington Queen. We walked down a steep, dark staircase, at the bottom of which stood a heavyset bouncer all in black.

'How much?' Mami asked.

'Three thousand for him, two thousand for you.'

'All you can drink?' I asked, handing him the money.

He nodded and stamped our hands.

Mami put her coat in a locker and sealed it. On the walls around us there were pictures of celebrities visiting the club. In Melbourne these sorts of walls contained local TV personalities. But here they were all Hollywood's biggest stars—far too many to count.

The bar was staffed by two foreigners, both black and muscular, and the floor around it was packed with fittingly beautiful patrons. Off to the left was a dance floor which was filled to capacity. Some people danced in tight-knit groups, others alone. The lighting was low and there was a rustic, almost dirty feel to the place, like a cavern.

I ordered two vodka shots and beers as chasers.

'Why did you do this?' I yelled to Mami as we battled our way through the crowd, looking for a place to sit. We were nudged and bumped by waifs, drunk Japanese youths and big, thug-headed foreigners. My beer splashed onto my shirt as the music changed, and the people on the dance floor thrust their hands up and whooped. The venue was so overfilled it had come to a near standstill.

'Do what?' Mami shouted back over her shoulder.

'Bring me out?'

'I've told you. Because you're honest.'

'But—' I let a sumo wrestler pass with difficulty, then another. Both nodded their heads in thanks. The surrounding mass of bodies pushed me against Mami. My hand came to rest on her thigh. Our mouths were almost touching and I worried my breath was bad. 'But,' I tried again, 'why are you so desperate to hang out with someone honest?'

Mami shrugged. 'I'm tired of all my usual friends. And they're probably just as tired of me. They're rich. We all attend the same events and we all know the same people. I can tell you every word they'll say before they even say it and they can likely tell you the same about me.'

'And I'm different?'

'Very. I can detail myself to you. You're like a diary. You're not confident enough to try and play me, to lie, to be cruel. That's important because either I find people I can trust or I sit at home on my own. New people are a risk—men especially. Who wants to be some foreigner's exotic Japanese fling? Not me. I'm not saying I'm asexual. I'm just saying I don't want to be some dickhead's doll.'

The three foreign men who had been listening to this monologue, nudging ever closer to Mami, now looked away, eyes moving on, darting from woman to woman. Mami had, I suspected, raised her voice especially for them, because she now leant in and placed the tips of all five fingers to my elbow.

'This might sound mean and I'm not sure I should tell you, but basically I was looking for someone with no clue.'

I pulled my arm away. 'That was mean, yeah.'

'Wait, let me finish.' Mami took my arm back. 'In my world, my normal everyday world, everything is a competition. Every last thing is a contest. It's the same in your world, I'm sure. But we inhabit different worlds. In yours, wherever it is and whatever it is, I'd be lost. I'd have no idea. There'd be no way for me to know about it because I wasn't raised in it. At the end of the day we all only know one world—the one we grew up in.' Mami paused, thinking. She took a large gulp of beer as if satisfied with all she had said, then, swallowing, seemed to change her mind. 'Unless we're moved around a lot by our parents,' she added, 'which I wasn't. Not at all. Do you understand what I'm trying to say? I'm not saying it very well. A shame.'

'I think I understand.'

'Maybe you do. Maybe that's why you're in Japan. Maybe you're not ready to compete in your world so you're holidaying for a while. I don't know. I don't actually care.

All I know is, you know nothing about my world. That, and you can't keep anything from me. Two things which make you perfect.'

'For what?'

'For telling the truth to.' Mami, clearly tired of talking, peered down at her beer and suddenly frowned. 'Why am I drinking beer?'

I thought about my world in Australia, while Mami gave her beer to a Spanish-looking man and battled to order another vodka. There was nothing about this world of mine that Mami would not have understood. It occurred to me that the worlds she referred to were not staked out by borders, but by money. She had only used countries as an analogy to make herself understood without being cruel. And if I was a poverty-stricken pet project, a convenience, then presumably at some point she intended to cut me free.

She returned and, determined not to be angry with her, I struggled to convince myself I was a friend—a unique confidant and respite from her pressured life.

'I shouldn't have explained it,' she said, inspecting my face and handing me a drink. She looked over the dance floor. 'I want to leave.'

'You want to go home?'

'No, I just want to leave.'

We walked to a Family Mart convenience store. As we stepped inside two store clerks chimed their usual welcome. One was straightening magazines, the other standing behind the register intently filling out a docket. Evenly spaced fluorescent lighting had chased out all shadow, bathing the store in the sort of light more commonly encountered midway through a sunny morning.

'What are we doing here?' I asked.

'Getting supplies. Drinks.'

'To drink where?'

'Out in the street.'

'Classy.'

'Classier than that club you took me to.' She pulled off one ruby-red shoe and inspected its base.

'Are you drunk?' I asked.

'A little, I think. I get very drunk very easily. But that's not why I'm holding my shoe up in the air. It's got a stone in it. I'm sure of it.'

Mami turned the shoe upside down and flapped it but nothing fell out. With a sharp, satisfied nod she slipped it back on and dragged me across to the brightly labelled drinks fridge, filled with the usual Japanese beers and liquors.

She pointed to a pre-mixed gin and tonic. 'Tell me, Noah, have you ever stolen anything? Even something cheap?'

'No.'

'And why not?'

'It's wrong.'

'At least you're consistently dull. That's what you said about the train ticket.'

'So why ask me now?'

'Why?' Slightly unsteady, Mami looked at me, her eyes glazed. 'Because you're going to steal this gin and tonic. In fact, now that you ask, you're going to steal seven things from this store.' She held up seven fingers. 'Seven exactly.'

'I am not.'

'You are. You can ask why again if you want.'

'Why?'

'Because if you don't, I'm going to.'

'You're drunk.'

'What a rude thing to say. Shall I get started selecting my seven things? She slurred her words slightly. She was far more drunk than I had realised.

'Let's go, Mami. I'm sure they both heard everything.'

'Who? The store clerks? If their English was that good, they wouldn't be working here at … what time is it?'

'Well past midnight.' I started towards the door. Mami did not follow, but I went ahead and left anyway.

I sat outside on the pavement and tried not to think about her. If she got herself arrested, that was her problem. I could not be involved. I was not, after all, Japanese, and my father did not own a string of expensive hotels. He was struggling just to keep a car. There would be no fancy lawyers for me, no golden get-out-of-jail-free card.

When she failed to exit I stood and casually peered into the store. Mami had taken a basket and now floated down the aisles, occasionally placing things into it. But mostly she seemed interested in chatting with the sales clerks. One nodded and disappeared out back. Then the other followed, hurrying to meet the first. Without paying any attention to either, Mami rounded the end of an aisle and kept on walking. She passed straight through the front doors and out onto the footpath with the basket clasped in both hands.

It was the most brazen act of thievery I had ever witnessed.

'Now,' she said calmly, 'we run until we're completely lost.'

I felt angry and elated all at once, running. Delinquency had never been a strong point of mine, but I took to it well enough. I wrenched the basket from Mami's arm and followed her blindly. She pelted along on her high heels with amazing poise, especially for a drunk woman.

We finally slowed at a fish tank full of ghostly grey albino carp and stopped to rest on a metal staircase. Rusted out and with a heavy chain hanging across it, this staircase—like the building it belonged to—appeared unused. We slipped under it and sat sucking up the humid night air. My throat was gluey and my chest hurt. Mami glanced sideways and suppressed a smile. Then, without speaking, we both began to laugh, the sound echoing hollowly in the narrow, built-up street.

'I'm crazy?' Mami asked incredulously. 'You enjoyed it far more than me.'

'Tell me,' I said, trying to calm myself in order to articulate the question, 'when you jumped in that moat did it feel like this?'

'No.'

'No?' Still grinning, I shook my head. 'If you ask me, that's a bad deal. You jump in a moat to feel better and when you climb out, *maybe* you do. I'd want to be sure.'

Mami's smile faltered. 'You didn't ask me that. You asked if I felt like this. This is nothing. After the moat I felt invincible.'

'So it did work?'

'For a while. Until it was bad again and I needed

another ending. That's how it is. Sometimes you get given an ending, other times you have to make one.'

'By jumping in a moat?'

'I don't expect you to understand. You only ever get to see me like this. But I'm incredibly good at ending things.'

'It certainly seems—' I paused. A random thought had struck me. 'Fuck.'

'Fuck?'

'Cameras! The store would've had cameras. They would've been everywhere.'

'So?'

All pleasure at having committed a successful crime now turned on me. My stomach felt as if it were full of putrid milk. I stared at the basket. 'Throw all this crap away.'

'Calm down,' Mami said.

'They'll identify you, Mami. They'll fucking identify you, and then they'll identify me. Maybe you'll be okay, being Japanese, rich and clearly fucked in the head, but I'll be put away. They can hold me without a charge here. Do you understand what I'm telling you? We're in real trouble.'

Mami only grinned. 'I stole this basket full of nothing. It's mine. I'm not throwing anything away.'

I started at the concrete surrounding my feet, furious.

'Stop snorting and listen,' Mami said abruptly. 'Forget the cameras. They're nothing to worry about. If anyone ever asks you—which they won't—we met just before we walked in. You hit on me and I said no. Perfectly believable. Then you left and after that you don't know what happened. Noah, you're in the clear. And for what it's worth, so am I. Look at me. Look at this make-up. There were only two cameras in that store and I know where they both were.

I never went near them and I certainly didn't look at them. I've been doing this for a long time.'

She bent to withdraw two cans of gin and tonic from the basket, gave me one, then upended the rest of her booty onto the footpath. Drinks in hand, the aluminium still cool beneath our fingers, we stared at a splashing of potato chips, chocolate and beef jerky. I edged a few items around with one sneaker.

'To you,' she said, opening her can, then mine.

'To me?'

'For being funny.'

I took a grumpy swig.

Without drinking herself, Mami pulled out her mobile phone and pressed a button. She gave detailed instructions to the cab company in Japanese and, putting her arm under mine, hoisted me up. I took another quick swig.

'I organised a rendezvous with a cab driver I know,' she said seriously. 'Don't worry, we can trust him. But you're right, we'll need to lie low until all this blows over. There's a safe house I know. Well, a hotel really. It's perfect for—'

'I can't, Ma—'

'No names,' she said, gently putting a finger to my lips and then slipping it into my mouth. I was too confused to resist. To mask my discomfort I tried to look fed up, but in the end only went cross-eyed. Having felt the backs of my teeth, and ignoring my grunts of protest, Mami left the finger in place until at last we spotted the cab.

The First Breakfast of the Summer

The sun rose slowly. We both sat cross-legged, drunk, toes against the floor-to-ceiling window. Below us Tokyo was already in full swing. Faint car horns reached us. People marched. It felt like another world connected to me only by the loosest of threads, and my earlier panic, my fear at this world, at its omnipotence had—thanks to crime and alcohol—been replaced with a soft contempt for the supposed strength of societies, which sooner or later fell and were forgotten. I had snuck past the hotel front desk into a new world high above it all, a world entirely without rules.

'I have whisky,' Mami said, standing and stretching. 'I don't normally drink whisky but I feel like it. I'm not at all tired and I'll get a hangover if I stop drinking without going to bed. Did you know today's the very first day of summer? At least, I think it is. I'll change out of this and we'll have whisky for breakfast.'

Mami showered while I flicked through her heavily scratched CD collection, selecting something classical and sliding it into the machine. When she heard this she stuck her head out the bathroom door and, drying her face with a hand towel, frowned.

'Can you get the whisky?' she asked. 'Everything's right above the bar. Choose whichever one you think is best. There's ice in the fridge.'

'Do they restock that bar every day?' I asked, thinking about my last visit.

'Every week, I think. Why?'

'Just wondering.'

Mami started to close the bathroom door, turning back towards the mirror.

'One other thing,' I said. 'Why do you cram everything into this one room?'

'So I know where it is,' she called, eyes following my reflection. 'I don't have time to search the whole place.'

'But why not have it—'

'Just get the whisky.' She shut the door, voice suddenly muffled. 'I'll be out in a minute.'

I crossed to the bar, stepping behind it. I slid out the bottom section of the refrigerator and found ice in a plastic tray. Not knowing the first thing about whisky, I dropped the cubes into a metal bucket on a stand. Next I ran a finger across the bottles. The second to last was a single malt, which I seemed to recall was a good thing, so I set the bottle on the ice in the bucket.

It occurred to me to call room service. I had no idea what went with whisky, and chose strawberries, potato chips and cheese sticks.

'Certainly,' said the man on the other end of the line in crisp Japanese. I hung up, walked back to the bar and poured myself a frothy beer.

A moment later there was a knock at the door. I stared at it, amazed.

'Room service?' I called, but there was no answer. Hurriedly carrying the bucketed whisky over to the window, I shouted, 'Just a minute.'

Mami stepped from the bathroom, now dressed in baggy pyjamas. There was another loud knock.

'Who's at the door?' she asked.

'Room service.'

'What did you order?'

'Chips and cheese.'

'What a truly strange breakfast. And you've put the whisky on ice, I see. A lovely touch. I'll get the door in case it's that maid.'

She put on a long, white dressing-gown, did it up at the waist and walked to the door. I collected a pair of tumblers from the bar and, with nothing left to organise, flopped down at the window. Mami clicked back the lock.

'You must be Matilda,' she said after a pause. 'Please, come in. He's over at the window.'

Thinking back on it now, it ought to have been far more unpleasant. Tilly stepped inside and, scratching the back of one hand with the other, crossed to the window at which I sat. At first I remained seated, staring up, mouth open. Then I jumped to my feet. She looked tired, pale and weak. Her

eyes crawled over the whisky bottle, the tumblers and ice
bucket, but she said nothing. Mami, meanwhile, leant
against the wall beside the door, one leg crossed over the
other, hands behind her back. She did not turn off the stereo
or fidget, but remained perfectly still.

'Hi,' Tilly said.

I tried to smile but could only grimace. 'You're back.'

'I am, yeah.'

It was difficult to know what to do next. My feelings
were tangled. I wanted to run and stay put; wanted to
protest my innocence and apologise; wanted to ask Tilly
what right she had to spy and offer her a drink. As it was,
the last urge won out.

'Whisky?' I asked. Tilly let out a sharp laugh and
swung to look at Mami, who pushed herself up off
the wall and smiled. A warm smile, it did not gloat but
it did not apologise, either. Nor did it make light of the
situation. Instead it simply offered up courtesy—or
the potential for it—like a window through which Tilly
was as welcome to climb as throw a rock. Tilly seemed to
understand all this in a single, perfunctory glance, as
women do.

'Whisky would be nice,' she said, voice flat. 'Do you
have a spare glass?'

Mami nodded and retrieved a third tumbler from the
bar. Though pleasant and natural in her movements, there
was a coldness in her eyes when they caught mine. Clearly
she wanted everything discussed later—argued elsewhere,
far away. She took charge of the whisky, pouring it into the
glasses and scooping ice from the bucket. The sound of her
long-fingered, beautiful hand chasing this half-melted ice

like a tyre on gravel was, until she decided to speak, the only sound in the room.

'This is an Irish whisky,' she said as she passed a tumbler to Tilly.

'Is it?' Tilly peered into the glass without any real curiosity.

'A single malt,' I said, because it felt like a safe enough thing to say.

Tilly crossed the last few feet to the window and peered directly down. With every tick of the wall-clock behind us I expected her to spin and pitch the thick-based tumbler at my head. Thrown accurately and with a modicum of force, the thing held the potential to kill me. But she refrained.

'I decided to surprise you,' she said. She embedded these words in a sigh. 'After talking to you on the phone I decided I wanted to come back, whatever the cost. A mistake.'

I shrugged weakly. Somewhere behind us I heard Mami answer the door, murmur in Japanese and scratch a pen across paper. She brought the room service over, set it down in front of us and carefully removed the silver lids.

'I got in late last night,' Tilly continued. 'By the time I made it to the hostel, to our room, you weren't there.'

'Your keys,' I said, remembering Tilly had left them with me. 'I'm sorry.'

Tilly turned to Mami. 'I sat against the door for a few hours. Then, worried, I woke up our new neighbour to ask if he had any idea where Noah might be. He suggested here —"as a long shot". He had an envelope with your address on the back. When I asked him what Noah was doing in a hotel room he clamped up, seemed to think he'd said something wrong. Curiosity got the better of me after that. I'm sorry to have intruded.'

Hands trembling, Tilly took a gulp of whisky. She scrunched her eyes and swallowed it. Mami offered her a glass of mineral water.

'I'm sorry,' Tilly said, ignoring the offer, 'but I don't think we've met.'

'We haven't, no. I'm Mami, a friend of Noah's.'

'Matilda North.' Tilly dolefully eyed the whisky in her tumbler then poured the rest down her throat. 'I've been away.'

Mami was unflustered. 'Which is why we haven't met, I'm sure.'

'I'm sure. May I have another glass of whisky? I've finished this one.'

Mami nodded and smiled. I had the sense that under very different circumstances the two girls might well have liked one another. I watched as Mami pulled her long hair into a pony tail and tied it off with one of the countless rubber bands she seemed able to produce at any time. She poured out a hefty whisky and carried it to Tilly.

We all sat and sipped quietly at our drinks.

'Beautiful morning,' Tilly observed coolly.

I stared out over the Imperial Palace. Looking to distract myself I traced the moats glimmering in the early morning sun. It was an exceptionally clear morning. Often the sky above Tokyo was a smoky white in summer, too bright to stare into and yet simultaneously depthless and depressing. This morning, though, it was perfectly blue. A number of birds flew in formation, stretching away then collapsing back in on one another, like dough. They swung in close to the hotel, only to be drawn back towards the green of the palace grounds. Mami took out a pack of Mild Seven cigarettes and lit up, the acrid smoke filling my nostrils. I thought about her jumping into the palace moat, her thin arms flailing, her mouth open but soundless, her eyes wide, her legs kicking, her clothes climbing up her tense body. The sudden thought caused a smile.

'What are you smiling at?' Mami asked, the question like a slap.

'It's an odd hour to be drinking whisky.'

'It is that,' Tilly said, nodding sombrely. She was looking drunk.

The smoke from Mami's cigarette ran along the window. I watched it, wanting to smoke myself. But I refrained, refilling my glass instead. My second whisky tasted smoother and softer than the first. It fell down my throat and into my empty stomach like hot soup. Tilly, long-faced and without ever looking at my tumbler, matched me sip for sip. Sometimes she even managed two to my one.

I sensed an obligation to speak but nothing—no particular topic—was forthcoming. I felt like a soldier lying between two opposing trenches, out in no-man's-land, faking dead. One false move and I would get it between the eyes, if not from one side, then from the other. Or both. That was karma after all—well, karma according to Harry, who certainly had gone and fucked me over for no apparent reason. What would he make of the energy waves surrounding me now? Did I care?

I refilled everyone's drinks. We kept staring out the window, growing increasingly drunk and saying nothing for fear of an explosion. Mami stood at one point and changed the CD to jazz, but otherwise we were still.

Finishing her third whisky, Tilly, who normally never drank, stood unsteadily. The movement was abrupt and she thrust her hands out to the glass window to keep her balance. I leapt forward to pull her back from it but she somehow found the coordination to push me flat on my back. The hand that was still on the glass squeaked loudly when she pulled it away.

She rubbed one ear confusedly. 'Sorry,' she said. 'Really, I am. My balance is off. I should go.'

'I'll come with you then,' I said, doing my best to smile.

Tilly shook her head. 'No, just give me your key. You should stay.'

Mami jumped up.

'No, he'll go with you. Thank you for visiting, though.' Very uncharacteristically, she bowed, holding the show of deference for a few seconds before straightening. As if in reply, Tilly casually reached out and shook her hand.

Mami again smiled. 'It was a pleasure meeting you, Matilda.'

'I'm sure it was. But he'll stay here.'

Before I could determine what to do, Tilly let herself out, taking my key with her. She shut the door softly and left me staring drunkenly at strawberries, chips and cheese.

Mami went to bed without a word. She was not angry, simply disinterested.

Limbo

To return to Japan, Tilly had accepted a three-month position at a university, running classes for students who wanted to study English but who could not include the subject in their Engineering degrees. Since she already had accommodation in Japan, she turned down the company's fully furnished, outrageously priced apartment. She did, however, accept a return economy airfare, signing a contract which stipulated she would reimburse the cost of this if she failed to teach for the full three months.

I learnt all this when I finally dragged myself home from Mami's hotel, determined to salvage a little dignity by telling the truth.

'There's no way I'm changing all my plans,' Tilly said when I knocked on my own door and found it to be locked.

'I'm not asking you to,' I said, slotting the words in beneath a hinge. I had a jagged headache and wanted only to rest up for an hour before work. Syrupy Japanese medication, bought and gulped down on the way home, had only teased the pain in my forehead, provoking a sustained roar. I might just as well have gulped ink.

'Tell me about that girl.'

'She gave me a short massage once,' I said. 'That's all. That's the only physical contact there's ever been.'

Tilly unlocked the door and wrenched it open. 'Where?'

'What?'

'Where did she give you this massage?'

'That's not—'

'Point!'

Hesitantly, I pointed.

'You've got to be joking.'

The door slammed shut in my face with a small gust of air, as if from a set of bellows. The lock clicked back in place.

'I feel like a fool,' came a small wailing admission.

I gave up on honesty. 'I'm not interested in her, Tilly.'

'You really think I'm an idiot?'

'No. Can you open the door?'

To my surprise, Tilly did. Exactly enough to eyeball me with one fearsome eye. I backed away and lowered my head.

'I'm sorry,' I said.

'What am I supposed to do now?'

'We'll keep on sharing the room. Platonically.'

She snorted. 'You mean you don't want me to kick you out? This was my room, remember? You moved in here.'

'Fine,' I said. 'I'll move out then. Is that what you want?'

'Don't put on that haughty crap with me. You wouldn't last a night sleeping on the street. You'd be back again by morning.'

'You're right.' I did my best to look hangdog. 'I can't afford to move out. I don't know what I'll do but it's my own fault. I deserve it.'

Tilly opened the door a fraction wider. 'I'll let you stay one week. After that I expect you gone. Clear?'

'Thank you. That's kind.' I took one step forward, hoping to get in a nap, but Tilly shut the door, only to open it again and continue, 'And for this one week—which I can't believe I'm offering—I'll be in the bed and you'll be on the floor. And I'm throwing out this damn ticking wall-clock of yours which I can't stand. And when I'm tired the light goes out. Those are my conditions. Understood?'

'Understood. Can I come in?'

'Are you sorry?'

'Of course. I feel absolutely awful.'

'Good.'

And she slammed the door shut again.

I gave up on going to work and went instead to a local Yoshinoya restaurant, toying with a large bowl of *gyudon*. Propped up at the horseshoe-shaped counter I lifted strips of beef with my disposable chopsticks and dropped them back down onto the cold, tacky rice. The place was filled with other miserable men and we all tended to our depression without looking up except to order beer.

The first night under Tilly's new terms we both lay awake listening to one another breathe. I felt like a trapped cockroach. I dared not move, dared not rustle a sheet for fear of disturbing Tilly's pretend sleep. Once, quietly, I whispered her name, but she ignored me and deepened her breathing. In absolute desperation I passed the night trying to think of places I could move to. I did sum after sum inside my head. I concocted mock budgets. I lowered my sights. But as light crept into the room, birds chirping and dogs yapping back at them, I was no closer to a solution than I had been at midnight. I simply did not have the money for a down payment. I had blown most of my savings on an air ticket home and the loan to Harry.

A few hours later, to make matters worse, I managed to get myself fired.

It happened in Suzuki-sensei's class. Suzuki-sensei was a smelly sycophant who liked to hitch his denim jeans up around his nipples and show off his understanding of Western culture. He always gave me conflicting instructions in a single laboured breath, delivering hesitant, shy, raspy little soliloquies, sentences glued together with ineloquent *and*s.

The moment I arrived he went though the lesson plan with me.

'And then you say "hello", and then I will say "hello", and the first thing for you to say is "hi", and I say "hi", yes, and we will start the lesson, and you can decide when and to start? Can you? Okay. And you should decide the greeting and do it for me now.'

He turned to the class. 'We are welcoming Mr Noah again today.' He turned to me. 'Mr Noah …'

I stared at him blankly.

'Please,' he said, putting his palms together and pointing at me with the tips of both hands, his thin, gawky body circling around two gargantuan shoes.

'What?' I asked.

'Please,' he said again, 'like we discussed.'

'Hello everyone,' I said.

'Hi,' corrected Suzuki-sensei with an irritating little laugh and nervous tilt of the head.

Bored, the second graders wriggled like worms in heavy dirt.

'Please say, "Now we go",' said Suzuki-sensei.

'Now we'll go.'

'Now we go,' he corrected softly, before darting to the back of the room to attend to something.

I walked around class, down rows of battered wooden desks. 'Now we go' had set them working. No doubt it had all been organised before my arrival. I was like a mayor, called in at the last moment to cut the ribbon and left to smile and shake hands. Students wrote busily, erasing their words just as soon as they wrote them. Others slept or stared into unseen worlds.

In no time—as always happened in Suzuki-sensei's classes—a number of the less imaginative male students started poking their index fingers into my bum, shouting something unintelligible in Japanese. Most teachers who work in Japanese primary schools have battled with this game. I ignored it. But when one boy with bleached hair and a bony finger scored a perfect bullseye, holding up his hands like a sports star, I lost my cool. I spun, stuck out my foot and upturned his chair in a single, swift, calculated movement. He was meant to stand but he was a slow boy and far lighter than anticipated. The chair's small backrest somehow ended up coming down on the back of his head, just above the neck.

'Fuck,' I said dropping onto my hands and knees and doing whatever I could to placate him. But the boy was bawling by this time, all his bravado gone. Suzuki-sensei hurried over, and it was clear to me from the look on his ill-aligned face that he had witnessed my attack.

'I'm so sorry,' I said. 'I'm sorry, I—'

'Please, I will help him now, and you will help him now, and the nurse,' said Suzuki-sensei.

I did nothing to help, though. I was of no use. I stepped out of the classroom, shocked, into the barren white corridor. Through the open sliding door I could see the student slowly stand up, gazing around confusedly as if he had been mugged. I felt a new disgust for myself.

Suzuki-sensei stepped out of the room a few minutes later and shut the sliding door behind him. He rubbed at his chin but said nothing at all. His eyes had always contained a certain contempt for me, but now they gleamed with something bordering on ferocity.

'Come, Mr Noah,' he at last said. 'This ... this is ...'

Suzuki-sensei led me to see the principal, a short, stocky man who had often been good to me. All the previous principals lined the walls with identical expressions in identical sized photos with identical portrait frames. A woman brought us green tea and the principal lit a cigarette. Suzuki-sensei did the same. The two men talked for five minutes in solemn Japanese. Occasionally the principal would nod and glance my way, but mostly he ignored me. He sat with one fat leg over the other on a large swivel chair. When Suzuki-sensei fell quiet the principal shook his head, clucked his tongue and picked up the phone to place a call to a Mr Yamamoto. That was all I understood

—the name. When this finished, he again spoke to Suzuki-sensei, who turned to me dutifully.

'The principal wants to say thank you.'

'Thank you?'

'Thank you,' said the principal.

'Thank you and no more,' said Suzuki-sensei.

'Thank you and no more what?'

Suzuki-sensei frowned. 'No.'

'No?'

'No more … ever.'

'No more what?' I asked.

The principal clarified something with Suzuki-sensei in Japanese and they both nodded, as if maybe between them they had worked out the cause of our communication difficulties.

'No more work,' Suzuki-sensei said. 'Thank you.'

Both the men pulled their suits taut like a final word on the matter. And feeling their decision to be perfectly fair, I did not argue. I stood slowly, unsure what to do.

'Then I'm fired?' I asked dumbly.

They stared at me.

'I'm sacked? No more? Bye-bye?'

'No more, yes,' said Suzuki-sensei, reverting back to his language-cassette English. 'Thank you, and I'll see you around.'

Both men stood and bowed.

I was escorted off the premises by the tea lady, who had, I think, heard the whole conversation and looked like she wanted to beat me to death with the broom that she held at a perfect right angle to her dumpy, middle-aged carcass. At the gate, however, she managed a half-hearted smile, obviously confident I would go quietly after all, and let down the broom.

'Thank you for all of your hard work,' she said in formal, ritualised Japanese. Without waiting for me to reply she hurried back inside, dusting off her hands as though she had just taken out an especially foul bag of rubbish.

This was not the first time I had lost my temper and attacked a far weaker aggressor without thinking. There had been another incident, and in the days following my sacking it resurfaced from the ever-shifting murk of my memory, seemed almost to bob beside me like a buoy, one I had weighed down to keep from looking at and which, having freed itself, now shot to the surface. I was thrust back to my final year of school, surrounded by boys who were well-off and whose looks advertised it; boys whose respect I had craved since joining the homeroom in Year 7. I could smell their designer deodorants and hear their talk behind me as though still in that homeroom. I could hear Mr Baldini reading the daily notices with his faint Italian accent, occasionally dropping in lacklustre jokes which aroused little or no response.

On this particular morning it was raining and I was worried about my hair—I had dyed it black and straightened it with my mother's hairdryer, convinced my usual russet curls were the cause of my unpopularity.

Finally one of the boys behind me noticed.

'Tuttle's fucked with his hair,' he said to the room at

large. 'Dyed it. And you know what?' he added, effortlessly adopting a lisp, 'I think he's straightened it.'

'Fuck, he has,' said another with genuine unease.

I turned to find them reclining in their plastic chairs, hands propping up pretty heads. One or two held a faint smile—more condescending than warm. I wanted to stand and leave. The whole room was looking at me. A chuckle spread.

Perhaps noticing this, a bored boy from the group behind me stood and whispered in Wang's ear. Wang?! Fucking Wang was a twit—the class parrot.

Wang peered up at the boy, puzzled. The boy repeated himself. Mr Baldini put down the notices and eyed the room over his glasses, aware something was up. Wang let out a nervous laugh, put one finger in his mouth, then another, then looked at me. He stood.

The room hushed. I felt a sudden and fierce hatred for them all. Wang unceremoniously scratched his flat, trousered bottom. All eyes were on him and, self-conscious, he rubbed an ear against his shoulder. I kept my head down.

'Wanna, wanna,' he stammered. Everyone fell silent. 'Wanna go on a date, beautiful?'

The room exploded into laugher and no one heard the sound of my chair being thrown back as I leapt to my feet and punched Wang hard in the face. Being slight he sailed backwards and collapsed in a heap between the rows of desks. The clatter of this furniture was implausibly loud. I stood, poised to strike again.

No one moved, not until Mr Baldini stormed towards me, grabbed my arm and dragged me outside into the rain.

His eyes bulged white. 'That was the cruellest thing I've seen any one human do to another. You're pathetic. From day one in this class all you've worried about is what those stupid boys think, and you've never had the guts to be kind to a soul. As long as you're this scared of being unpopular, you're better off where there aren't people. Now get out of my sight and explain all this to the principal while I check you didn't kill that poor boy. I hope you're expelled on the spot.'

A few months later, having endured a suspension negotiated by my father and finished my exams, I took Mr Baldini's advice and moved to Japan. I had thought a lot about his choice of words and decided the number of people around me was not nearly as important as being alone—alone and defenceless, like Wang.

The summer was torturous. I cannot recall any one thing about it that was pleasant. Despite resolving to move out of Nakamura's and separate myself from everyone I knew, I no longer possessed the strength. It seemed with age I was becoming increasingly weak. Perhaps there was merit in all my father had said. Perhaps I was a loafer, a dropout. I liked to believe I was holding out, waiting for something without knowing what. I liked to believe I was finally testing myself. But now I was unsure. What had changed since that rainy school day? I kept thinking of the look in Suzuki-sensei's eyes when he joined me in the corridor, of the tea lady with her broom, of my father. Tilly, watching wordlessly, alternately despised and worried about me.

I mulishly refused to enjoy the steaming hot days, the meals I ate or the sudden abundance of free time I found myself with. It took Phillip weeks to get me to accompany him to Shinjuku. When I finally did—wondering all the while as to the contents of his hiking pack—he led me into Kinokuniya, a bookstore with a floor for foreign books. *Gaijin* of all colours, shapes and sizes drifted silently between the densely packed rows.

'Do you think she's gone and kicked it?' he asked, examining a 700-page guide to better sex.

'What?' I asked vaguely.

'You're thinking about it again, aren't you?'

'About what?'

'All of it,' he said.

'I can't sleep, can't concentrate. It's all just—'

'You wanker. Snap out of it, Tuttle. You're becoming a real fucking bore. All I've heard for ages is what a shit you are. How awful the world is, that it could spawn and weave something so wretched as you. It's all said and done. You can't change it. Tilly's fine, the kid you hit is fine, and you're free to fuck Mami, which is what you wanted in the first place, isn't it? No harm, no foul. Things have a way of working themselves out.'

Phillip leant in and lowered his voice. 'What are we all here for in the end? To have fun, right? To eat, drink, screw and experiment. So live a little.' He tapped a tangled position sketched inside the book. 'Like this guy. This guy's got the right idea.'

'Who kicked it?' I asked, ignoring the picture.

'Nakamura-san.'

'What makes you say that?'

'Her apartment.'

'What about it?'

Phillip rolled his eyes and held an ancient Chinese position up to the light for a better look.

'You've only been staring at that apartment since you were sacked. You haven't noticed anything odd?' he asked. 'Like the fact it's empty?'

'It is?'

'She's gone. All that's left are two plastic slippers on the balcony. That's it. You look through the windows when the sun's right and it's empty inside. There's not a plate, cup, chair or anything.'

'She's probably moved.'

'No,' he said.

'I'm sure she has.'

'I've got a funny feeling about it, Tuttle. You get to her age, you get that fixated on beating the shit out of your bedding every day, and you're waiting to shuffle on upstairs. You're not thinking about buying a brand-new apartment in Asagaya.'

'True.'

'She's dead,' he said flatly.

'Maybe.'

For a moment I wondered about my rent and, as a follow on, if there was a room in the hostel I could move into without anyone being the wiser. Then Phillip's backpack nudged me as he returned the sex book to the shelf, in turn knocking me into a girl of perhaps six who hugged a small handbag and peered up with a look of distrust.

'What's with this backpack, Phillip?' I asked.

'For me to know and you to find out, Tuttle.'

'So you keep saying.'

'Come on.' He glanced at his watch. 'Let's get out of here. It's time.'

Phillip led me from the store into a muggy, late summer dusk. The heat showed no sign of letting up or of being swept from the city by a sea breeze. The buildings acted as walls and locked the air into a sweltering steel box, sealing it with airconditioning exhaust.

'God I hate this city,' I said to myself. People bumped me, bouncing me off walls like a pinball. I almost tripped on a stack of porn magazines and their owner, a toothless bum, grinned. He gestured for me to buy one with a brown, sun-weathered hand. I shook my head.

Phillip—letting the backpack slip from one shoulder—led me onto a large, semi-enclosed pedestrian bridge near Shinjuku Station. From here we could peer down one of Shinjuku's widest and busiest thoroughfares. At its distant end, at right angles, were three skyscrapers, each a little lower than the last, their tops forming steps. As the sun set, metal and glass everywhere had taken on an almost blue hue. There was, however, still enough natural light to mute the narrow backlit advertisements which—in garish pinks, reds, blues and greens—ran up the sides of every building, detailing the companies within. Delivery trucks and cars idled beneath us, waiting for a change of lights. And every footpath swarmed with people, many of them silhouettes in the half-light.

I stared at customers queuing for a meal outside First Kitchen while Phillip gently set down his pack and pulled out a box held together with sticky tape. I watched him tear at the tape and toss it aside, flapping it off his fingertips.

'What's in there?' I asked.

'A biplane.'

He pulled away the last of the cardboard and packed inside were indeed the components of a biplane. He worked quickly, snapping the sections together until he was holding in one hand a canary-yellow plane with a red plastic propeller and two tiny metal machine guns. Kicking the backpack aside he began to wind the propeller up. People crossing the bridge either hurried on or stopped to watch.

'You can't be serious,' I said.

'Look at the street, Tuttle. It's the widest street on earth. It must be a hundred metres across. And it just goes on and on.'

'But the engine—'

'There isn't one. The propeller's on a rubber band.'

'Still …'

After winding it up Phillip released the propeller and flung the plane from the bridge. For a moment it was beautiful, this one small balsa craft flying silently over so much clutter and chaos, so much metal. There was something immensely graceful about it. The setting sun glinted over its taut, painted wings. Phillip watched it closely and made no attempt to run.

'What about these people?' I asked, not taking my eyes off the biplane, which held straight and level. 'They saw you build it—throw it.'

'Worry, worry, worry,' Phillip said. 'They're Japanese. They're not going to do anything.'

And he was right. Around us, as if they had come simply to see the plane, people took up positions and watched it fly. Likewise pedestrians down below began to notice it, mouths ajar. Although tiny, the yellow biplane was so alone in the vast space above the road and between the endless walls of buildings it seemed to catch people's eye. It continued to fly in a straight line, over crowded intersections and upturned heads. More and more people saw it and nudged those beside them.

Slowly at first and then with increasing speed the plane began to lose altitude, finally dipping sharply. A few people moved towards it and Phillip laughed. A second later the thing exploded—a sharp, far-off pop and puff of white smoke. Balsa rained dimly in the growing dark. I saw one man duck and then rise cautiously, and when I turned my head we were again the centre of attention.

'C'mon,' Phillip said. 'We could have the eyes of the whole city on us in a moment.'

But I only smiled. For some reason I was suddenly relaxed. I saw the biplane had already been forgotten by most.

'Walk this way,' Phillip hissed. 'Act normal.'

No one chased us. Laughing, we toasted the historic flight with pints of Guinness in an Irish bar, toasted it as if we were aviators, two pioneers. But later the drink turned on us and we sat arguing about the details—distance, height, the volume of the explosion—until we tired of each other's company and went our separate ways.

I burped quietly without meaning to and smelt the sushi I had eaten for lunch.

Nakamura-san had indeed vanished.

'Hey,' I said to Tilly, who lay on her bed pretending to read. 'Nakamura-san's gone.'

She nodded without looking up. 'Weeks ago, Noah.'

'And …' I drew the word out, 'I can't find a room to rent.'

'Keep looking.'

'No. I mean—'

But Tilly checked her watch, swore and sat up, face groggy.

'I have to work. Can't you step outside while I get changed? Actually, go find something to do.'

'Why?'

'You're bugging me, standing there like that. Do something.'

'Like what?'

'Like find somewhere to live.'

I ended up watching Japanese TV for half an hour and, returning to the room, found that Tilly had left for work. I stood at the window, staring across into Nakamura-san's apartment. I thought of the morning Mami first appeared, of the winter cold and Nakamura-san beating her futon. Even then her apartment had lacked personality, lacked life. Now, though, it was all bare concrete, nothing more; the lime-green balcony rail was the only obvious colour. The rooms were both hollow and I stared into them for close on a minute, morose, until I resolved to break in.

The sliding door had two small, rectangular windows at its top, one of which had been left open for ventilation. It seemed possible to exploit this and I set my mind to doing so. Apartments like Nakamura-san's—which required hefty, non-refundable deposits—were usually vacant for months before being let. I will not deny my pending eviction drew me to the place like a cat to fish, but there was something else too. This gloomy space across the two-metre alley seemed to be in communication with an equally hollow void somewhere deep inside me. The two were acting like magnets, this sense growing only stronger as I wrenched up my window and climbed onto the sill.

But the height of it all gave me cause to pause—to think. Height—zooming up at me, faceless, depthless, wrapping itself around my heart and tugging lightly so my body recoiled backwards in panic—had to be considered. My toes curled around the sill's edge and my hands gripped the sides. I crouched there, window digging into my back, worried I might faint, worried I might topple forward like a dead bird from a branch.

In the end it was to avoid exactly this unceremonious death that I took a sharp breath and leapt out into midair. I came crashing down onto that lime green rail, wedging it between my chest and upper arms and scraping around with both my feet until one found a hold. I was too scared to take a breath. All the impetuous bravado that had facilitated my leap was gone. It was only a fear of being spotted from the street below that gave me the courage to pull myself over the railing, from which position I flopped like a hooked fish onto the cold concrete and resumed breathing.

After a minute's rest I stood and checked for witnesses. There were none. I tried the sliding door but it was locked. Whoever had locked it, had done so quickly, however. The bottom lock had only been slotted halfway into the groove on the adjoining door, leaving the handle sticking out at a seventy-five-degree angle. All I had to do was slide some-thing heavy like a hammer through the open top window and drop it onto the bottom lock to flick it open. I picked up what little I had at my disposal—plastic slippers. I turned them over in my hands, one after the other. Both were heavier than expected, their bases thick. I decided to try to use them. I poked one through the open window and let go of it. But it missed and fell with a thud onto the tatami matting inside.

'Shit.'

I picked up the remaining slipper and repeated the process. The toe struck the handle squarely and I heard the latch fall open with a dull clunk. When I tugged on the door it slid back without difficulty.

'Ha.'

I quickly picked up both the slippers and dropped them back onto the balcony before stepping inside.

The largest room smelt of cleaning products. I guessed that someone—maybe even Nakamura-san, if she was still alive—had cleaned the place from top to bottom before departing. There was no dust or grime. I stared at the white walls, at the beige cupboards and wood-veneer ceiling. I wandered from empty room to empty room—the living rooms, the kitchen and shoulder-width bathroom.

Here, standing over my missing landlord's immaculate toilet, I urinated while trying to decide what to do next; I had not devised a plan beyond getting in. Where was Nakamura-san? It made no sense. If dead, was someone else going to take over the hostel? Were we to be evicted? Or was she perhaps coming back?

I returned to the first of the living rooms, sat down on

the tatami and took a deep breath. These living rooms were separated from one another by nothing more substantial than thin, patterned sliding doors. I traced the pattern with my finger—an oriental scene featuring ducks in flight. I should have been scared, afraid of being found out, but I had no such concerns. For the first time in weeks nothing distracted me. I flopped onto my back and lay still, staring up at the fake grain of the wood-veneer ceiling. The lampshade and bulb had been removed from the light fitting and I suddenly felt sure whoever cleaned the apartment was never coming back.

Then a remarkable thing happened—I slept.

I am not sure exactly how long I slept but when I woke it was dark, which meant it must have been three or four hours at least. It had been years since I had slept so long without stirring, without jolting on the strings of muddled dreams. Confused, I rolled onto my side, aware of a tingling in my arm. I sat up and this same arm flopped into position beside me, lifeless and heavy. I had to wait for it to recover its full movement before standing, stretching and walking through the kitchen—past the deep, silver, distinctively Japanese sink and mounted hot-water unit—towards the front door. I opened the in-built, metal mailbox and, as hoped, found two identical silver keys. Without any hesitation I snatched one up, shut the mailbox and opened the door.

I locked it behind me and, pocketing the key, walked back towards the hostel, passing the old man and his even older dog on the way. As always, the decrepit animal was circling, making tentative attempts to raise its tail and lower its anus over the gutter. Its back legs shook precariously and the old man, smoking a cigarette and holding the leash with both hands, casually propped the creature with an equally shaky foot.

Harry had no intention of paying me back. He had the money—this much was obvious because he was frequenting a variety of ritzy snack bars and often bringing back the hostess from the first for sex. Sometimes, lying awake at night listening to Tilly snore, I would hear him with this girl. She had a piercing, put-on giggle. Harry always used Japanese with her, having somehow picked up a basic command of the language in mere months. Then they would fuck—loud, raucous, pounding sex that never failed to wake Tilly, so the two of us could stew on things we would have preferred to forget.

To Harry, I was invisible. He left the hostel early every morning and stayed out late. If he did run into me, he was too busy to talk. And never once did he raise the matter of money. I lay awake most nights thinking about how much I hated him, polishing the barbs I planned to fling given half a chance. But I always put off challenging him. I needed him on side. Without that there was no hope.

Around the hostel everyone discussed our missing landlady. They feared not for her, her fate, but for themselves. She could have been trapped in a well and I doubt any one of us would have thrown down a rope without first receiving a guarantee of accommodation. The more talk there was, the less credible the information. Eventually it was concluded, and generally accepted, that we had no idea where she was. No one dared put out rent in case it remained uncollected or was stolen. And in time most expected to be evicted or at least notified of a change in ownership. But no word came. It was as if we had stepped out of the vast economy surrounding us.

I began regularly crossing the alley to Nakamura-san's apartment, using it as an escape. Perhaps inspired by Harry's progress, I often took a Japanese language textbook with me. Lying on the tatami I would try to study. I never stuck at it for more than ten minutes and afterwards shut the book, fell backwards and slept. Something about the place invariably put me to sleep. Never a light, fretful sleep, but always a deep, refreshing slumber that could last hours.

This odd routine might have gone on for the full duration of Tilly's contract were it not for three Japanese men in summer suits. They were standing just inside the entrance of the hostel upon my return from an especially satisfying snooze. One was obese and it was clear that his pants were causing him discomfort around the groin. He was unashamedly sorting things out, making complicated adjustments while the other two tacked up A4 signs.

I paused to read one.

Due to the change in of ownership in this lodgement, this will be collapsing in eight weeks from today (the date above written inward.)

'Fuck,' I said.

I stormed to Harry's room and hammered on his door. He answered, chest bare, looking sleepy.

'The money, right?' he asked with a nod.

'Right. Give it to me now, in full, or I'll go to the police. Time's up.'

He rubbed at the mat of black, coarse, curled hairs coating his bloated little belly and stretched to his full five-foot-nothing.

'You'll have it tomorrow. My apologies.'

And, like that, without another word, he shut the door.

'It was stupid of me, wasn't it?' Tilly said, sliding half off the bed.

'What was stupid?' I asked.

Her voice fell to a mumble. 'Coming back was stupid. Everything's changed. Not just us, but the whole hostel. Half the tenants who were here last time are gone. And now they're just going to tear it down. It'll be like it never existed, like *we* never existed.'

I shut my book—Harry Potter and the something's something. 'I'm glad you came back,' I said without conviction.

Tilly slid the rest of the way from the bed, ending up with her back to it. 'Of course you are. You're thrilled.'

'I am. Honestly.'

'Anyway,' she said, taking a sharp, tense breath. 'We can't rent this room much longer and I don't see any point in forcing you out ahead of a demolition. You might as well stay until we're kicked out.'

She seemed to have more to say, so I waited.

'I think I came back to Japan to break up with you,' she said. 'I wasn't going to tell you that, but it's bothered me. All along I was planning to leave you. Even back at the farm, waiting for the train. Only it wouldn't come out then.'

'I see.'

I stood and took two steps to the window. The heat had given out to a typhoon. Dark clouds whipped across the sky at an unnatural pace, gusts of wind whooped excitedly around the tallest apartment blocks, and the alley below dripped loudly.

'Is all that okay with you?'

'Well it has to be,' I said, surprised by my anger.

'I guess it does.'

I had expected we would talk about things in more detail, but Tilly stood and left, looking miserable.

Hours later the storm reached its peak, or what I guessed to be its peak. Tilly returned and said nothing as she prepared for bed, following the steps she always followed and which I had come to know well. While she applied moisturiser to her face—more patting than rubbing it in, her mouth ajar, her eyes on the ceiling—the hostel grunted in the frenzied, inconstant wind. Rain marched across corrugated iron and continued surreptitiously to leak in beneath the window sill. I watched Tilly return her toothpaste and other toiletries to a cheap plastic case.

'What?' she asked. 'Why are you watching me?'

'You look pale.'

'I do?' she said without interest.

'I'm worried about you.'

Holding the ends of her baggy nightgown together she stepped over me and crossed to the door. There was a dark, apple-shaped bruise just above her ankle.

'I'm putting out the light.'

'Okay.'

I was lying in jeans and a T-shirt on the thin, uncomfortable futon she had set for me on the floor. In the dark she stepped back over me. I could tell from the sound of her walk she was again holding together the ends of her nightgown. This seemed pointless, since I could see nothing anyway, but I shut my eyes out of courtesy. It saddened me to have to do it. I had once known her body so well and she had never been shy. Often during the previous summer she had performed her nightly routine wearing nothing at all. Everything she had to hide—freckles, a birthmark and a faint, cheap tattoo—I had seen.

I fell into an uneasy sleep and woke at some indeterminate point in the night to discover the typhoon all but gone. Tilly was sobbing into her pillow, a wretched sound that cut out when I coughed.

This unacknowledged sobbing continued for weeks. We fought during the day and missed each other at night. Even the fighting changed. Whereas once we had been able to say anything, we now watched our every word, aware there existed matters we could not address without the two of us quickly coming to hate one another. We knew too much and could wound too deeply, and instead fought about inconsequential things—wet towels, disposable razors, toe-nail clippings, hair, post-it notes and even stock cubes, which I accused Tilly of stealing. The two of us seemed always to be on the edge of a cliff, waiting for the tussle that would send us over.

Perhaps because of this tension, Tilly fell ill. She took a week off work and I, exhausted, moved into Nakamura-san's apartment. I reasoned Tilly would right herself in my absence. She would not let me nurse her and I was therefore only a cause of fatigue.

I had been crossing to the apartment regularly, but rarely took much in the way of personal belongings—a book or a magazine at most. But after Harry departed without warning, leaving no forwarding address, I began to take food and stay for days, leaving this item or that behind until most of my belongings were secretly stowed in the apartment's numerous cupboards. There was a real risk of being caught and I was careful to check nothing had been moved whenever I arrived. Night after night I slept from dark until sun-up and felt I was living dangerously, that there was some modicum of autonomy in my life.

One afternoon, collecting things for the apartment, I found Tilly ankle-deep in bloodied tissues. All this blood had come from her nose, and when I asked her how long it had been bleeding she only shrugged and said, 'What do you care?'

This reply caught me off guard. 'You can break up with me and still be nice, you know.'

'You think this is breaking up?'

'You said you wanted to, that you've wanted to since Australia.'

'Yeah. But it's words, isn't it? Go somewhere, stop showing up pretending to give a shit. Why can't you just leave me alone? Why can't you vanish?'

Her eyes, when she looked up, contained a trace of tears, and her face was drawn and tired. 'Please,' she said. 'This is exhausting, Noah. There are no nice break-ups.'

Later, I sat staring at her dark window. I wanted to hold her, but could not. Did I believe she had come back to Japan simply to break up with me? No. Why return for so long? And why plan to share a bed? It made no sense. I suspected now that with every push Tilly was inviting me closer, but I did not want to look at it. Not like that. Not now. Not at all. Holding on to her was as scary as letting go.

The Deconstruction

A week passed, then another. Tilly recovered from her illness and returned to work. I saw her head out each morning. By this time I was used to the apartment. I was living there in earnest—sleeping there, showering there, even keeping a toothbrush in a cup there. Tilly knew where I was. Occasionally she would catch sight of me moving around behind the dark glass and peer through. I liked this. I had not lost her, only found an adequate limbo. I soon forgot even to fear losing her.

Lying on my side in that empty room between naps I often thought of my father. Who can say why he came to mind? Maybe it was because I was breaking the law simply by being there, and he had always promised to turn his back on me if I broke the law in any serious fashion. Looking back, that had been something of an idle threat. He had not abandoned me when I hit Wang. If anything, he had saved my skin. But long before that he had clearly explained why I had to behave better than most children my age. I was not simply a son of God, but also the only son of a priest (or ex-priest, thanks to my mother). People expected more from me because, morally speaking, I had been given more.

Growing up I had lived by my father's rules and never questioned his beliefs. Yet they sat inside me now like a lump of metal, forced in and wholly foreign. The more I thought about it, the more I came to thank Nakamura-san's apartment for enabling this realisation—my breaking into the space, my choosing to be at ease within it, my sleeping soundly on the smooth tatami. Day by day, as alone as I could bring myself to be, I sensed I was cutting the lump out, cutting it out messily and with little idea how to get at it, but it was certainly coming out. With no one there to watch, to judge, I had the time and freedom I needed to grope inside, to prise back muscle, tissue and fat, fingers wet with blood, and get some sort of a grip on it.

One night at dusk—the dreariest hour of every day when I would drink a beer and cook a bowl of noodles with an egg—Phillip visited. He was irritated by my hermit-like existence and wasted no time telling me what to do.

'Look at yourself. For fuck's sake get some sun, Tuttle. You're such a pasty, sad-looking fuck. I'd throw you money if I saw you on the street. When's the last time you left this place? Do you realise it smells like shit?'

I only shrugged.

'Where are you sleeping anyway?' he asked, flicking a light switch repeatedly, despite there being no bulb. 'On the floor?'

'Yeah.'

'Get a job. Jesus! Get some cash—a life. You're losing your mind here.'

'I'm fine.'

'You need to get out. That Japanese couple I met—did I tell you about them? The pair I went to Guam with— they're up for fun. There's a group of us and—'

'I can't afford it.'

'Someone's driving. There won't be a cab fare.'

'I'm not going.'

Phillip shook his head sadly, handsome chin on his chest. 'Fine. Stay here, read, toss off and feel sorry for yourself. I've tried.'

He left half an hour later—after splitting a pack of noodles with me—and he must have said something to Tilly because she visited well after dark, timid, like she expected to find the apartment full of rats. I was just out of the shower and wrapped in a towel. She nodded at my stomach, which was full of noodles and flabby from lack of movement.

'You've put on some weight.'

'Some. Surprised to see you here.'

'Yeah, well, I'm feeling a bit better than the last time we talked. Phillip says you don't get out much.'

'No.'

'When did you last go outside?'

'A while back.'

She put her fists on her hips as though prepared to wait all night for the answer.

'Friday.'

'Four days ago! To do what?'

'I don't know,' I said defensively. 'To see a friend, get some sun. Why does anyone go out? More to the point, why does anyone care when I go out?'

'To see Mami?' Tilly asked. She rolled her eyes. 'I know all your other friends, Noah.'

While I had gained weight Tilly had only lost it. At the farm I would have thought it impossible for her to get thinner, but now she was quite skeletal. I wondered momentarily if she had an eating disorder. Her face looked drained, her eyes tired. There were two pronounced bruises on her left forearm, both reminding me of the one I had seen on her ankle.

'Just how is Mami these days?' she asked coldly, sitting on the tatami. 'Such a nice girl.'

'I don't know.'

'Not your type but—'

'I'm not seeing her.'

'You mean you're not screwing her?'

'No.'

Tilly only smiled. 'No? No, you don't mean that? Or no?'

'No, I'm not seeing or screwing her.'

'Just friends then.'

'Do you want me to write it for—?'

'You can't live here, you know,' Tilly said, cutting me short and standing. 'It's not yours.'

'I know.'

'I said you could share the room with me until it's torn down.'

'Yeah, but you wanted me out as well.'

Tilly flinched. The movement, little more than a blink, was hardly perceptible but I felt certain I had seen it. She ran her hand through her hair, which was still quite short

'When will you move out?' she asked.

'Of here?'

'Yes here. Where else?'

'I won't.'

'Then you can't be helped.'

At that instant I thought of Celeste. She had not mentioned that after love there was always something. And this was it, the something. It was both a comforting and horrible discovery, two people staring at one another across a room, both realising they might well live without one another, that they might make a chop of it, but that they would always be hopelessly tangled. Even if they never saw one another again.

At a loss for conversation, Tilly talked about her job, admitting she wanted to give it away.

'Then leave it,' I said.

'The airfare.'

'I'll pay it.'

She laughed. 'With what?'

'I'm serious,' I said sadly. 'I can find the money. Let me pay for it.'

Her face hardened. 'Pay for it to get yourself off the hook, you mean?'

'No.'

'What then? To keep me on it?' Tilly stood up and crossed to the front door. 'I'll think about it,' she said. 'In the meantime, get out of this apartment. It's got a bad feel to it. You'll go mad in here.'

The bang of the door behind her rattled the kitchen walls.

Within half an hour I was asleep, but it was not the usual sound sleep. I dreamt that one of my teeth had broken in two, that the middle was filled with a sort of tasteless, toothy honeycomb. I kept running my tongue over it, over the sharp-edged, inverted crater, trying to smooth it until I eventually woke, highly agitated. It was well before sun-up. I showered and stood out on the balcony, staring across into Tilly's room.

I found the courage to call Mami. I began meeting her on Fridays in a small, out-of-the-way coffee shop in Odaiba. It was the demolition of the hostel that had convinced her to meet me. The moment I mentioned it, she declared she wanted to see it, that I could not under any circumstances let her miss it. I should have known she would be interested in all the dust and destruction, in the misery and tears. It was Kaketa to a tee.

The demolition started far earlier than anyone anticipated and was a slapdash affair from the first clang of a hammer. The labourers all wore matching tracksuits and talked to one another in mumbles. Not without trepidation I watched them from behind the curtains of Nakamura-san's apartment. They never seemed to work unless a man with dark glasses and a missing finger visited, and were always smoking and gawking at passing women.

Something about these labourers was not right. They looked nothing like the government road workers up a nearby street who operated in clearly defined teams with set, whistle-toting leaders. Cheap new signs were put up around the hostel notifying tenants of 'The First Stage'. These signs did not specify (at least not in English) what the first stage was, only that it would soon be followed by a second and maybe even third stage. Tenants were left to work out for themselves that the so-called first stage was nothing more sophisticated than a stripping of the building for anything of value—planks of wood, slabs of carpet, posts, tiles and even bricks where they could be pulled free.

The last warm rain of the summer drew me out of hiding. I wandered from street to street without a care and watched it. It came late in the afternoon and steamed on hot, tiled roofs. It muddied dusty gutters—filling them with leaves and other litter—flooded cracks in the older, narrower roads and caused pets to seek shelter. Then it was finished, just like that. What had been a hard, driving, cleansing rain became a dribble and then nothing at all. The summer, one of the worst of my life, was over.

When I returned to the hostel I saw the rain shower had shooed off most of the workers, whom I thought of as the Deconstructionists since they were tearing the building down in reverse, working from the finishing touches back towards the foundations. The last of them—two men and a sour girl—departed in a souped-up van with black windows, fenders, flashing lights and a stereo thudding deep inside. Watching them flick on a blinker and pull out into the street, I decided to have a look inside the hostel. Though I did not especially want to bump into Phillip or Tilly, or anyone for that matter, curiosity overcame me. What had these Deconstructionists done? I strolled to the front door and stopped dead. The hostel's innards had been callously excised. It seemed the Deconstructionists, though lethargic-looking, were far more serious about their work than I had guessed.

I started in cautiously. Almost all of the internal plaster was gone and numerous wires were exposed. Power points were cavities in walls. There were no taps in the two bath-rooms. And here and there light-blue plastic tarps had been put down in the corridors to catch a powdery grit.

The place was dying, no question about it, and un-surprisingly many of its old tenants were gone. They had simply vacated their rooms and left the doors ajar. Without anyone living in these rooms they looked larger and cleaner. I passed Harry's and saw it was empty except for an old clock.

Tilly called out from next door and I heard her move.

'Oh,' she said, appearing at the door. 'It's you.'

'Who did you think it was?'

'A worker.'

'A Deconstructionist?'

'A what?'

'That's what I've been calling the workers.'

'I see you're still not doing anything, then.'

Since this was not a question, I did not answer. Tilly, who looked ill again, with big, dark bags beneath her eyes, retreated into the gloomy room. She climbed back into bed. Everything smelt of sleep and there were a number of pill bottles on the table which I guessed to be vitamins. Beside one of these lay a wad of cotton wool. When Tilly saw me eyeing it she again climbed out of bed, put all the bottles in a drawer and shut it sharply.

'Vitamins?'

'Mostly. Cold and flu tablets, too.'

'Can they just slowly force you out like this?'

'Yes.'

'Isn't there anything you can do?'

'Well, I could break into a nearby apartment and set myself up there, I suppose.'

I ignored the snipe and adopted a stern look. 'But this work they're doing is dangerous. Wires, asbestos and stuff.'

'Asbestos and stuff? The only people at risk are these … what did you call them?'

'Deconstructionists.'

'Right. If they were legit, they would have evicted me. But they're amateurs. I saw one guy hammer his finger out of shape yesterday. He ran off howling. And now, at the first sight of rain, they've all packed it in. Not that I'm complaining. It's the first quiet I've had in days.'

'They're not trying to be quiet?'

'Of course not. They're gutting the place and they want us out, so they're doing it as loudly as they can—and as messily.'

'Well, I've made my offer, Tilly.'

'You're serious then?'

'Yes,' I said, miserable at the thought of her leaving. 'Have you decided?'

She shook her head.

'I'm happy to pay for everything,' I reiterated.

'I know. But I don't think I can accept it.'

'They're tearing everything apart backwards!'
Tilly glanced up. 'Like you.'

Midway through the following morning the apartment
doorbell rang. Having asked Phillip, Tilly and Mami to
knock seven times when visiting, I froze. Sweat coated my
forehead. The sun glared in through the fuzzy kitchen
window, beneath which I had been making a sandwich.
I put this meal aside and tiptoed to the alcove just inside the
door, peered through the peephole and realised, with a new
sense of finality, just how well I had trapped myself. Two
Japanese men stood in pristine, creaseless uniforms. No
matter the angle I could see nothing much more than their
heads and upper torsos. They appeared rounded and
distant, and there was nothing familiar about their smudged
faces. They talked to one another for a moment, apparently
in two minds. One kept glancing at his feet, as if maybe he
had something there.

'Go away,' I whispered softly. 'Go on, fuck off.'

But they would not. They continued to linger, talking.
I watched them intently. What was it that was below my
field of vision? Was there a third, unseen party? Nakamura-
san maybe? She was short enough—but dead. I had
accepted this as fact. When one of the men tried the door
handle I panicked, certain I had forgotten to lock it. Stepping backwards onto a shoe, I fell sideways and crashed into
the wooden shoe locker. The sound of this clumsy collision
came and went as sharply and incongruously as a gunshot.

Then someone knocked seven times.

I put my eye to the peephole again, frowning.

'Tuttle, you hermit nut fuck, open the door. I'm in trouble here.' Phillip's voice.

I opened the door, careful to leave the chain on just in case there was a last, remote chance of escape. One of the uniformed men peered in through the gap and I saw a stretcher with a body laid out on it. I could only see the outline of a hand beneath a blanket, but guessed it belonged to Phillip.

At this, I shut the door, flung off the chain and wrenched it open again. My haste was dictated more by curiosity than concern. Phillip looked glum. Heavy white bandaging covered most of his skull and face. The rest of his body was pinned beneath the blanket which, though he wriggled and winced, he could not loosen.

'What the—' I said.

'Accident.' He tried to shrug.

I helped wheel him in, apologising for the delay and talking in a garbled fashion about a very important phone call, but the ambulance men appeared not to understand English.

'What accident?' I asked Phillip.

'We almost hit a kid on a bike.'

'Almost? So he's okay?'

'She.'

'She then. She okay?'

'We don't know.'

'We? Who's we?'

'Later, Tuttle. Not now.'

The two ambulance men wheeled Phillip into the living room and peered around—looking, no doubt, for furniture, somewhere to set him down. I gestured to the two blankets I had been using as a bed and they nodded. Their bemused faces turned suspicious.

'You didn't hit the girl, did you?' I asked.

Phillip winced as he was set down on the tatami, a surface hardly softened by blankets. 'No. I don't think so.'

'What did you hit?'

'A shop.'

'A shop? Shit.'

'Went straight through a window into something— a steel foundation, I think.'

'So the police'll be coming?'

Phillip shook his head. 'Don't worry about it, Tuttle.'

One of the ambulance men glanced at me when I said the word 'police', but did not ask questions. Together with his partner they moved towards the door.

'Where's the pillow?' Phillip asked.

'There isn't one. You just had it made it into a bed.'

One of the men carried a CB radio, which squawk-ed. He ignored it and tried to speak to me in rapid Japanese.

'Yes,' I kept saying without having understood a word. 'Yes, yes.'

The radio squawked again and he cut off sharply, either listening to the CB or realising I could not under-stand him. He was an intelligent-looking man in his mid-twenties with wire-rimmed reading glasses. I had the impression the ambulance work was service to his com-munity. I did not trust this do-gooder with my secret and wanted to finish Phillip off myself, stab him with my butter knife.

'Insurance,' the man said in broken, hesitant English, nodding towards Phillip.

I groaned.

'I don't have it,' Phillip said. 'That's why I checked myself out.'

'You did what?' I asked.

'I can't afford further treatment.'

'Have you had any treatment?'

'No, Tuttle. The fucking bandages are for looks.'

After the effort of saying all this Phillip lay still in his makeshift bed, staring at the roof. One whole eye was covered in gauze and I worried about the extent of his injuries. The other ambulance man, far thicker-looking with a friendly face and the soft, pleasing aroma of cheap cologne, now handed me a bottle of tablets. The bottle rattled and hearing the sound Phillip held out a hand. I looked down at it, opening and closing, and then to the bottle, but the man who had given me the tablets shook his head.

'Not to two,' he said, having as much difficulty with English as his co-worker.

'Not to two?'

'Not to do, no. Two.'

'Do what too?'

'One two, every two.'

They gave me further hopeless instructions and let themselves out.

'Pills!' Phillip yelled.

I walked back to the living room and rattled the container loudly.

'Were you driving?'

He shook his head.

'Who was? Who were you with?'

'Forget it, Tuttle.'

So I returned to the kitchen and sat stacking up loose change that had amassed, sorting it into useless little piles. I could not decide whether to move out. I needed more information. After a few minutes Phillip proved himself predictable.

'Pills!'

I took three pills through to him and held them just out of reach.

'Fucking give them to me.'

'Tell me everything and I will. You can OD on them for all I care.'

He waved me off, but his eyes betrayed desperation.

'What happened to your room?' I asked.

'I moved out a few days ago.'

'You didn't say goodbye?'

'You hardly ever said hello. Anyway, I was going to. Today maybe.'

'But instead you drove into a building?'

'Yeah.'

'With who? Who else was in the car?'

Phillip sighed loudly. 'The couple I went to Guam with. I guess I've been seeing a lot of them. They'd taken me in before all this.'

'And?'

'She's hurt. He's not. The girl on the bike ... I don't know.'

'Were you drunk?'

'And the rest, yeah.'

'The other two?'

'Yeah.'

'Who drove? Which one?'

'He did.'

'And the police, will they be interested in this?'

'I don't know. Maybe.'

'They'll have this address.'

'So don't answer the door,' Phillip said irritably.

For a moment I said nothing, pacing the room. 'Why the fuck did you come here, Phillip?'

He tried to roll over, away from me, but it caused too much pain. 'We'll hide. It only has to work once,' he said. 'Then we'll run.'

'You'll run? Like this?'

'I'll do my best if it means not getting arrested. Now give me the pills and fuck off.'

I ignored his pathetic attempt to intimidate me. 'Would they arrest us do you think—for being here?'

'Yeah,' Phillip said, without giving it much thought.

'Then we should move.'

'To where?'

I handed him the pills and he chewed and tried to swallow.

'Where?' he asked again.

'Wherever. Away from here.' But saying this I thought of Tilly and did not press the point.

Phillip fell asleep. I crossed over to the hostel to see what assistance I could offer Tilly. Even before I entered I could tell the Deconstructionists had returned. It was the noise and dust. It spilled out into the street from doors and burst from holes in walls. There was the usual clatter associated with destruction. Drills screeched and jammed, hammers thudded and an angle grinder squealed before it was let to chew into metal.

Inside, sections of corridor wall had been reduced to skeletal wooden frames. The ceiling was being pulled out, and I noticed tangled wires and makeshift-looking rusted pipes which all took an indirect route to their destination.

Tilly was at work. Tracking down a pen and an old receipt I left a note for her. She was to visit me ASAP, since she could no longer stay in her room. On the way back to the apartment I passed the old man with his even older dog. He looked mildly annoyed. I had the impression he knew I was squatting in Nakamura-san's apartment, and when I bent to pat the dog he abruptly pulled it away.

I took the stairs two at a time and, a moment later, sat down beside Phillip and asked him if he was hungry. He looked to be in pain and immediately wanted pills.

'Two,' I said, standing to collect them from the kitchen.
'Four.'

'Only two for now.' I brought him the tablets along with water in a small margarine container, and he swallowed the lot greedily. 'You should eat,' I said.

'Eat what? More noodles? No thanks.'

With the curtains drawn the room was dim and depressing. I had bought a bulb and was using the ceiling light, but it was hardly adequate. In fact, the whole place had lost its appeal. It had begun to feel like a prison. Outside, Moaning Man, who I had not heard shout for months and presumed long gone, let out a groan and kicked something—a wall. The sound echoed in the alley. Wanting light I pulled back a curtain and watched him drift by below, angrily smoking a cigarette, face scrunched in pain.

Mami was immediately drawn in by the misery of the accident and my report of Phillip's suffering.

We met in Ikebukuro rather than our usual Odaiba coffee shop, and she dressed up for the trendy district. She wore a knee-length skirt, the material grey-green, heavy and patterned by texture rather than colour. It accentuated the sharp curve of her hips which sloped into a completely bare stomach, all abdominal muscle and ribs. Much of her upper chest was exposed, too, covered only by a white, bra-like top and an open, sheer, chocolate-brown cardigan. She made little effort to hide any aspect of herself when she sat down in front of me, crossing long, svelte legs. She leant forward to tap her cigarette in the Starbucks ashtray and people stared. In a city of prim women reluctant to show even a strip of skin between pants and shirt, Mami had decided to wear nothing more than a bikini top and towel. Were it not for the exquisite fabrics, she could have been at a beachside café.

'I'll take care of Phillip,' she said. 'Nurse him.'

I put down my caramel macchiato and shook my head.

'He'd love that. But I've got it under control. It's just a few pills and—'

'No. I want to.'

'Why?'

She shrugged. 'I'm bored. It'd be interesting.'

Neither of us finished our coffee that first Friday after the accident, pushing our way out of the store. Mami wanted to start on her new project at once and so we returned to the apartment. Phillip, a little shaky on his feet, was in the kitchen trying to make a sandwich with the same limited ingredients I had used prior to his arrival. He noticed Mami and ran his eyes down her full length.

'What the hell's she doing here, Tuttle?'

Mami smiled patiently. 'Me? I'm going to be your new nurse.'

'I don't need a nurse. I have one.' He clucked his tongue and curtly added, 'Nice outfit, though.'

Mami glanced down. 'You like Prada? Does your present nurse dress like this?'

'Tuttle? Could do. Wouldn't surprise me.'

'And you like him in it?'

'I wouldn't,' Phillip said carefully.

Mami reached out and softly ran two fingers along the length of his jaw. 'That settles it then. I'll be better.'

Phillip frowned, perhaps remembering Mami's noodle snub. Eventually he shrugged his compliance.

At that moment, Tilly appeared at the door, still thin and pale but more energetic than I had seen her in weeks. I let her in and Phillip rolled his good eye. 'We're trying to squat here,' he said.

She stared at the bandages. 'What happened to you?'

'Nothing.'

Mami stepped forward. 'Hello,' she said.

Tilly nodded a reply and quickly turned to me. 'I got your note. What do you want?'

'Good. Let's go for a walk?'

'If you had fifty thousand dollars, what would you do?'

'Tuvalu,' said Tilly without hesitation.

'What?'

'It's an island—a string of them.'

'Where?'

'In the Pacific.'

'Why go there?'

She smiled. 'Why do I have fifty thousand dollars?'

'To make conversation. You haven't said a word the whole way here.'

'As I recall, Noah, you invited me. I've been waiting for you to tell me why.'

'And now I'm waiting for you to tell me why Tuvalu.'

Tilly entered a small civic park and took a seat on a creaking swing. It was a narrow park hemmed in by apartment blocks and filled with pine-like trees which cut out the light. The dusty ground undulated unnaturally, almost as though it were a golf course, rising up at its highest point to a half-moon which supported a drink fountain and toilet block. A nearby sandpit spread like a tentative weed to just beneath our feet. Two children took turns to jump and argued over the results.

'See that tree?' Tilly asked.

'Which one?'

'The thick-trunked, spindly-topped one near the toilet.'

'Yeah.'

'It's a cherry tree.'

'I hate cherry trees. I hate the week they bloom—
everyone obsessing over them, taking pictures with their
phones. What's relaxing about thousands of people packed
into a park, queuing to peer at petals?'

'Someone at the hostel—a Japanese girl—told me this
tree's at least a few hundred years old. And there are others
a thousand years old. That makes me wonder how many
people have stared at them. How many people have stared,
exactly as we're doing, then vanished into the memories of
their children, and then altogether? Look how thick that
trunk is.'

'People are remembered.'

'Are they? Remember the ambulance when we first
met? The man on the stretcher?'

'Vaguely.'

'In a few hundred years—just the age of this tree—
there'll be no proof he lived. That's the size of time.'

'You're changing the topic.'

'Because it's as good as anywhere,' Tilly said with a
frustrated shrug. 'Tuvalu. That's my reason.'

'That's it?'

'That's it.'

'That's not a reason.'

'It is. Once I was in a hospital. I was watching midafternoon TV. You know what it's like at that hour, all kids'
shows—educational stuff. The one I was watching had a
segment on Tuvalu and I've never forgotten the place. It
wasn't a remarkable show or anything, not at all. The pre-
senter did a dive, went to a village and stayed in a bungalow.
But to me, then, it looked like somewhere to go. Somewhere

to want to go. Everyone has a place like that. A dream land or life they're working towards, however vaguely.'

'Why?'

'Because without it we realise we're obliged to die wanting.'

'You don't think you're being just a tad melodramatic?'

'Am I? Some people probably have more than one Tuvalu in a life. It changes as they grow. Or maybe they get to the first and find it's nothing like they imagined and need a new one. You must have had at least one?'

'Maybe it was Tokyo.'

'No.'

'No?'

'You're here because it's the perfect place to be alone—no one pushing. You can hide out, be as selfish as you like.'

'And you? Why are you here?'

'To be alone,' Tilly said, 'but for different reasons.'

For a moment we were both quiet. I sat staring at the cherry tree, thinking about my place in Tokyo, which was no place at all.

'Tell me more about Tuvalu,' I said finally.

'I guess for me Tuvalu's always done the trick. I've never been anywhere near it. I've never even studied it. For all I know it might well have sunk. But that one word's taken on a meaning all of its own.' At this she grinned. 'Don't look so puzzled. Haven't you ever once looked into the future and pictured a different life for yourself, made it a destination in some abstract way? A place in which you're content and from which you never look forward, except maybe to hope for more of the same? You must have. You're just not telling.'

'No.'

'Maybe you're busy making one?'

'I don't think so.'

We watched the children take turns to jump, leaping ineffectually and falling well short of the sticks they had set down to determine points.

'Why don't you just go there?' I asked.

'No.'

'A moment ago you said it was the first thing you'd do with—'

'—fifty thousand dollars. Exactly.'

'I think you should see what's there and get it out of your system. Do it before it's too late, before someone's sitting here, staring at this trunk, thinking about you.'

Tilly shifted on the swing and frowned. 'I don't want to.'

'Why not? What's the point of a dream without trying to live it?'

'I didn't say it was a dream, not exactly. It's similar but different.'

'I don't have a Tuvalu, granted, but if I did I'd sure as hell make an effort to go there.'

'I think I know what your Tuvalu is,' Tilly said sadly.

'What?'

But she ignored the question and went on. 'It serves a purpose as it is. Perhaps once, perhaps in that hospital, it was somewhere I wanted to go. Now it's just what it is.'

'Which is what?'

She shrugged. 'We all have to look forward to something, don't we?'

'But if it's fake, why—'

'It's not. It's real. That's the problem. There is no perfect place to live. If all I knew was satisfaction it'd soon develop colours, shades, some of which I'd take to calling dissatisfaction since they're not half as pleasing as the original. After a while those differences would feel very severe to me and I'd be back where I started. I'd be back here. And knowing that, in order to keep Tuvalu I have to keep away from it. Anyway, if I really believed I was going there, going to find a Tuvalu, I'd never live. I'd live only in waiting.'

'So how do you keep it and keep away? By lying to yourself?'

'In a way. And by accepting this is life. I'll be me anywhere. I just sometimes picture the place and pretend it's still coming. It's my answer to this tree, to what I said before—the size of time.'

I felt irritation at her pessimism. 'I don't agree.'

'Then you haven't worked it out yet,' Tilly said, standing.

Tilly seemed upset with me for asking so many questions about Tuvalu, for laying it bare like some dead fish, and I never got around to asking if I could help with her living arrangements or flight home. She returned to the hostel and did not even give me a parting smile as she walked past the builders, dust and scattered nails, and on into a barrage of noise.

I wished I had kept my mouth shut.

When at last I stepped into the apartment Mami, fully dressed but with wet hair, was just stepping out of the bathroom. She looked at me blankly, as though perhaps

I had entered a house in which I had no clear business, in which she was the wife and I was a common thief. Then she averted her eyes and roughed up her hair with a towel.

'You're back,' she said casually.

'That's right.'

I walked past her into the room where Phillip lay on his makeshift bed, one leg crossed casually over the other, both his hands up behind his head. He did not seem to be in pain and I guessed he was drugged. He looked sleepy and his T-shirt was lying crumpled beside him. He was bare-chested and began to play with what little hair was growing back from an old photoshoot shave.

Mami touched me on the shoulder and said she would return in the morning. She left quickly, not bothering to listen for people outside. I heard her say good evening to someone, then the muffled sound of her feet taking the steps two at a time. The door banged and I moved to lock it. For a moment I stood perfectly still in the alcove, then I resumed my old post at the entrance to the living room, staring at Phillip.

'Tuttle …' he said dreamily.

'Feeling better?' I asked.

'Much, much, much …' And his voice evaporated like a fog into morning sunlight.

Then came the final destruction of the hostel.

We watched it from the apartment, realising that the deconstruction was over, that the place needed to fall in on itself and be forgotten.

The Deconstructionists worked like termites, sawing, hammering and drilling until the building was set to collapse of its own accord. I sat with Tilly, Mami and Phillip on the apartment balcony and watched the bulldozing. The hostel toppled in on itself neatly, almost like a house of playing cards. There was no great dust cloud or explosion, and precious little left to bemoan. No one said a word for a while. We were not sad, nor happy. We were like rats on a life raft, impassive so long as we were safe.

Deep in the rubble I saw a corner of the old vending machine—a sort of burial at last. It surprised me to note the Deconstructionists had left it, unsparing as they had otherwise been. The cats circled the ruin cautiously and eventually stepped into it, gingerly moving over jagged steel edges and splintered wood. Even without the building standing they appeared at home, weaving in and out of crevices.

'What will become of them?' Tilly asked our party on the balcony.

'Soup,' said Mami.

This, as it turned out, was not wrong. Two days later Tilly called my attention to the killing of the cats. By the time she rushed me to the scene, half were dead. The other half—some fifteen-odd animals—were being herded into a corner by five men with shovels.

It was a hot, dry morning, a remnant of the summer. Out of breath, Tilly pointed to the dead cats. They were battered out of shape and lay in small pools of bright red blood. Here and there tufts of fur floated across the concrete. I looked from one cat to the next. Four stark, white eyeballs had popped whole from battered skulls creating a cartoonish sense of alarm, and yet others had burst, forming flaccid sacks which drained a transparent, tear-like liquid into damp fur.

'It's a massacre,' Tilly shouted at me, voice panicky. I had to nod. The scattered carcasses lay in a five-metre-long court. Anyone could see this dead end had been purposefully selected for the gruesome task at hand. It had been sealed off at its open end with miscellaneous building products such as plywood and corrugated iron. Those cats awaiting their turn beneath the shovel circled and hissed while steadily moving towards the back wall.

'Don't you see what they're doing, Noah? Do something!'

The men raised their shovels in anticipation, their chests heaving, their rigid faces dripping sweat. I watched them move further and further forward, but action seemed beyond me. The sun glinted across the base of a shovel, blinding me. One or two of the cats hissed and the men shortened their steps, lowering their heads a fraction and exchanging glances. When it finally happened Tilly hit me across the shoulder angrily, fist clenched. I heard her screaming at them but the men ignored her, lining up the cats one by one and bringing their shovels down forcefully. They only raised them as high as their shoulders. Sometimes a shovel would smack concrete, other times there would come a thud.

In the end, the hairless cats and the kittens held out longest. The former were, as Tilly had insisted long ago, the strongest and smartest. They seemed almost to run with their eyes up, looking for shovels. They also knew to vary their speed and direction. The kittens, not nearly as smart, only survived because their rat-like bodies made them a hard target. The last three cats were killed messily and completely without compassion.

Tilly did not stay to see all this. She stormed off after watching a man scoop up a kitten with his shovel and heft it into a wall. He was close to the barricade and she spat on him as she passed. He stared at her, then at her white, bubbled saliva on his jacket, and finally wiped himself clean with a handkerchief. Tilly walked away without a word.

Escape

Phillip and I took work in hotels—work procured by Mami. We taught English to the staff and occasionally helped out with the foreign guests, but neither one of us could get more than twenty hours a week. Initially Phillip embraced this sustained state of poverty as he had his previous hiatuses from clubs and drugs, throwing himself into high-rep weights. But when this particular hiatus did not end he began to despair.

There was no question of him modelling, even after the bandages came off. There was a nasty gash crossing his face. It started to the right of his hairline, crossed his forehead, passed between his eyes just above the nose, and ended in the middle of his left cheek. It was healing well, though the scar would require plastic surgery. Slowly, we watched the swelling and bruising surrounding it falter and vanish.

But there was another injury too, one Phillip rarely discussed. He had sustained a bruise on the top of his head. This bruise had faded, but well after everything seemed back to normal he continued to suffer debilitating headaches. If anything, they worsened with time. To my way of thinking, the blow to his head and the headaches were linked, but Phillip would not concede the point. He self-medicated with painkillers which he became all too adept at conning from doctors citywide. Somehow he avoided going to hospital and paid only what he had to for an almost constant supply of drugs. Anyone could see this was a patch-up job but Phillip would not listen. Medicated, he did sit-ups and push-ups until exhausted.

Meanwhile, Tilly was gone. I could feel it. There had been no sign of her since the killing of the cats, and those things she would never have parted with—a photo of her mother on a plane, her passport, her leather wallet, a faulty silver watch and a Soseki novel—were all missing from the pile of belongings she had left just inside the apartment door.

Faced with this reality, I thought about striking out for Europe, for a cheap but somewhat central city—Bratislava, say—where I could start over. But even if I could find the money and arrange a work permit, Tilly's abrupt departure and refusal to say goodbye had rattled me. I was suddenly reluctant to be any more alone than I already was.

Our eviction—or escape—from Nakamura-san's apartment marked the start of colder weather. It took place on a dim, rainy day. Tokyo had pulled in all the bedding which normally hung from its countless identical balconies, and the dripping apartment blocks were hulking and drab without colourful splotches of linen. In the end it was probably our use of the amenities that was our un-doing. The police appeared at our door at around one p.m. I heard the doorbell and crept to the peephole. Phillip followed, making unintelligible gestures.

'Who?' he hissed.

'Police.'

'Shit it.'

The doorbell rang a second time. Outside, the two officers exchanged comments. Phillip signalled that we should escape via the balcony, then changed his mind, whispering that there might be a police unit in the alley below and anyway, it was too high. He was woozy from painkillers regardless. I agreed it was a bad idea.

The police rang the doorbell a third time. We both pulled back from the tiny peephole. The handle moved, but luckily the door was locked.

The officers, grumbling softly, started back down the staircase.

'This is our chance,' I said.

'How?'

'If they had a key they'd already have used it. More than likely they have to go to the landlord for it. We wait one minute, then we run.'

'We've got to pack.'

'We've got one minute.'

Together we bundled up our various belongings, mine into my suitcase, Phillip's into his backpack. When he dropped his passport in, however, I grabbed it back out and thrust it into my little pack, along with other essentials, mostly documents. We limited ourselves strictly to clothing, blankets and food from the fridge. Finally we hoisted it all up, dropped the keys into the sink and paused in front of the door to listen.

'Nothing,' I said. 'Is there anything left here that can identify us?'

'My pills!'

'Do they have your name on them?'

'No.'

'Then forget them.'

'No.'

Phillip searched both the living rooms then returned, sagging beneath his backpack and out of breath already. I threw open the door and we ran. One or two people pruning pot plants stared, but no one said a word or tried to stop us. We ran for five minutes without seeming to go all that far. Reaching a large road we tried to flag a taxi. Two cruised by but neither stopped. Back at the apartment we could see a police car pulling up. One officer started towards the building without looking in our direction, but the other noticed us. They hurried back towards the car and climbed in. A second later the lights flashed and a knife-edged siren sounded. The car jolted forward out of the car park.

'We're in trouble,' I said.

Our situation was unfavourable but not impossible. We were standing at a T-intersection with traffic blocking our path. There was an alley ahead leading to a far larger, far busier road a hundred or so metres up. We had one chance.

'If we can cross this street and cut through that alley to the main road up ahead, we might beat them through the traffic. We could get a cab before they catch up.'

'Not a chance,' said Phillip dejectedly.

'No, it's possible. Come on, dump your pack.'

We both sprinted across the street into an alley, sealed off from traffic and loosely lined with wooden fences. Phillip's voice echoed off each slat differently. 'They can't prove it was us, Tuttle.'

'They can. The neighbours can identify us.'

'Shit it.'

Halfway up the alley I turned to see the police car stuck beside our luggage at the pedestrian crossing, and I let out a whoop. My arms felt heavy and cumbersome, and my legs began to protest. I kept having to pull the little pack up onto my shoulder as I ran. Ahead, cars, trucks and taxis flicked past, all oblivious to our flight. I could smell carbon monoxide.

As we exited the alley, gasping for air, I ventured a quick look behind. The police were crossing the intersection, siren still blaring, and pulling up at the alley entrance. My heart sank as I grabbed Phillip by the shirt and dragged him along the busy street to a bus stop. I casually waved one arm, trying not to look desperate. But when I turned Phillip was waving with both, as though signalling a far-off plane.

'What the fuck are you doing?'

'What?'

'Act normal.'

The police were in the alley now, running. In the distance I heard shoes on concrete. Whoever was coming was serious.

I was about to give up when a taxi veered sharply left and skidded to a halt in front of us.

'In,' I said to Phillip, who only nodded.

The driver smiled. He was a young Japanese man with long oily hair—not at all the typical Japanese taxi driver. There was no comb-over, no starched white gloves.

'Where?' he asked in English.

'Anywhere,' said Phillip.

'Shinjuku,' I cut in. 'Shinjuku Station.'

'Okay.' The driver put the car into gear and activated his right blinker. There was a steady stream of traffic and for a moment we went nowhere. I glanced back. There was no one there. Then the officers appeared, both lurching as they ran and out of breath. They stopped dead at the main road and looked left and right. One pointed towards the cab. I snapped my head back to the road, watching the driver who, with one eye on the rear-view mirror, tapped his index finger on the steering wheel. His mouth was curved in a smile, and without warning he punched the accelerator.

I let out a lungful of air.

For a while we worried our bags might have contained something that could identify us, but we could think of nothing inside them that did and no one tried to contact or arrest us. Not that anyone could have. We took time off work, checked into a cheap love hotel under false names—after convincing the manager we were straight—and became invisible to the authorities. Not even we knew where we were.

From here we moved into a far smaller box, taking a room on the eighth floor of an apartment block in outlying Saitama prefecture. The elevator was broken and we were only allowed to stay for two months, filling in for foreigners holidaying in Eastern Europe. Mostly it was an awful place to live. Entering, you stepped into a dark, narrow hallway which led past a sink and bathroom to a room the width of a sedan. This room ended in a frosted window, jammed shut.

Phillip slept in a three-foot-square loft above the hallway, a sort of tube he slid himself in and out of and derived a sense of privacy from. The loft was accessed by a ladder and Phillip, once nestled inside, would pull it up and lean it against one wall. He also had a small curtain, rarely open. As far as I could tell he spent most of his time up there high on grass—God knows where he got it— shivering on the fetid mattress.

We both returned to work, and on my days off I tried to get out and walk. There was a factory nearby and I made it my habit to watch bored, blue-clad workers letting themselves in and out of a small gate, all punching timecards. Judging from the smell, this factory made vinegar. It was a raw smell, almost like a detergent, which sanitised the indistinct smog of outer Tokyo.

Though I e-mailed Tilly daily, she never replied.

In between missing Tilly I also missed Mami. I had fallen out of touch with both and, though I could not contact Tilly without another flight home, it was always in the back of my mind that I could find Mami.

One cold cloudless pre-dawn, unable to sleep in the new apartment, I commuted back to the familiar Tsukiji fish markets and wandered beneath yellow bulbs with green tin shades and alongside jobbers pulling carts, cigarettes hanging from their down-turned lips. These were men so tired of tourists I felt like a ghost in their presence. I followed the long reflections of the bulbs on the wet concrete, moving between cluttered, boxy stalls and squeaking polystyrene to the tuna bidding, where I was told to hang back by someone in uniform. I was thankful to be away from the endless sameness of square-box living, no longer surrounded by a stranger's belongings. Here there was again that modicum of mess, chaos and clutter that I missed about the hostel.

I found my way to Tsukiji Station—to the Naka-Meguro-bound platform, where I waited for a train and thought about the sarin gas attack of several years ago. Some foreigner had told me the story and every time I stood on the platform details returned. The train had come to a halt here a full five stops after the release of gas at Akihabara. People had collapsed from the doors. Although one passenger had kicked the deadly package from the train at the previous stop, Kodenmacho—where it killed four passengers waiting on the platform—a puddle of sarin remained inside on the floor of the carriage. Eight had died and hundreds were injured. As always, the thought made me nervous.

I travelled on to Roppongi, wandered in the stark remnants of the previous night's unfettered festivity, then took the Toei Oedo Line to Shinjuku. From Shinjuku, finally aware I was circling in on someone, I found my way to Tokyo Station, enduring Phillip's unscarred face beaming down from countless JR posters. The smiling man featured bore no resemblance to the sour dope addict I now lived with. He was the old Phillip. Staring at the ad I was struck by how little I knew him. He came without a past, as if born fully grown.

I snuck into the hotel and took the elevator to the twentieth floor. Mami at first refused to open the door. When finally she did she looked like a wrung-out dish-cloth, face pale and sagging.

'What are you doing here?' she asked. 'I thought I made it clear.'

'Made what clear?'

'Made it clear I'm busy.'

'With what?'

'What does it matter what? What do you want?'

I had not expected this greeting, and thus had not prepared an excuse. I said the first thing that came into my head. 'I wanted to talk to you about Phillip.'

Mami frowned. 'What do I care about Phillip?'

'Aren't you his nurse?'

'Do I look like a nurse?'

I shook my head, biting at the inside of my lip. 'Can I come in for a moment?'

'Do you need to?'

'It'd be a lot easier, yeah.' I gave the impression of great solemnity to aid my chances and stepped inside. I crossed to the bar, dropped my jumper over it and groped for something to say about Phillip. Again it occurred to me how little I knew.

'He's been smoking grass.'

'That's it?' Mami asked. 'What's that got to do with me?' Her voice was clipped, rude. She kept her arms folded over her chest, distancing me. Her face conveyed distrust and her eyes jumped over the room as if wondering what it looked like to another.

'Well, you were interested,' I said. 'Now I don't know, I, ah—'

'Is that everything?'

The room looked messy and neglected—completely unlike it had on my previous visits. Clothes were scattered about as if Mami had been putting them on only to take them off and drop them. Judging from the number of garments, this had been going on for days. I counted five or six room-service trays piled high with dirty dishes. The curtains were drawn, the ceiling lights dimmed, there were magazines open everywhere, the TV was fuzz, and there was a hole in one wall roughly the size of a basketball.

'Are you okay?' I asked.

'Of course.'

'You just look—'

'What?'

'Nothing.'

For a moment not a word was said, then Mami threw up her arms. 'Oh for God's sake, you feed a stray dog once and it really does follow you for the rest of your life.'

'I don't deserve that.'

'The hell you do, Noah.' Mami was furious with me. 'Go on,' she said. 'Shoo.'

'Not until you tell me what I've done.'

'You?' She laughed.

Oddly, at the sound of this laugh, I felt compassion rather than anger. 'Then what's this all about? Something's wrong. What?'

'Nothing.'

'Tell me, please.'

'It's nothing.'

'Just tell me.'

'I did, you idiot!' Mami screamed. She seemed almost like a child. Then, inhaling sharply and letting the air out in a longish sigh, she composed herself, snatched up the TV remote and turned the volume to full. The static forced me, against my will, to yell.

'Please, I want to help.'

Ignoring me, Mami began flicking through channels. On one a man with an absurdly large microphone cracked a joke and the studio audience roared. She kept flicking until the TV reached Video 2, a narrow slot of dark, expectant silence at which she threw down the remote and pressed buttons on the DVD player. She skipped chapters until Audrey Hepburn filled the screen. Regal, Audrey presided over a hall packed with people—journalists. It was *Roman Holiday*. The journalists were codedly explaining to the princess that, while they would treasure time spent with her, they would never print a word of it nor seek to impose again. She could resume her old life without interruption.

'She escapes,' said Mami. 'She wanders out into the world and they pose as guides, these men. But finally they know the game is up. She has her life to think of. She hates it. But she has it all the same and people demand. People always demand.'

'I've seen it.'

'Then why am I explaining it to you? Why are you still here?'

'Maybe I don't believe you really want me to go.'

Without the slightest hesitation Mami picked up the TV remote and threw it at my head. It struck my chin, deflecting into my shoulder. My body remained rooted to the ground while Mami relaxed palpably, letting out—of all things—a hiccup. I turned and stared at the remote, now off in a corner, the batteries askew.

'Now shoo,' she said again, softly, even sadly.

I left quickly, wiping a little blood from my lip and carefully closing the door behind me. The maid I once yelled at was in the hall with her full trolley. She frowned and stepped back, and I unhappily nodded hello.

I had no idea where to go. I took trains until at last I found myself outside Tsukiji-Shijo Station. I was back at the fish markets, seemingly drawn to them, as if the hostel was still home and Tilly still in reach. The jobbers had sold their fish to retailers and packed up, and the concrete was being watered by a tanker truck, front nozzles jetting white and washing away the morning.

A typhoon struck the following day. Tired of being cooped up in the airless box I worked at getting the window open. It took me twenty minutes of hefting and swearing but it finally gave. Fresh air buffeted its way inside. Above me, clouds sped past at three or four times their usual speed, and below people lost umbrellas or had them fold inside out with a faint, far-off whoop. Stray dogs—their noses down, tails up—scurried for shelter. Buildings howled. And liberated plastic bags took off down empty streets at speed, tumbling and seeming always to look behind as if on the run.

Halfway through this storm Phillip arrived home. He was saturated but his eyes seemed alert. 'Look,' he said, opening the palm of one hand. 'Stems. I bought stems.'

'For what?'

He only grinned and, closing his hand, stretched. He looked inordinately tall and I noticed he had the beginnings of a belly.

'Stems for what, Phillip?'

'Grass, of course. What the fuck else would I grow in here?' Yawning through a smile, he wandered into the kitchen and I heard him open the fridge. I could picture him resting his weight on the door, eyeing my food.

In a strange about-face, Mami invited me to the Artist's Café high atop Tokyo Dome Hotel to celebrate her birthday. She sent the invite via work. At first I decided not to go. But her offer ate at me until I relented.

When I arrived at dusk, having taken a glass elevator to the top of a forty-something storey hotel, Mami was smiling and holding out an ornate envelope. She handed it to me, then led me towards an elegant bar with two uniformed staff.

'I'm breaking with convention,' she said, head tilted as if asking me a question. When I frowned her smile warmed. She ordered drinks and gestured for me to take a seat at a narrow glass bench with headphones and a steel footrest. This was built against a floor-to-ceiling window and

afforded me a superb view of the city. I could make out
Tokyo Tower and a far-off ferris wheel even before I sat,
perhaps the same wheel Mami had taken me on.

'How are you breaking with convention?' I asked when
she arrived at the bench with two whiskys and a plate full
of nibbles.

'You haven't opened the envelope?'

'Not yet.'

'It's my birthday and if it wasn't for you, well, I'd still feel
awful. Throwing that remote helped me somehow, even
though it was a despicable thing to do. I'm surprised you
even came tonight. But you did. So instead of receiving a
present I'm going to give you one. That's only fair.'

Mami gestured to the envelope. I opened it and found
a thin wad of 10,000 yen notes. I at once shut it and
handed it back.

'A thankyou is perfectly sufficient.'

Mami placed it back in my hand. 'No. I insist.
Anyway, it's not my money. It's my father's and he'd want
me to give it to you. It's how things need to be.'

'Why?'

'Why? I don't like to be indebted to a person. My
family doesn't, either. This way we can put it behind us—
as though it never happened.'

I again handed back the envelope. 'No thanks.'

'Pure madness.'

We sat in silence for a moment staring out over the city.
In the last light of day it was square and grey and cluttered.
The buildings were packed tightly beside one another, like
old boxes in storage. Boxes on boxes, extending out
endlessly. The glass deadened all sound. I watched great fans

turn lazily inside the rooftop airconditioner and thought how unlike the hostel this was, how unlike the little street Mami had stood in, squinting up and telling me to ask more questions. Back then I feared her entering my life. Now she was excising me, cutting around and beneath me like a tumour.

'And in addition to this gift—which will only be left here if you don't take it—I'm going to find you somewhere to live. You'll pay the rent but I'll act as a guarantor and pay the deposit. All you'll have to do is move in.'

'I won't take it. None of it.'

'You will. Just watch.' And without another word, Mami dropped the envelope on the floor and left. I called after her but she ignored me. The eyes of the staff followed her out, curious. I suspected they knew who she was because they grouped to discuss the visit as soon as she was in the elevator.

For a long while after Mami's departure, I remained. I sat staring out the window at the city, watching familiar red bulbs pulse on tall buildings while trains slid into a station immediately below. They came from opposite directions but stopped perfectly in line, time and time again. Nearby, a Mitaya store, the brightest in the area, demanded a degree of attention hardly befitting its size. And to my right, dwarfed by distance, sat Shinjuku, a lump, like an ant nest burning from the inside out.

I had come to associate this height, this detached over-view of the world and its workers, with Mami. I decided it was a perspective I should never have known. Having stepped from my own anxious poverty just long enough to recognise the endless possibilities before me, the vast panorama of adulthood, I had marooned myself between two worlds.

I picked up the envelope on my way out and buried it deep in my coat pocket. Perspectives aside, there was rent to pay.

Tinkerbelle's Treat

Growing marijuana gave Phillip something to think about, distracting him from his daily headaches. He was in and out of the apartment like a bee, researching one horticultural detail after another.

I did not share his enthusiasm. The size of the project and Phillip's intention to sell the crop to a mystery buyer worried me. I researched Japanese drug laws on the internet but found little information that was concrete. The reliable sites were all in Japanese, the remainder posted by past and present foreigners. Though I did not trust the latter, they were clear on two points—Japanese law made little or no distinction between marijuana and heroin, and growing it was tanta-mount to dealing it. Which meant a hefty prison sentence.

When Phillip purchased tubular fluorescent lights and installed them without permission, I decided there was a need to put an end to this new hobby. I interrupted him as he read from a book on hydroponics, purchased in the English section of Kinokuniya.

'You know,' I said, keeping my voice calm and level, 'you never told me where the stems came from or who it is you plan to sell this crop to.'

'It's a need-to-know basis, Tuttle.' Phillip put the book down, collected his wallet and keys, and crossed to the apartment door.

'Bugger that,' I said.

'What?' He looked irritated at not having escaped before my objection.

'I share the risk.'

'Relax. You know the guy.'

This surprised me. 'Who?'

Phillip opened the apartment door as if about to leave but did not step out. It was raining and I could see large drops falling as straight and fast as darts. Unlike in the rainy season, this rain was cold. Suppressing a shiver Phillip pulled on a windbreaker with one hand.

'Harry,' he said at last. 'You know, from the hostel.'

'Where is he?'

'Why?'

'I'm curious.'

Phillip looked sceptical as he pulled on the hood. 'If you screw this up for me, Tuttle, I swear I'll—'

'You'll what?' I glared at him but then quickly thought the better of it and almost smiled, allowing the faintest hint of a laugh to fall into my words. 'For God's sake, I won't screw anything up. Trust me. Now where is he? I'd like to catch up with him.'

Phillip thought a moment, then answered in a murmur almost lost to the rain. 'Tinkerbelle's Treat.'

'What?'

'It's in Musashi-Urawa. That guy's making a name for himself. The rumour is, he owns the place. Now keep your mouth shut and remember there's money in this.'

'Fine.'

Phillip let himself out, shaking his head. Rain dripped loudly, coldly, until the door banged shut and the silence of the kitchen leant in to hear my whisper. 'Son of a bitch.'

Tinkerbelle's Treat was a bizarre building, just bizarre enough to be a success in Japan. The country was funny that way—it was the perfect place to launch a ludicrous business. Like, for example, theme parks modelled on Dutch towns, or the ride at Parque Espana, where people become the bull in a bullfight. There was always a new novelty waiting to grab the attention of a population raised on bright lights and kitsch replicas.

I was lucky to find the place. After taking a commuter train to Musashi-Urawa Station I asked locals for directions, but no one had the first idea what I was talking about until one man grinned and pointed down a featureless street. He mumbled instructions in shy, broken English. I thanked him and within a few hundred metres passed the barn he had described. A sign, situated above a huge American flag—flapping like a rug in the strong breeze—read 'Tinkerbelle's Treat—Authentic American Hostesses'.

I had waited only one day to find Harry. I had no plan for getting back my money beyond asking him for it and again threatening to go to the police. Somehow, never having dealt with unscrupulous, thieving, drug-dealing people, I imagined he would feel bad and offer up whatever he could. In each wood-framed window there were fluorescent lights promoting American beers—Bud, Miller, Coors Light. I could hear the bass of a stereo thumping to a rock song and on the balcony a carpenter was cutting lengths of timber with an electric saw while another stacked them. Without doubt Tinkerbelle's Treat had been built to a theme. There was a balcony and railing, an ornate doorbell, a letterbox and space for a front lawn, now sprinkled with seed. The more I looked at it, the less barn-like it seemed. It was a prairie cabin.

I ignored the workers and rang the bell. Behind me the electric saw wound out. I stood waiting. Finally Harry appeared, short as ever and dressed in a suit with a shiny tie strung loosely around his flabby neck. He was perfectly relaxed, giving the impression he considered me a close friend. He stuck out his hand and I could not help but shake it.

'Let's go for dinner,' he said.

'Fine.'

'I know a good place. Grill your own meat sort of a thing. You'll love it.'

The automatic glass doors slid back. A woman in her early fifties came rushing to assist us, apron around her middle, notepad at the ready. She showed us to a table and, as soon as we were seated, reached to the side and turned a knob. The burner in the middle of our table flared beneath black coals and she stood expectantly with her notepad until Harry ordered two Kirin beers.

'I want that money,' I said while we waited.

'I know.'

'Do you have it?'

'I've said I'll give it to you.'

'But you haven't, and it's time you did.' I was doing my level best to sound assertive.

A young girl of five or six in a floral dress entered with her mother, distracting the waitress from our drinks. We sat watching the two women—obviously old friends—talk, while the girl stood facing the counter, head turned towards us. Her eyes drank us up without revealing an opinion. She might have been staring at a television. After they left we received our drinks and clinked them wordlessly.

'So why won't you pay?' I asked.

Harry leant in, elbows on the table. I had the uneasy sense he was enjoying toying with me, like a cat with a grasshopper, unwilling to kill it outright—letting it go and swiping it back.

'The world to me,' he said, 'is nothing more than opportunities, and you're not an opportunity.'

'Let's confine this to the money.'

'I am confining it to the money.'

'I'm serious, Harry. Don't give me the run—'

'You're not worth repaying, not yet.' He gestured to the waitress. 'Let's eat,' he said.

'I know about Phillip, about the grass—what you're up to. It only takes a phone call.'

Harry's face lost its levity. 'Listen to me, Noah. For whatever—' The waitress arrived and, not understanding a word, waited by our table for an order. Harry glanced at her, but decided to go ahead and finish what he was saying.

'For whatever reason, you've cut yourself off from this world. You know next to no one and you don't seem interested in getting to know anyone. That's why you're no opportunity. I don't have any need for some kid who sits around staring at his cock all day. You understand? Whatever use you were, I've used. I'm talking plainly now. You somehow want to make yourself of use again, well, maybe you'll see the money sooner rather than later, but you never, ever fucking threaten me. I'll pay you when I'm good and ready.'

He turned to the waitress, smiled and placed an order in effortless Japanese, adding in English for my benefit, 'It's just for one. My friend has to go.'

I sat for a moment, trying to think up a powerful reply. But I lacked the courage. All those nights planning my invective, and I only stood and walked out of the restaurant. The doors peeled back for me—chimed. Outside the last of the sun glinted in my eyes. Cars roared past too fast for the narrow roads.

Then something struck me hard from behind and the pavement smacked my skull, grazing my face. Someone kicked me sharply in the stomach. Trying to look up I caught sight of the carpenters from Tinkerbelle's Treat, before both men climbed into a car and pulled out into the traffic.

The Winter

So began the winter.

I remember thinking, sitting on the train home from Tinkerbelle's Treat, that the season ahead could only improve. I stared out over apartment blocks—thousands upon thousands of staircase safety lights. Somewhere a giant strobe was sweeping the sky and I found myself following it up, down and around. The stations stopped and started. In the carriage I could feel everyone's eyes on me, my face. Presumably it was still bleeding. I could taste blood on my lips and took care licking them clean.

A middle-aged woman would not avert her eyes, even when I stared her down. Others glanced or shared whispers. At home I would have been a ghost, everyone afraid I might stand and hit them. But here I was a spectacle. And no wonder. The train carriage looked like every other. A few boys tended to their streetwear in darkened windows with the fastidiousness of young women. Ugly salarymen read about computers. Make-up-smeared girls typed messages into mobile phones from which dangled cheap toys and tacky plastic jewellery. A bum rubbed at his hands and explained something to himself. Dull men in plain clothes read porn. And attractive women scowled as if they would have their looks forever. There were no children.

Above all this, like an exhaust, lingered an oppressive unease, a nastiness that got into the blood and filled the brain with malice. To blot out the middle-aged woman I pulled a newspaper from the luggage rack. I could read nothing more than the date—two days old. I flicked through the dense pages, scanning pictures. There was a crane, a boy in uniform, a politician and a Bangkok freeway which came to an abrupt halt in midair. Finally I turned to a society page only to find myself staring at a photo of Mami Kaketa. She was with a man. There was no doubt in my mind it was her. I tried to read the article but it was hopeless, so I asked the girl to my left if she spoke English. Startled, she waved her palm rapidly and dropped her head. Same with an old man with gunk at the corners of his lips, though he stiffened stupidly like a hare hiding in a mown field.

It was my stop and I had to get off. I dropped the paper into a bin, deciding it was nothing important, and did not give it another thought until my hotel shift the following day, where it was still news.

It turned out Mami had stolen something—a bag. She had been caught on video trying to smuggle it out of Takashimaya. Oddly, though an accomplished thief, she had set off the store alarms and was taken in for questioning by a security guard who wasted no time turning her over to police. A co-worker of mine with frizzy hair and a degree in English Literature from a top Japanese university raised the matter as we stood in the kitchen, waiting for the same order.

'It's a shock,' he said.

'What?'

'Kaketa-san.'

'Why?'

'She was—how do you say? Royal. Famous. No, not famous. Almost, I think.'

'She was? I didn't know.'

'But you had heard of her?'

'Yes.'

'Then you see.'

I did not explain how I knew Mami.

'Yes,' he went on, 'the media in Japan, they used to say the perfect girl. Rich and pretty. Clever maybe, too. Always I think pretty people are clever. Clever ugly get the money to do the sex with pretty people.' He paused. 'Et al.,' he added.

'What will happen to her?'

'Trial. But she had run away. It was on the news—NHK. She had run far, far away. Maybe Hokkaido, the top Japanese island.'

'Why not leave the country?'

He shrugged.

'Here at this hotel, I hear she has no money from her father now. Or maybe she likes snow. There will soon be snow.'

I hardly slept for a week. I walked quiet streets, peering into yellow-lit apartments. I felt incredibly lonely and it was this which eventually led me to call Tilly a little before sun-up on a Saturday morning, having walked and sat on benches all night and waited in vain for the sun to rise from the top of an austere parking lot. How could it hurt to be civil, I reasoned, to take an interest in an ex-girlfriend? Was she home?

I found a phone, purchased a card and dialled Tilly's number, which was still deep inside my wallet. The call rang out and, nervous, I dialled again.

Mr Willoughby's voice was sleepy.

'Mr Willoughby?'

'Yes.'

'It's Noah Tuttle. I was wondering, is Tilly there?'

There was a lengthy silence in which I pressed the cold plastic receiver hard against my ear, waiting for a reply.

'Matilda?' he asked.

'Yeah.'

'Who's this?'

'Noah Tuttle.' I worried about the early hour. 'I didn't wake you, did I?'

Another pause.

'She's dead,' Mr Willoughby said, before quietly hanging up.

I was astounded. I had to know more. Even if more was only a scrap, a single word. I had to know *how*.

For days I dialled Tilly's number, always getting the busy signal. More often than not I would think about that one tail-light, about the day I found a seat on the train without bothering to say goodbye. It was by no means the last time I saw Tilly, but it was the moment I most regretted. Somehow in my mind that was the point at which I abandoned her; the point at which I finally took her for granted. Perhaps it was even earlier than that. Perhaps it was from the beginning. But it was the tail-light my mind skipped to whenever I heard that long tone.

Once or twice I slumped and tried to cry but, sober, the tears felt forced and unearned. I had no idea what to cry about. Without knowing how she died, she was not dead. At least not to me. Over and over I would expect her to answer, to discover she was alive and merely extracting revenge for the cats.

In between dialling I tried to go on with my life as before, but my hatred for Tokyo only intensified. At work I came close to shouting at customers. My thoughts bubbled threateningly like lava and I became yet more racist in my outlook, lumping the Japanese in together and hating them all with an equal, unjust ferocity. I had, of course, never made any effort to integrate myself into Japanese society, but now took Tokyo's disinterest in me, in my loss, as a rebuke.

It never occurred to me to leave, however. There was nowhere to go. Instead I acquired sleeping pills and dog-gedly tried to take up drinking. The two threw my life out of focus like a snapped antenna. I was fired for not being able to add up change and for vomiting on a computer keyboard. I was always either drunk or ill, rarely bothering to leave the apartment. I stole Phillip's grass and smoked it in the bathroom, regularly exiting to dial Tilly's number, until eventually it was disconnected and replaced with a Telstra 'Out of Service' message.

This bout of booze, pills and self-pity came to an end outside a love hotel near a foreign shot bar called 'The Munroe'. I had been drinking whisky since around midday when, just on dusk, a woman sat beside me, a woman with an old, scar-pink cut that caused one eyelid to sag slightly. Japanese, she had a solid roll of fat around her middle and was perhaps forty but still retained a certain unmistakeable attractiveness. She said nothing for an hour or so, just sat and drank whatever I did. Eventually I think I bought her something—a pack of cigarettes, maybe—and we did our best to chat across two languages, mincing up the grammar of both. Twice the barman warned her off, whispered in her ear that she was drunk, that she ought to go home, but this did not stop me kissing her. We rented a love-hotel room and I vaguely recall sleeping with her, sex that became almost violent towards the end as we both struggled to finish. Horribly drunk I sobbed afterwards, and she lay hugging me until our hour was up and we found ourselves back outside, roughly dressed. She took my hand and shook it, then hobbled on high heels to a pedestrian light, waiting patiently for it to turn green before crossing the street and vanishing into a dark, leafy park full of concrete dinosaurs.

Ten minutes later my misery swirled up into a solid

fear. I vomited and, slumping onto the concrete and staring disgustedly at the mess, resolved to go home at the first opportunity. I had too many questions.

Home

The girl beside me was nervous. She wore a tight top which revealed her navel and enabled me to visualise, with some certainty, the shape of both her breasts. Whenever the plane shuddered these breasts bounced and the girl clutched the inside of the window as a rock climber might a mountain face—with sheer force of pressure. During turbulence her nasal breathing shortened and she shut her eyes. I must have sat staring at her hands for half the flight. Either that or at the girl in front, on whose head a tiny brown ant walked in muddled circles, lost amidst the black, coarse hair.

We landed safely and I was once again in Melbourne. My new backpack was searched by customs, after which I was let into the onset of summer—T-shirt weather. Women's arms and legs were on display and everyone was wearing sleek sunglasses.

This time it was Celeste who picked me up, driving me to her house, where my mother had prepared a roast. Oddly, it made all the difference to me to see my mother. I had not thought about it flying over. She was just someone who was going to be there, a stepping stone on my journey to the lavender farm. Perhaps it was the food. It took my mind off death. I tried to relax, battling a headache and feeling an obligation to actively participate in the conversation. My mother drew talk from me carefully, like worms from arid ground.

We discussed the lingering impact of the coalition war in Iraq, then Celeste's artwork—mostly about a piece called 'Fork' which, she reminded me, she had been working on at the time of my last visit. It was the can-opener project. She had welded them all into a giant fork, she explained, watching me, my face. I nodded blankly and she dropped her head.

'It's crowding fucking back of the house,' she snapped angrily, jabbing at her downcast head with one thumb. 'No one gets it.'

My mother caught my eye. 'Given a can,' she said softly, 'people so often have nothing more than a fork.'

'And so,' said Celeste, looking up and holding out both arms, 'furk!'

'I see.'

'So stupid an idea. So many openers but too smart.' She scrunched her face up. 'Too smart, too simple, *ne.*'

'I still want to see it,' I said.

'You can buy it. Buy it and melt it.'

'If it's all the same, I'd like to see it before I buy it.'

This improved things markedly. Celeste brightened, nodded and shrugged. 'I am sore,' she said. 'Ignore me.'

We ate in silence, until my mother felt it time to once

again draw me out. 'So,' she said brightly, 'tell us all about Japan, Noah. We speak so little.'

'Japan's okay.'

'You and your girlfriend,' asked Celeste distractedly, as if it was any old question, 'still fucking?'

'No.'

She cocked her head. 'Why no?'

'Tilly returned to Australia.'

'Ah … lust but no love,' she said, voice a mumble.

I did not reply, stood and cleared my plate in the kitchen, afraid that I would say something nasty about the first piece of artwork I saw. My mother joined me. She gave me a hug, which I suddenly realised she had not done at the front door.

'Celeste reacts badly to people being inside this house. She feels exposed. Everything she's done with her life since returning to Australia's here. Also …' she said, hesitating.

'What?'

'She doesn't like being the third wheel.' I suspected my mother was blushing. 'It's a shame,' she continued, 'that Celeste's like this, that this is all you see. She's fantastic when it's just the two of us.'

'She was nicer last time.'

'She wasn't. She'll calm this time, though. At the moment she's just nervous.'

'A third wheel,' I repeated. The words were not exactly a surprise but it was still bizarre to hear them.

My mother smiled. 'It must be strange for you. I remember being a child, looking up at my parents and thinking they're different to me, that they've stopped making mistakes. You always tried to look at me that way.

I saw it and I let you. But you're not a child anymore, Noah, and I'm here with Celeste. Now that you understand, perhaps you could go easier on your father.'

I felt a flutter of panic. 'I …'

My mother smiled and ran her fingers through my hair, roughing it up.

'Now come back out, will you?'

'I was only stacking my dishes.'

'I know.'

But Celeste, having heard whispers, was determined to pick a fight. 'You cheated?'

'She's dead,' I said. 'That's why I'm home. She died.'

After this no one spoke. My mother had an awful look of pity in her eyes, unaware that Celeste had been correct. Celeste, meanwhile, looked perplexed. She eventually stood and refilled her wineglass, which, being a large glass, she emptied half the bottle into. Without another word she left the room. I could hear her heavy tread on the ceiling above, pacing.

'Well,' said my mother, throwing down her napkin, 'that went much as expected. I'm sorry about Celeste. And about Matilda. What a terrible thing to have happen. Was it some kind of an accident?'

'I don't know. That's why I'm home. To find out.'

'You're going back to her place?'

'Yeah.'

An eighties pop song started to blare upstairs, bass causing the crockery to shudder.

'I really am sorry,' said my mother again.

'Stop saying sorry.'

That night I thought of Tilly and there was no comfort

in the little sleep I managed. It was all sweat, muscle ache and dreams.

The following morning I wandered down to Celeste's shed, wanting to make peace. I found her inside, dressed down in pyjamas and cutting one-inch lengths of fencing wire from a large coil before straightening them in a vice.

Behind her was one half of Tokyo's Imperial Palace. I recognised it at once and caught my breath. Made entirely from lengths of wire it included the buildings, gardens and moats, and shimmered beneath a bare globe hung over it specially. I marvelled at how Celeste had created the illusion of water and even greenery with nothing more than wire.

'Amazing,' I said, momentarily forgetting everything.

Celeste's face brightened. 'It will stand as long as the real one,' she said. 'Toughest Aussie wire.'

'I want to buy it.'

She beamed at this, cutting off a length of wire for me to inspect. I tried to bend it with my hands but could not. Seeing this, Celeste held up the tools she had been using and explained how she constructed various aspects of the buildings. I noticed she used large maps and I asked her what she could tell me about the moats.

'No information,' she said. 'I have maps for the buildings and for the gardens. And for where moats are. Nothing else. Why?'

'I know a girl in Tokyo who says she jumped into one of these moats—right here.' With a finger I pointed to where Mami claimed to have jumped.

Celeste let out a sceptical laugh and shook her head hard and fast—like a child. 'Not possible.'

'I didn't think so. She says things, this girl, things that are hard to believe.'

'She sounds bad.'

'Maybe.'

'But you like her?'

'No. Not like that.'

Celeste shrugged and returned to her work, a slight smile on her lips, like a last comment I could not rebut. I had no interest in rebutting it; I thought about Tilly and the journey ahead.

'So,' Celeste said, 'will you please your father?'

'What do you mean?'

'Live with him, go to university, get a job, get a wife, leave him for this new wife?'

'Put like that, probably not. Who told you he wanted me to do all that?'

'Your mother. Once your father, too. He came here for lunch. They both fighted—fought. Mostly it was about you. That's odd, no? You are in Japan and you don't care, and they are here. They need to talk and they use that talk on you, they spend every word on you.'

I watched Celeste return to her work. 'And what did my mother say?'

'She said you will come home.'

'When?'

'When you are tired of alone. Then you'll marry here.'

'So they talk a lot, Mum and Dad?'

'Only about you or bills or selling things.'

Celeste seemed pleased to say this. She held my eye

and, almost out of spite, I shifted the conversation from my family to hers. 'What about your children?' I asked.

'What about them?'

'Do you see them?'

Celeste glued a piece of metal in place—a part of the guardhouse I had stopped to inspect shortly after Mami tried to hang herself.

'No,' she said. 'They have lives. I have this life. I hear sometimes, they hear from me. We are close but really we don't know anything. They left home like me. We talk on the phone but they tell me nothing. When you do not see someone, when you do not see eyes, it becomes easy to lie to and hard to see a lie, I think ...' Celeste stopped talking to glue two pieces of wire, both belonging to the guardhouse. Only when each was safely in place did she resume our conversation. 'I was in Japan. They chose jobs, my children. I wanted to be involved in the lives. I had a husband but he was a risk man.'

'A risk man?'

'He loved the risk. If he had everything, he would risk everything for more. He was in construction.'

'What, a speculator?'

'Construction man.'

Frenziedly, she flapped one hand and scraped glue from the edge of a finger. 'He bought old buildings and made them better. Or he made buildings from nothing. Or he made money just to make buildings. He always wanted to make something big. I loved that. He was a dreamer. But not really dreaming about me, I knew.'

She ended up biting the dried glue from her finger.

'In Japan gambling is difficult. Without casinos it's

difficult. You have to go to the yakuza. You have to go to secret casinos. Little. My husband did not like that. He liked to gamble always, every day.'

Celeste shook her head. 'He gambled at work, with work. He looked like a good salaryman. I was always embarrassing when people came to dinner. I said too much. My cooking was bad. He liked to pretend but he was all risk. When he did projects he made them too big. He always wanted to win. We were rich. Then we went broke the first time and the second time, and I said, "goodbye love".' Celeste waved her long-fingered, glue-free hand at me.

'The children were at the university then. In and out like our money. Then back in and they got angry. This is not fair, they said to him. He was sad and he was with other women. I knew this but I did not want to prove it. I did not catch him because I did not want to. The children left us, all going to different cities. They were angry about the university, about the money. Only my husband was left—to get old together *ne*, but he did not like this idea. Also, I did not like this idea, not his way. He slept with some young women. One was our daughter's friend. I screamed. He went to parties. I stayed at home. I sat on the floor calling my children, leaving a message, leaving another message. The bad time. After it, I took a lot of money. I left. He agreed and I was very lucky because soon he went broke again. His buildings had a problem—they fell. Maybe he's rich again now, maybe not. Maybe he has more children, maybe not. I don't know. I don't think about it. He's a risk man, so I stay here. I stay away. I don't need risk. I don't need his crazy life. This is enough.'

'Do you regret it all?'

'No. Nothing.'

'Why not?'

'Dreams you must chase. Maybe they leave you, not like you think, but after they finish you are somewhere new. Like chasing an animal.'

I was impressed with this response, and to note Celeste discussed her own lingering disappointments with the same almost thoughtless candour she did mine. She gave up on the Imperial Palace, setting down a largish pair of pliers.

'Let's drink tea,' she said.

I followed her upstairs to the kitchen. My mother had gone to tennis. She played every Tuesday and was the top competitor in her division. I had had no idea she was so good at tennis. I wondered, watching Celeste strain the tea, what else I did not know, what other things my mother had done before marrying my father and being saddled with me. I had an idea of her as a young woman, but now saw that it was garnered from a handful of stories which she herself had chosen to tell. She had had the luxury of being able to edit her own past, tailoring it to fit her present. I thought of her words the previous night, and of my father.

We carried our tea to the balcony and sat in silence watching a willy wagtail hop along the rail in a series of flighty, nervous bounces. It was careful to keep one eye on us at all times, as though expecting an attack.

'Mum seems very happy staying with you.'

'Thank you.'

'Have your children seen this place?'

'Yes. Once each. Maybe it's like a job for them now.'

'You must miss them.'

'Of course. That's why I make my art. A long time ago

it wasn't needed. I had my children. They were my art. I did everything for them. Maybe too much, maybe not. I was like three mothers.'

An hour passed, which we filled talking about everything from coffee to confetti, then I stood and pretended to stretch, watching the bird—which had come and gone throughout—resolve to take off and flap ineffectually towards the city. Tilly came to mind.

'I'd better get on and pack,' I said.

'Where are you going?'

'A bit of a road trip, but I'll be back by Friday. Thanks for the tea.'

'A pleasure.'

I stepped into the house, then turned. 'I'm going to go and see Tilly's father. What should I take him?'

Celeste beamed. 'I will arrange Japanese flowers.'

I travelled early the following day, using yet more of the money Mami had given me, and arrived at Mr Willoughby's farm around midmorning. It was a cold day despite the clear sky. I paid the taxi driver and took the long path in. The air was clean and cool, and there was more green in the fields than I remembered. Blue smoke wafted horizontally from the chimney. But as I got closer I realised it was all wrong. It was not the same house. It was the old shack. I quickened my pace and was soon standing inside a scorched section of earth the size of a basketball court. Littered with blackened bricks and charred stumps, it was all that remained of the house in which I had stayed.

I kept on towards the shack, where unseen birds chirped lazily in shrubs. The ute was parked out front. My presence went unnoticed until a cat came out to greet me, running its long body over my leg. I nudged it with my foot and it cantered towards the ute, pausing underneath. I could not remember if there had been a cat the first time or not.

Setting down the Japanese flowers, I knocked on the door, then cupped my hands at a window to peer inside. Before I could see anything I heard the deadlock turn. I stood straight, brushing lint from my jumper. I was nervous, so nervous my hands trembled, but I dared not bury them in my pockets. I completely forgot the flowers, which were off to one side, out of sight. The door opened and Mr Willoughby appeared, looking frail, almost unsteady on his feet. The whites of his eyes were bloodshot and he had the skin of a sober drunk—flushed red and layered with a fine film of sweat. He was wearing only a dressing-gown.

'You,' he said. 'I didn't expect you.'

Silently, the cat slipped around him and on into the shack.

'I tired to ring but—'

'Disconnected. They hooked the line to this place right after, but it never stopped ringing. I cut it off.'

I swallowed gloomily as Mr Willoughby pulled his dressing-gown tight and tied the belt with a bow.

'You'd better come in. That sun's got no heat.'

The kitchen was a mess and filled with acrid smoke, like a fog.

'I'm having trouble with the chimney. Dead bird in it, I think. Can't get a fire to take.'

Mr Willoughby clicked the kettle and spooned coffee into two mugs. When it clicked off he filled both, yawning. 'No milk,' he said.

'That's fine.'

In one corner of the kitchen the floor was littered with once frozen, finely diced carrots, peas and corn. I took a seat at a rickety wooden table.

'What happened?' I asked.

'The house? Fire.'

Before I could ask more Mr Willoughby excused himself to get changed. When he returned, dressed in jeans and a shirt, face shaven, he explained he was going shopping. I offered to accompany him into town but he shook his head and started for the door. 'No, I'll go alone. How about steak?'

'Steak?'

'For dinner.'

'Great.'

'I'll be back in a couple of hours. Make yourself at home. It's comfortable enough. I'm almost done moving in.'

When the ute's diesel engine faded, I crossed to a small bookshelf and flicked through a work about Russell Drysdale before picking out a larger book, *The History of South-East Asia*. Published in 1959 it finished with a chapter discussing European domination. I replaced this carefully and, after some indecision, began reading Graham Greene's *A Burnt-Out Case*. I read all afternoon. Two hours became four, four eight. Darkness fell. On my third visit to the bathroom I opened one of six stacked cardboard boxes and found it to be full of empty whisky bottles. It was no surprise to find the same in the other five.

I took a shower. Above the recess, between heavy, full bottles of shampoo and conditioner, there were intricate spider-webs. When I splashed them they shuddered. Afterwards I dried myself with my T-shirt, then put it on wet. Back in the living room, clocks ticked. Even here there were too many clocks and a piano.

I thought about Tilly and tried to piece the puzzle together, but I still needed answers—certainties. Without these the trip was in vain. I began to wonder if Mr Willoughby was perhaps giving me a chance to leave quietly. It seemed plausible, then possible, then probable. He had not said anything explicit, but where was he?

Mr Willoughby finally returned a few minutes before ten p.m. I heard the ute, then headlights ran over the living room. Oddly, there were no dogs to bark.

I helped him in with the shopping. Although characteristically stooped he looked a little stronger, and drunk. He lurched under the weight of the shopping bags and twice avoided looking me in the eye. When he spoke his voice was a mumble, as though his sentences had no real importance. We set up a lantern in the backyard and barbecued three steaks. We drank beer and did not bother with vegetables. We said little. After the beer ran out we swapped to whisky, served straight. Around us the night wind delivered far-off sounds. This wind had been reassuring all afternoon, but now it seemed impatient, like it wanted me to speak up. Mr Willoughby lit a cigarette and offered me one. I nervously accepted.

'So we both want information,' he said, surprising me. He stood and crossed to a window, staring inside as the wind flung his hair about.

'How did she die?' I asked. 'Was it in that fire?'

'Leukaemia.'

'Leukaemia?'

'Her third time. The first two bouts she battled when she was still just a teenager. She didn't tell you about it, did she …'

'You mentioned she was sick.'

'True. I did.'

'And the fire?'

'An accident.'

I remembered the story Tilly told me on the phone and it occurred to me Mr Willoughby had probably lit it himself.

'How long had she been sick?'

'This time not very long. The first two times everything was about survival. Her mother died of cancer, as I think you know, and I was determined Matilda wouldn't. To you that might sound natural, but it's not. Not at all. It's selfish.'

Mr Willoughby loosened his shirt which had bunched a little around his potbelly. 'Let's get inside,' he said. 'It's too cold.'

I followed him indoors, and in one corner the cat that had snuck in sneezed gingerly. It appeared with the subdued pride of a magician from behind the piano, stretched its body and strode to Mr Willoughby, who reached down to pet its ball-like skull.

'With Matilda's mother I was confident. Being confident was my job. No matter how crappy some piece of news—some doctor's honesty—by the time I repeated it there was a positive spin on it, an angle no one had thought of. I still believe she needed me to be like that. Never mind that she died in inches, died in the sort of pain you could only begin to understand by lopping off your arm at the elbow and dunking it in this whisky. In and out, day after day.' He cleared his throat and took a sizeable gulp. 'Five a.m. comes, goes. That's when you hold your breath, hope for a miracle. You go along and here and there even get your hopes up. We're halfway through. Not in the clear, no, but halfway. And half of nothing is nothing. I couldn't have tortured the poor woman better if I tried.'

'I'm sorry.'

'Naturally I approached Matilda's illness the same way. It was something I could do. She was young and she believed me. If I said it wasn't going to come back, then it wasn't. But it did, as leukaemia often does, making a liar of me. It shot my credibility to bits. The second time she didn't want to hear a word out of me, like it was my talk that jinxed us to begin with.'

Mr Willoughby, taking another long gulp and putting the tumbler down, misjudged the coffee table. Glass banged loudly on wood.

'By the time the symptoms showed up a third time it'd been years. Statistically she was in the clear.' He coughed. 'I told myself it was a whole host of other factors, nothing to do with leukaemia. This was before you first came to stay. She returned with the results the day you arrived, told me while I pretended to fix the ute.'

'I had no idea.'

'I didn't agree with keeping secrets, but it was her call, not mine.'

'She chose?'

'After you left,' Mr Willoughby said, 'there was a leak at the hospital. Not the staff I don't think. Someone must have overheard something and it spread around town. People avoided us in the supermarket or gushed with sympathy. Matilda hated both. People get nervous around death. The hint and history of it.'

Mr Willoughby shooed the cat off, and it made a point of strolling away at its own, unhurried pace before settling near the piano. 'She saw more specialists in Melbourne, getting all the details into a pile. It became clear the odds were stacked against her. We talked about you, about telling you, but she decided to keep you in the dark. It was nothing personal. More that you were the last person alive who knew her well but didn't know a thing about the leukaemia. She liked that. She began to talk about Tokyo, about returning. I droned on about treatments. That was the pattern of talk in this house. Eventually she decided to forego treatment and take that short-term university job. That was all it was ever meant to be. Three months of a normal life, then she was going to return. When she got back a little early she let me believe she'd told you everything. I presumed you'd decided to stay put.'

I said nothing.

'I'm Catholic. Sometimes I think life—all life, any life—is worth fighting for, much like I used to. Maybe I've never deviated from that view, only made this one exception. You saw me with those stupid bloody frogs. I like to think I can save things. But surely when some-one's going to die, when they truly want to die, it's cruel to stop them.'

'You helped her?' I ventured.

Mr Willoughby's eyes clouded and he shook his head. 'No.'

'She did it?'

He nodded.

'How?'

'Gas. There was an old gas tap in her room. She must have knocked it open and gone to sleep.'

'Where were you?'

'Melbourne. I had to see about a loan and stayed the night. She rang me at the hotel. Cheery. Chatty. After the call I couldn't find my sleeping pills but I stayed put. Best not to drive at that hour. I told myself it was nothing.'

'She had them?'

Mr Willoughby shrugged.

'I only know what the police told me. The gas would've rendered her unconscious. She would never have known she was choking.'

He drained his tumbler and flicked it into the centre of the table.

'What caused the fire?'

'They think she put clothes on an old, faulty electric bar heater. By the time they started smouldering she was most likely dead. The medics all agreed. She never felt a thing. A farmer a few kilometres away claims he saw the lot go up. But he's a worse drunk than me and a liar from birth, so who knows. Newspaper carried it as an accident.'

Mr Willoughby pulled the glass back and filled it to the brim, standing as if about to retire. He stood there a moment, in two minds.

'I never told the police, but when I came down here to this shack, the place had been tidied up ready for me and there was a swag rolled out in the back room. I found a note inside. She wanted me to start over. Build a new house by hand, fill it with a new family. I'm yet to get started but she wrote down exactly what it should look like.'

I felt incredibly guilty, listening to this without explaining my role in things. 'You said you wanted information from me. What do you want to know?'

He waved me off. 'We're too drunk now.'

The following morning I sat on the edge of my bedding, collecting up scattered, unsettling recollections of the night past. I had not felt myself drunk climbing into the sleeping bag, nor when crying into the pillow, but now my head throbbed, my mouth was parched and I felt a familiar nausea in the pit of my stomach, a churning that threatened to swell into a wave at any second. Angry with myself for not having told the truth when I had the chance, I pulled a towel from my bag and set out for the bathroom. The shack was chilly. There was no way to escape the cold breeze which swirled down the hallway with the peculiar aimlessness of a bored teenager, meeting with even colder air when I opened the bathroom door. I yanked the creaky, narrow window shut, noticing the morning outside was all fog. Grey and thick, it had draped itself across the farm. Trees were black and skeletal, and whatever animals there were seemed intent on observing a short silence.

A tacky plastic gauge on the wall read six degrees. Nevertheless I showered and, shivering, climbed back into the previous day's clothes.

To my surprise, Mr Willoughby had cooked me an English breakfast which we both ate in silence. The static-prone radio was tuned to ABC talkback, the volume low. I heard only snippets about the Beatles' first Australian tour before he cleared the plates and put them in the sink. Clicking the radio off, he coated the dishes with detergent.

'So, what will you do? Will you go back to Tokyo?'

I thought of the last time I ate breakfast with this man, of Tilly, the tail-light and her telling me she had planned to break up with me on the platform. I had no idea where I would go.

'Maybe,' I said, watching him run cold water over the oily plates. Even with detergent it sheered off, hardly breaking the grease. He washed each plate in turn then, picking up a tea towel only to toss it aside with a tired sigh, spun to face me. I sat dead straight. His voice, when at last it came, was surprisingly soft—gentle, even—but I remained determined to answer everything he asked directly and honestly. I owed him that much.

'Why did she come home early?'

'I cheated on her.'

He only nodded. 'Did she say goodbye?'

'No.'

'She left without saying a word?'

'Yes.'

After that, silent, he started on the drying, taking enormous care with each plate while I sat debating whether or not to stay still, help or make my excuses and leave. He did not seem angry. Sad, but not angry. The last plate took him an eternity.

'Get your bags and I'll meet you outside,' he said, setting it down. 'There's a midmorning train back to the city.'

'Okay.'

'Bring it all out to the ute.'

'Listen, I'm sorry.'

'There's no point in telling me you're sorry. I'll meet you outside.'

There was nothing left to say. I collected my belongings and started through the thick fog, headed for the ute. Mr Willoughby was in the driver's seat, alternately wiping condensation from the windshield and trying to start the motor. When the engine refused to turn he hit the steering wheel with the palms of both hands and swore. He kept hitting, kept swearing, the ute bouncing slightly, suspension creaking. Blunted words thudded against the closed windows and I looked away, wanting to give him privacy. He seemed not to know I was there. Against the shack, near the front door, I noticed the Japanese flowers. They were best left there. And without a word I stared into the fog— the world a black and white silent film—certain, given time, I could find my way.

I travelled from this silent film into a colourful, cataclysmic storm, complete with lightning and thunder like wobbling sheets of aluminium the size of the sky. The rain from this storm drenched me in the course of walking from the train station to Celeste's house. I was pleased to get indoors, to have a long, hot shower and sink down in front of the television.

I watched it without taking much in—something about getting bogged vehicles out of sand, a church service, then parts of a local football match. I closed my eyes and pictured Tilly sitting beside me, her hair short, her smile restrained.

'It's so odd, but I can't wait to get back,' I had her say.

I retired to my room and lay down on the western-style futon bed with a book titled *Kings and Queens of England and Greater Britain*. It kept me occupied for a few minutes before my thoughts began to skip. I could not stop it happening. First I thought of Mr Willoughby. The man seemed unlikely to start over. His Catholicism ought to have helped him but I doubted it would. Then I thought of Tilly. I wanted to warn her that he was drinking again and apologise for the killing of the cats. I stood up. I sat down. I missed her. I felt like speaking aloud, speaking directly to her. I wondered if there was any chance she could hear me, any chance she could simply have slipped into another room as the Henry Scott Holland poem insisted, but there was no other room, no heaven. Far away a car alarm sounded and was silenced, and it occurred to me that I would probably want to speak to Tilly for as long as she lived inside me, malformed—or more likely romanticised—by faltering recollection. I rolled over to shut her out, but again pictured her with short hair.

Finally I sat with my back against the door and thought of my father. What a diet of sanctified fairytales he had raised me on. And even now, when I most needed them, they were useless. Yet I did not feel anger towards him.

Instead, oddly, I recalled the afternoon he met with the principal regarding Wang. I had always assumed my father arranged this meeting to request my expulsion. But I had not been expelled and now I was unsure, especially following my mother's comments. Had he perhaps requested an exception? Clemency? Had he striven all along only to protect? It was hard to imagine, but plausible.

Standing, I noticed a Murakami novel on the shelf. The photo on its cover was from the collection in Mami's hotel room. I reached for it, stared at it, then tossed it aside and crossed to the window. Rain zigzagged down, filling the pane.

Suddenly I needed to walk. I let myself out of Celeste's, marched through the rain to my father's apartment and lingered outside for a minute, thoughts still skipping around. Then I pressed on into the dripping night. In one street a long, quiet line of oaks stretched endlessly ahead, and I sat against the first one I came to and stared up through the canopy. The sky was dark and empty. I could not find the moon, stars or even a cloud.

I began to think about staying in Australia. It was my mother who put the idea in my head. She took me shopping with a credit card I had not seen before and spoke to me through a curtain while I tried on new jeans I could hardly do up.

'You know,' she said, 'your father thinks you'll move back.'

'To Australia?'

'No, back into the apartment.'

'Why would I do that?'

'I'm only telling you what he said.'

Having given up on the jeans and folding them as best I could, I pulled back the curtain. The store was busy. *Geijin*—which is how I had come to think of Anglo-Saxons—browsed racks and chatted aimlessly in pairs or similarly dressed female clusters. My mother held up an almost purple T-shirt.

'What do you think?'

'No.'

'Do you want to try another store?'

'No. Let's go.'

She replaced the T-shirt and sighed. 'I've put you in a bad mood.'

'No.'

'I have. Talking all about your father and going to university.'

'You hadn't mentioned university.'

My mother smiled. 'Hadn't I?' She turned serious again. 'We worry a little is all. We'd like to see you with a degree because the two of us battled a sort of poverty all our adult lives and it doesn't need to be that way. You can take steps to make sure you're comfortable and uni is an obvious one. I don't care what course you do. Aren't you treading water in Japan? Maybe that's a mean thing to say, but your father and I agree. It's time to come home and start your life, your real life. In fact, your father said Anna—you know, the Livingston girl—has a spare room in a share house. He wasn't keen on the idea, and perhaps it's already filled, but wouldn't you be happier there with people around you? You've been through a lot. Maybe you should slow down.'

'I'll think about it,' I said, wondering how I could slow down any more than I had. I was not hurt, but more pleased—pleased the two of them had talked and had taken such an interest in me.

Over time the decision to study more or less made itself. My mother and Celeste began to talk as though I would start in March. I spoke on the phone with administrative staff and academics, and wandered the windswept Monash University campus. Most students seemed to be on holiday. Those who were still around sat and drank coffee, studied or pasted up political posters. It was all very subdued.

Following school this scene might have appalled me, a continuation of study, but now it appealed. There was freedom in it and I was tempted to sign up, put my name down for something utterly useless. Something from the Arts department that, though I would never use it again, I could sink my teeth into and pass many a lazy day debating. Greek tragedy, Bolivian feminism, anthropology, dinosaur-hunting—what it was hardly mattered.

Then came Mami's letter, and I never once phoned or went near a university again.

Dear Noah,

I had someone contact you about new housing. They spoke with Phillip who gave this address. I hope you don't mind my using it now.

Letters aren't easy things to write. Not for me, anyway. Whenever I write a letter it always ends up as a listing of facts, emotionless. This will too, no doubt, since there is so much to put down starting with this. I fucked Phillip. You'll remember

*the day. Didn't you think it a little odd, me coming out of the
bathroom with wet hair?*

*Maybe you know. I think you knew as I stepped from the
bathroom. So I'm writing this in explanation and also as an
apology. I'm trying to write to everyone I've ever cared for and
been cruel to.*

*I've not slept with many people—three (that I've chosen).
I do other things, find other ways to please. I don't really like
sex, the position it puts me in, and I want to make it clear I
didn't plan to have sex with Phillip. When I felt his hand, his
finger brush my inner thigh, I fully expected to laugh at him.*

*But I kissed him. I let one of his hands crawl up my back,
up my neck into my hair, tugging at the roots. I let his tongue
inside my mouth. I straddled him, pulled his pants down and
had him remove my clothes. I helped him get his blind, stupid
cock inside, felt his pig-headed fingers grope for my nipples.
Looking back on it now I'd say it was his injury. He pretended
he was enjoying it, pretended he was up to the task, but he
wasn't. The way I was doing it hurt him. I could tell. I could see
it and adjusted in increments until he was in agony. I left him
unfinished. He won't get a letter. But you get this one.*
Mami

Niigata

The cold air inside the gangplank caused me to teeter between the plane and Japan. I was done with the place and yet was allowing a girl—or the invention of a girl sculpted between transient meetings—to reclaim me. She was an illusion. Common sense told me Mami Kaketa was a bad bet. But it was beyond my control since I was in love. Being in love was the easiest way forward, perhaps the only way forward. It gave me a focus. And while it did not excuse past actions, did not excuse my treatment of Tilly or give me a true end to her, it provided an explanation. Mami was no fling. I had not abandoned Tilly for a quick screw. I had to believe that. Love, so long as it was love, was messy and beyond anyone's control.

And yet nothing is ever clean. Stepping from the plane I had the sense I was returning not to Mami but to Tilly. The charred remains of the farmhouse had not erased her quite as she had hoped. She lingered in my thoughts, danced around them. As had been my habit for weeks I thought of cockroaches, of the smell of insect spray, of freckled pale skin and red pubic hair, of a round woman waiting by an ambulance, of skinny stinking cats and smattered blood, of ghostly lace curtains, chopped wood, a huntsman spider, a knock on the door and light across long-burnt carpet. This was how Tilly spoke now. And unless I ignored her, unless I forged ahead, I feared she would speak forever.

In the customs line a middle-aged woman behind me bumped me every time we took a step forward. She seemed to be using me as a marker, a yardstick to indicate the end of the queue. I scowled but she only stared back un-comprehendingly, her face taut, her make-up thick and hard. The man in front of me constantly pulled denim jeans up to his bellybutton, outlining two flat bum cheeks, and it was not difficult to envisage what sort of a bum his wife stared glumly at before bed. Without warning, he turned to face me.

'This line is for Japanese,' he said. His voice was loud and confident despite his heavily accented English. To re-inforce his point he held up his Japanese passport and thrust it towards me. In the photo, as in person, he had the flat, unsettling face of a man struck with a shovel in early infancy.

'You must go there,' he said, gesturing towards a long, winding line full of foreigners.

I was in the right line, being a temporary resident.

'Don't worry about it,' I answered simply, using Japanese. A few people chuckled at his meddling and he turned around, giving his jeans another hitch. We all took a step forward and the woman behind bumped into me. I fought off a panicky suspicion I had made a terrible mistake returning, and pictured Mami lying on her bed, the curve of her hip beneath her silk slip and her wide, beautiful mouth. A way forward.

Phillip was gone. The apartment door was opened instead by a British girl with an upturned nose and a dumpy little body. A second Brit—a tall, gangly man with wiry hair—appeared behind her protectively. He yawned as if just woken.

'Yes?' they both asked.

'Is Phillip here?'

The man stuck his head forward, frowning. 'Who?'

'You mean the boy we had stay here?' asked the woman.

'Yeah.'

At this the man, realising he was not needed, peeled back and ambled down the narrow hallway. The woman shook her head. 'He's gone.'

'Where did he go?'

The woman shrugged. 'I don't know, but he left a bag of things here for a friend. What's your name?'

'Noah Tuttle.'

'That's the one. You'd better come in and collect it then. We were thinking about throwing it out.'

Somewhere in the main room a child started to howl. I hurriedly collected my things, which Phillip had piled into a garbage bag, and let myself out. Dragging it all to a Denny's restaurant I rummaged through and found a scrawled note. All that was written was my name and an address for a town in Niigata prefecture, high up in the mountains. I realised Mami had extended her offer to Phillip as a matter of course.

'Shit ...' I mumbled, throwing down the note, 'she found us both a house.'

At first Phillip would not believe it was me.

'What's your hair colour?' he asked.

'Reddish.'

'Wrong,' he corrected, opening the door.

'Then why'd you open the door?'

'Because anyone else would have said red.'

'Why the paranoia?'

'Tuttle,' he said sleepily, pulling me inside and locking up, 'you can't be too careful these days.'

After this greeting I was surprised to find the vast kitchen devoid of marijuana. Instead it looked like any other kitchen, complete with all the latest conveniences. A microwave with more buttons than a stereo, a dishwasher, a fridge with a built-in ice dispenser and a knife set to rival any my mother coveted. The living room, too, looked perfectly normal: new tatami matting, two leather couches, a digital flat-screen TV, a coffee table and a small but flash sound system with the speakers on stands.

'All came with the place,' Phillip said with a laugh. 'We really got lucky with that Mami bird.'

I resisted the urge to ask him just how lucky he got with Mami.

'This place is a palace,' he went on. 'We each have a bedroom, only I'll need to sleep in yours.'

'Why?'

'Mine's occupied.'

'By who?'

'By what,' he corrected.

I rolled my eyes. 'You're not actually growing that shit, are you?'

Phillip only smiled.

I followed him into his room, the walls of which had been lined with black plastic. He had cut this from something—garbage bags, most likely—and taped it all up. At the far end of the room, built into the main wall, there was a fan, and at our end, in the door, a cat-flap-like device. Phillip quickly shut the door behind me and pointed up at six solid banks of fluorescent lighting.

'Cool tubing,' he said. 'Perfect set-up. And the plants,' he ran his hand over the rows of square-potted trees, 'all come from clones. That's how I got this up and running so fast.'

'Clones?'

'Yeah. Sections cut from trees. Stems. I left them in water until they grew little white roots, then transplanted them. I tell you, I'm good at this.'

'Well I want nothing to do with it.'

'You won't have anything to do with it. I'll run the whole thing. Your cut'll be for keeping quiet.' He patted me on the shoulder. 'I can't believe,' he said, 'that Mami offered to set us up. It's perfect. When I first saw that fan up there in the corner I danced, Tuttle. Honestly danced.'

'Yeah?' I asked without the least enthusiasm.

'Right now I'm making a deodoriser box for the exhaust fan so the neighbours don't smell all this flowering.'

'Good idea.'

Phillip was genuinely excited. 'It's not easy. People think it's easy but it's not. The heat's a nightmare. I've pretty much got it sitting at twenty-seven degrees in this growing room but it still rises and falls a bit. I've insulated it round the front windows and other spots where the cold was coming through. Then I just have the aircon running hot twenty-four hours. The fluorescent lighting helps, too, while the air moving through makes sure it doesn't get too hot. I crank up the aircon a little at night when the lights go off.'

'You turn off the lights? Don't they need light to grow?'

'It's darkness twelve hours a day, just like outside.'

'It's damn hot in here, Phillip.'

'I know. It takes a bit of getting used to. The best thing to do is step outside when it really gets to you. Wipes away any sweat.'

'It's zero degrees.'

'Exactly.'

I wandered to the far end of the room and back again, running one hand along enormous plastic pots.

'Still getting those headaches?' I asked.

'Yeah.' Phillip shrugged. 'Sometimes.'

'Seen a doctor?'

'No point here. They all do the same—give me those hopeless headache tablets that just clog me up.'

I said nothing, but I knew at that moment I could not live with Phillip long. I had to move on. He was no doubt still smoking himself into a half-stupor to counter pain, and it seemed likely he would pay for it with prison time. Why he was still in Japan was beyond me. There were better countries for a drug habit. But then again, he had landed an apartment without set-up costs and could expect absurdly high returns for any grass he sold. While it was stupid, it was not entirely irrational.

'You got brothers and sisters?' I asked.

'Yeah. Two older brothers.'

'What do they do?'

'They run the farm. Why?'

'Farmers?' I asked, surprised.

'Yep.'

'And your parents?'

'Why?'

'I was wondering.'

'Mum and Dad help my older brothers. It's a sheep place.'

'So they're all living happily on the farm, huh?' I laughed.

'What?' he asked, moving between the rows. The fluorescent lights hung from adjustable chains and, though a less than salubrious enterprise, I was impressed by Phillip's ingenuity. Everything was well built and looked sturdy and planned. There were sketches piled up in one corner— possibly designs for the deodoriser.

'What?' he asked again.

'Nothing,' I said. 'I shouldn't laugh because it's not funny. But I just never picked you as being of farming stock. Now I understand how you made all this.'

'No. I was never a farmer.'

'Well you are now.'

'Whatever. And don't be bringing people over, Tuttle. This has to be kept a secret.'

But Phillip, stoned or drunk or both, broke his own rule three nights later. He headed out after dinner while I watched TV. I waited up for him but finally slept fitfully, sweating like a roast duck until sometime just before sun-up when a girl put her ear to my mouth to check if I was breathing. I got a glimpse of her but pretended to be drowsy and then fast asleep. She had seemed young, possibly even a high school student, but she undressed and screwed Phillip in the kitchen, whimpering throughout. Later, when she finally left, Phillip hardly stirred.

'You're here,' he said at midday, groggily.

'Yeah.'

'You were here all night?'

'Where else would I be?'

'We didn't wake you though, right?'

'No.'

'Good.'

'What happened to keeping secrets?'

'A slip-up. She saw nothing.'

I left him there with his absurd crop and hangover and went out for lunch. It was a nice enough town despite the frigid mountain air. It was walled in on all sides by forested hills too jagged to climb and yet with peaks that never seemed far away. Most of the apartments and houses were simple two-storey jobs, and the hulking department stores at either end of town were the main hubs. They welcomed and farewelled the steady traffic which ground through on a smoggy four-lane freeway, exhaust multicoloured in the midafternoon sun.

I sat in a dim restaurant beside this freeway watching vans pass me by like little bread loaves. I felt like a tourist. I wondered what Tilly would have made of it all, then forced her from my thoughts. There was absolutely nothing I could do about Tilly now and I hated it, hated even to think of her. I tried to picture Mami. I remembered, of all things, the way she put her finger in my mouth, the way she led me home that night and her reflection in the bathroom mirror as she turned back to face it.

The Emperor's Bluegill

I decided to pay a visit to Mami's hotel. Although all reports had her as exiled somewhere in Hokkaido, the ease with which she had paid the deposit on and furnished our apartment nagged at me. If in exile, how had she been able to access the money? I had to know for myself if she was still in Tokyo.

When I asked for Mami at the hotel's front desk—I had been careful to dress well and use polite Japanese—a small, delicate woman with the first signs of greying hair led me to a couch, where she gestured towards a number of magazines. She said she would make a call. Stupidly, I presumed this call would be to Mami and so thought nothing of the man who appeared a moment later, smoothing down his suit.

'Noah Tuttle?' he asked.

'Yes.' I quickly stood.

'I am Mr Kaketa.'

Mr Kaketa offered his hand, which felt soft and moisturised against my own. He smelt all at once like fruits, plants and something almost chemical—no doubt the result of various shower and shaving products.

'Pleased to meet you, sir,' I said, staring blankly into Mr Kaketa's face, which was pleasant even without a smile. Though a man well into his fifties, Mr Kaketa had a youthfulness about him. His skin shone and his eyes were those of a far younger man. They were alert, the whites unstained by red tentacles.

'So, you're a friend of my daughter's?' he said without much trace of a Japanese accent.

'That's correct.'

'You want to see her?'

'If possible.'

'Sorry, no. She is no longer here. I'm not sure when she'll be back.'

'Where can I contact her?'

'You can't. She is what you might call … indisposed.'

'I see.'

'Tell me,' said Mr Kaketa, 'do you live in Tokyo?'

'No, Niigata.'

'Niigata? A long journey. I'm sorry to disappoint you now you're here, but please, travel back safely.'

He reached out and shook my hand before I could ask anything more. A beautiful woman was crossing the lobby nearby, her head up, her high heels echoing loudly, but she did not distract the staff from Mr Kaketa. They all watched him from the corners of their eyes with a mixture of reverence and fear. They seemed to work doubly hard now he was around, doing everything too quickly and half-running from one task to the next. When I let go of his hand, the woman who had seated me rushed over and led me towards the doors. I saw Mr Kaketa turn to walk to the elevators. He paused to answer a staff member's question, head down, staring at the marble floor as if it were a flower bed.

I decided not to take the bus back to Niigata right away, but to remain in Tokyo for a few hours. The trip down had not been cheap and, since I was now using the last of the money Mami had given me, I felt an urge to wring value from it.

Outside, unsure what to do with myself, I walked towards the Imperial Palace. I had the beginnings of a headache, which I attributed to dehydration. There was nowhere to buy water, but since I had no desire to turn back I pressed my hand to my head and trudged on through the East Garden, out onto the bridge on which Mami first told me about her 'feeling'. I envied the carp below, lazily thrashing along the same stone walls, churning up the same water without concern.

Behind me two boys, backs to the bridge railing, stared gloomily down at matching sneakers while their grandparents, motionless, gazed into the water. I nodded hello, then returned to peering from my side of the bridge. I stared along the moat to the tall, sharply angled wall Mami claimed to have leapt from. Again I pictured her jumping. And this time I could see it. She was calm. She did not flail limbs or open her mouth. She did just as she said she had, and when she hit the surface there was not a splash or sound. She was swallowed up.

I walked to the spot in question and, stepping across a low chain fence, crept to the edge to look over. Due to the angle of the stone wall the water seemed a long way off, a fifty–fifty target at best. I could never have made such a jump—not into unknown, murky waters.

'I would not jump in if I were you,' said a foreigner behind me. I spun and was amazed to discover the voice belonged to an elderly Japanese woman.

'I wasn't going to, actually.'

The woman nodded and took a step towards me. Her thin white hair and crumpled skin both outlined her skull: dimples on top, eye sockets like deep, dark pits, and the jaw so sharp it could have belonged to a dog. She wore a grimy kimono that might once have been red, and blue Nike sneakers. In her veined, rutted hands she clutched a framed photograph of a young Japanese soldier. His expression was arrogant, hers amused. I had not heard this woman approach and momentarily entertained the notion she was a ghost. But others were staring too, young people power-walking or jogging, housewives being pulled along by their family pets.

'I am Mrs Onoda,' she said, carefully stepping over the chain fence. 'How nice it will be to speak English with someone who understands me.'

'Nice to meet you.'

'Nice to meet you, too,' she said, putting the photograph down against a tree. 'And you are?'

'Noah.'

'Noah. A good name.'

'Thank you. Onoda's Japanese, right?'

'It is.' She followed my gaze down to the photograph.

'My husband, Mr Onoda. He's what I think you call a straggler.'

'He's still coming, is he?' I looked about for an old man and Mrs Onoda laughed heartily. She pulled the base of her kimono taut around hairy, stockinged shins, then nudged her husband aside and eventually laid him flat on the grass. In all my years in Japan I had never seen anyone—of any age—sit on the ground without first putting down some sort of a protective cover, even just a page from a newspaper, but Mrs Onoda went ahead and knelt anyway without regard for grass, dirt or insects, giving me a friendly, toothless smile.

'I am old but strong. I can touch my toes,' she said. 'He,' and she again nodded towards her husband, 'is three years younger. The straggler.'

'Straggler?'

'Never came back.'

'From the war?'

'Yes.'

'I'm sorry.'

'Oh no, don't be.' She waved me off. 'He didn't bother to come back. After it ended, he plain forgot. He was alive, they saw him, but he stayed away.' She nodded towards the Imperial Palace. 'Maybe he didn't believe the Emperor had surrendered. I was a translator then. English mostly—some German. I waited but he didn't come back. That's a straggler. You've never heard the term?'

'No.'

'You do know there was a war though, which is something.'

I smiled.

'It's so nice to speak English with someone who understands,' Mrs Onoda repeated. A butterfly swooped in low, busily sewing an unseen quilt.

'I'm on my walk,' she said. 'I am in a home. They think I've lost my marbles.'

'Why's that?'

'Because I don't speak Japanese to them, only English or German.'

'Can you speak Japanese?'

'Of course. It's my language. My parents were Japanese. They were ambassadors before the war.'

'Then why don't you use Japanese?'

'It's bad luck. Worse than bad luck. If I use Japanese people in the home die.' She paused. 'You don't believe that. I can see you don't. But they do. I spoke to Mr Miyake last Monday. On Tuesday they found him dead in his bed, cold as a rock. It's not the first time that's happened.'

'What did you say to him?'

' "Pass me the pepper." I was so tired of gesturing.'

'I'm sure it wasn't your fault.'

'He choked on a carrot.'

'I'm sorry.'

'You're quick to say that.'

I again smiled and decided to ask a question that had been bothering me. 'So why do you have the photograph?'

'Fresh air is the only excuse I have. Now and then I like to get it out.'

'So the air's for the photograph?'

'Don't look so sceptical. You're much too young to know everything.'

'I wasn't saying you—'

'Also, he likes the palace. He was from here, from Tokyo. I met him on the other side.'

'The other side?'

'Of the palace. What else would I be talking about?'

The butterfly finished its stitching and began a long, indecisive arc which took it up over the moat. Mrs Onoda, watching it, said, 'A butterfly in this cold!'

'Is it late for butterflies?'

She shrugged. 'Animals …' she said. 'You know, there are problems with the fish in these moats. I read about it in my newspaper, the English one they bring me. Have you ever heard of the bluegill?' She proceeded to curl a blade of grass around her leathery index finger, then sharply uprooted it.

'No.'

'It's an American fish. They breed well and eat anything. They're taking over the moats and a host of Japanese experts are trying to fish them out. The Emperor studies gobies, you see. Do you by any chance know what a goby is?' But Mrs Onoda did not wait for me to answer. 'It's a Japanese fish. It lives at the bottom of the moat in the mud. The thing is, the American bluegill eats the Japanese goby.'

'Eats?'

'Devours. It's a problem. They have to empty the moats. Nets are no good. Japanese fish experts have to pull the black ships out. It's a *joi* campaign.'

Mrs Onoda grinned at my confusion. 'But there's a secret,' she said. 'It was in my newspaper.'

'Oh?'

'The Emperor, he put them there.'

'The Emperor put—?'

'—the bluegill in the moats. That's right. They were a present.' She dropped her voice and glanced about. 'Because he liked fish—he studied them, even wrote books about them.'

'Oh?'

'They came from some American politician. My, could they breed. And eat. Now they put them in dry plastic bags, let them flap themselves to death.' With all this said, Mrs Onoda took a breath and puffed up her wan, wrinkled cheeks like a blowfish. I waited for her to release the air, but she did not. Three seconds became five, then ten.

'No, no, please don't,' I said. 'No, Mrs Onoda, please breathe.' I was about to call for help when I felt someone tap my shoulder. Looking up and shielding my eyes from the sun, I saw a panic-stricken woman in her early sixties standing with two policemen, both of whom talked to me in Japanese while Mrs Onoda ignored us all and blithely went on holding her breath. The woman hurried around behind Mrs Onoda (who I guessed to be her mother) and expertly depressed both cheeks with two loving but firm palms. The old woman exhaled and began to chuckle. She spoke to the four of us in English and the three above stared down uncomprehendingly.

'There are other foreign fish, too. Lucky those Japanese gobies like hiding in the mud.'

The two policemen, following the orders of Mrs Onoda's daughter, picked up the old woman as if she were a priceless artefact and led her towards a parked police car. Blue and red lights swirled silently, beams lost in the afternoon sun.

'Goodbye, bluegill,' she called out to me as they lowered her into the back seat and shut the door with a thud. 'Beware of plastic bags.'

Mrs Onoda's daughter collected her father's portrait and smiled somewhat feebly. 'Goodbye,' she said in heavily accented English. Then, swapping into Japanese, 'Really, thank you. She's my mother. She escaped again. She likes to walk.'

After they left, my headache, which I had momentarily forgotten, only worsened. Perhaps a plan was already circling in my head but I had not yet identified even the need for one. I had not thought one step ahead of finding Mami, whose letter I had bravely come to look upon as proof she loved me. I did not allow myself to question this assumption, flimsy though it was. Without it, I was lost.

Returning to Niigata, I began teaching English two hours a day. The rest of my time I spent reading. Though I did not care to admit it, like Phillip I was waiting for the cursed plants to grow. Outside the temperature continued to fall. Every night it was below zero and Phillip compensated with bar heaters and the aircon, which could be used to both heat and cool the room depending on fluctuations. I came and went without Phillip showing the slightest interest. He lay on his bed, staring at the ceiling, bong to one side.

As we moved into December, Phillip, satisfied with the height of the plants, hacked them down and strung them from the ceiling in tightly spaced rows. It became an eerie room to move through once he had cleared away the fertiliser bags, wooden frames and plastic pots—a sort of upside-down forest. Some four days later he set about removing the leaves. I watched him work but did not offer help. Then, once the leaves were off, he cut the buds free, trimmed them and laid them out on cardboard. They filled the floor, a carpet of buttons, and while they slowly dried he hauled woody waste high up into the hills to bury. Both jobs took about a week, after which he returned home with brown paper bags and blue plastic containers. He dropped roughly three inches of buds into each paper bag and once again left them to dry, the bags in neat rows like a miniature graveyard.

Yet another week of waiting crawled by, in which I taught English in cafés or set out for the hills. I became familiar with the hiking trails behind our house, sometimes walking all day up over peaks from which it was possible to see not just our town but four or five more depending on the weather. The silence of these forested hills appealed to me. There was never much wildlife but I had the impression a host of animals were following me from afar, curious to see where I was headed but too shy to show themselves plainly. In the canopy above, birds raised their usual alarms, and below, my damp sneakers squished and snapped long-dead autumn foliage.

On one such walk I came across an abandoned single-gear bike, the type popular throughout all Asia. It was not uncommon to find such junk dumped in these hills by people unable to afford to dispose of their belongings legiti-mately, and I thought nothing of hopping on it. Remark-ably, the thin wheels still had air and I was able to get it moving. It wobbled at first but as I picked up speed it became steadier, and I avoided branches and one or two rocks embedded in the path without difficulty. The simple, rusted metal frame transferred every bump directly into my lower back.

I was contemplating tossing the thing aside when I noticed two cats up ahead. One darted into the foliage but the other started running, keeping to the path and occasionally checking back to make sure I was not gaining. I pedalled furiously, enjoying watching it bounce along, and I must have chased it half a kilometre before it tired of me and vanished. By the time I tossed the bike into the trees I was bent double, gasping for air.

'What if my Tuvalu isn't a place?' I asked the ground, voicing a thought which had been in my head all along. I conjured cannons, Admiral Perry's black ships, my 'diploma' and Mami's happy words to me. 'It's an illusion, all these rules. We can do whatever we want.'

I stood straight and stared through the endless bare trunks, unconvinced.

From the bags, Phillip transferred the buds into the plastic containers, packing the dope in tightly and stacking it into the freezer. Two days after doing this, however, he found a fine sweat inside the containers and had to unpack everything. The miniature graveyard reappeared and remained a fixture until he was finally satisfied the buds were perfectly dry. My resolve weakened. Wanting the job done with I helped stack everything into the containers once again. We waited six days for the sweat to reappear and, when it did not, we toasted our success with imported beer. It was by this time five days till my birthday and seven till Christmas. I could feel an unseen, airless plastic bag closing in on the two of us.

This growing sense of doom was reinforced by an unexpected visitor. Phillip had gone to the nearby Lawson's convenience store to buy food when the front door buzzer sounded. I assumed that it was him, that he had forgotten his keys. With the grass in the freezer again, I did not bother to identify him. I simply opened the door.

I was confronted by an inordinately tall, thin man in overalls with a clipboard. He smiled and, holding his name badge at an angle for me to read, said something long-winded which I did not fully understand. I had him speak slowly and discovered that he worked for a power company—our power company—and that he had come to cut the power. It seemed we had not paid our bill.

'I didn't know we had a bill yet,' I told him, quite sure nothing had arrived. Though it was nearly impossible to know which mail was junk and which required urgent payment, I had been careful to check everything, hoping to avoid exactly this situation.

The man asked to come in. I stood back and he entered the kitchen, looking around, Thankfully, the doors to the other rooms were closed.

'No, it wasn't sent here,' he said, running a finger over the clipboard.

'Where was it sent?'

The man handed me his copy of the bill and began to sniff—not big sniffs, but secret sniffs he did not want me to notice. I ignored him. Running my eyes over the bill I at once found the Japanese characters I was looking for. A surge of excitement ran through me.

'Can I keep this?' I asked.

'Yes. And you can use it to pay.'

'What does this say? This bit?'

He leant in, squinting slightly. 'Where?'

'Here.' I pointed.

'Kaketa.'

'And this, beside it?'

'Mami.'

'And all this?'

'An address in Hakodate.'

'Thank you.' I paid him with the money I had been saving from my work teaching English, then led him outside. He got in his car, and as he drove away an absurd plan took shape inside my head, one I scarcely credited possible until it occurred to me that there was no other.

As a first move I asked if I could be the one to transport the grass to Tinkerbelle's Treat. Phillip, taking a long drag on his cigarette and trapping the smoke deep in his lungs, eyed me suspiciously.

We were walking down what was obviously once the town's main street, past closed roller doors and the sort of fashion shops that pop up in small towns all over the world —cheap, shapeless garments and sun-worn posters in the front window featuring models who could well have aged ten years since the shoot. Through the smell of Phillip's cigarette, I occasionally noticed the stench of human shit from the street's main drain. Barbers with twirling white, blue and red poles out front and yet more faded posters in their windows sat inside waiting for customers. Everywhere beneath the dull afternoon sun there was lethargy and silence.

'That's a turnaround,' Phillip said at last, after taking his time to figure out my possible motives.

'I want to earn my cut.'

At this he smiled. 'And just what sort of cut would that be?'

'I was thinking half.'

'You were? Well, Tuttle, that's a hell of lot more than I was ever planning to give you.'

'I know. But you need someone to cart it, right? You don't want to do it yourself, not if you're staying in Japan.'

'And you're not?'

'No.'

'Where do you think you'll go?'

'Home—uni.'

Phillip laughed. 'Drug money spent on an education.'

'I'm going straight.'

Phillip's caginess was all show. For days he had been watching, wondering how to get me to courier. Dropping his half-smoked cigarette into the open drain he pretended to be in two minds.

'Shit, Tuttle, I don't know,' he said. 'I'd have to ask Harry.'

'Tell him I want to make myself useful.'

'Why?'

'Just tell him that and he'll understand.'

'Is there something I don't know?'

'No.'

'There is. I can smell it.'

'Smell whatever you want.'

'Why should I trust you?' Phillip asked, surprising me.

'Because we're in this together.'

'The fuck we are. I grew it, Tuttle. People think it's easy but it's not.'

'True. But from a legal rather than a horticultural perspective,' I said patiently, 'it'll appear I helped. We were living together the whole time. I can hardly claim I didn't notice it.'

'Good point. Okay. Consider it a goodbye present.'

'Thank you. When will I move it?'

'This coming Monday, in the arvo. Don't fuck up.'

I took leave of him, pretending I wanted to shop, and rang STA Travel from a payphone, feeling a rush of excitement when the operator listed the various flights to my destination.

Next I drafted a letter and carefully copied the Japanese characters from the power bill onto the front of the envelope, praying it would somehow reach Mami in Hakodate. I wrote that her apology had been appreciated, that I had come into some money and was planning to depart for an undisclosed location, where I intended to relax for a few months before looking for work—something part time. I concluded all this with a heartfelt apology for being vague and assured her that I was perfectly serious,

encouraging her in one last crazy act to disregard her bail
and flee the country. This was a calculated proposal. Unless
my offer was absolutely irrational I had little faith Mami
would give it more than a moment's thought.

As a P.S. I added the most important detail of all—a
meeting point. For this I chose a Japanese-style hotel near
the airport, one I had found on the internet that did not
look too cheap or too expensive. I booked a single room for
Monday and Tuesday, paying with an old credit card which
still had a few hundred Australian dollars attached to it.
The payment went through without difficulty.

Monday, as it happened, was the day before my birthday.
Around midmorning Phillip removed the plastic containers from the freezer and packed them into a specially
purchased backpack.

'Time to go,' he said.

'Time to go.'

I picked up the backpack and let myself out. It was
heavier than I had anticipated and I thought about turning
back, reneging on my plan—I no longer had the nerve for
it. But the thought of Mami kept me moving. On the bus
down to Tokyo I stowed the pack in the underneath compartment and enjoyed knowing I could walk away from it if
discovered, deny any knowledge. Once we arrived at Tokyo
Station, however, I had to claim it and heft it up again.

The commuter train to Shinjuku was half empty. I sat
opposite a mother in a cheap suit and a girl of four or five in
a pink dress. Aside from the dress everything the girl wore

was a bright white: the hair bands wrapped around her near vertical pigtails, her collar, cuffs, stockings and shoes. She stared up at me unselfconsciously with two large brown eyes. Her chubby face and downcast but not unhappy mouth made me want to smile, but I instead clutched at my backpack and averted my gaze.

It suddenly began to rain. The millions of drops seemed to move almost horizontally. We were above a road and I peered through the water-streaked window down into a crowded street, where I caught the eye of a man smoking before he was gone again, before it was all gone again, replaced by city windows. Down the carriage an attractive, svelte woman with long, reddish hair typed a short message into her mobile phone and smiled at the reply, and a young businessman of perhaps twenty dropped his head and tried to nap. The backpack, even resting between my legs, sat heavily. No one paid me much notice. Certainly not the girl asleep beside me—one cheek scrunched against the rail at the end of the bench seat, yellow cashmere scarf threatening to suffocate her. She twice changed position and dozed on my shoulder as if she had known me all her life. I stared up at the colourful ads for magazines hanging from the carriage ceiling. Unable to read even a word my eyes jumped from one portrait photograph to the next while I thought about jail.

Intent to Sell

Shinjuku Station is the perfect place for an amateur drug deal. Millions of people travel through it and exchange packages every day, and I was not surprised Harry chose it. I was surprised, however, to be giving the drugs to a perfect stranger. Harry had described the man to Phillip who, in turn, had described him to me. The man would wear dark pants, a light-blue shirt and a leather jacket. He would have short, spiky hair and be carrying an English newspaper. He would be shopping for a tie at one of the tables set up outside the men's toilets, and would enter to urinate upon seeing me. I was to follow him in and stand at the urinal immediately to his right.

As I neared the drop my nerves got the better of me and I had to pause, my back against a wall, to catch some air. It was the wrong country to run drugs in, a country where some judges took pride in years of service without ever handing down an 'innocent' verdict, and where prisons attracted the wrath of Amnesty International. I was an idiot.

And yet there was my desire, bubbling below, willing me on and reminding me it would all be over in a matter of days. Without money I had nothing to offer, not even a crazy plan, and without anything to offer I had no right to expect Mami to follow me. Before starting on again I thought of Phillip, but decided I owed him nothing. Then my father came to mind. What would he make of a drug conviction? I hoped he would never know.

I took a deep breath and, pushing myself up from the wall, rounded the corner and passed the man with dark pants, blue shirt and leather jacket. He was apathetically holding up two cheap, ugly ties and, though he gave no indication of having seen me, he put them down and started towards the men's. Presumably he had identified me by the backpack and tight-fitting suede jacket Phillip insisted I keep on at all times.

I entered the men's, walked past the grimy white porcelain basins—without looking at my reflection—and took my place at the urinal beside the man with the blue shirt. He had obviously been waiting a while because I could hear a steady stream of urine. Hefting the pack onto the ledge I unzipped and took aim. This bathroom, which often had a queue, was not too busy today. It smelt of shit. I glanced behind me towards the pit-toilet stalls, then along the urinals to my left. It was only as I did this that I noticed the police officer, one of four evenly spaced men, pissing with obvious pleasure. Unsure what to do, I froze. Through the window at the end of the bathroom I heard a train pull into a platform. The announcer's voice crackled.

The man with the blue shirt did not look at me. He kept pissing, steam rising from his urinal. I gulped. When I tried to urinate nothing came. The man with the blue shirt, nodding almost imperceptibly, placed his newspaper on the ledge above the urinals. But at that moment two men zipped up and walked to the basins, affording the policeman a perfectly unobstructed view of all we did. He showed no sign of finishing up and kept glancing our way.

I was now pushing so hard I fully expected to fart, but there was not even a dribble, and I was about to give up, about to zip up and flee, when the man with the blue shirt smiled, casually took up my backpack and walked out. The police officer noticed at once. He nodded towards my backpack and I dumbly averted my eyes. He shook himself dry.

I truly had been left with my dick in my hand. Everything about the situation was terribly unpleasant. In a stall behind us someone groaned and farted. For a moment I contemplated running but something held me back. I tugged desperately at my zipper while the policeman did his own fly up without difficulty and collected his hat from the shelf above the urinal. He gave me a funny look and I was certain he was going to arrest me, but he shrugged and walked to the basins where I heard him wash his hands, humming.

I waited until his heavy tread was inaudible and then started for the basins myself, having to double back for the newspaper.

'I could walk away,' I said in a whisper, staring at my reflection in the mirror, both hands on the basin. 'Leave it and walk away.'

But realistically I knew the time to do that had come and gone. I turned on a tap and watched water run into the plughole. New men came in, others exited. What if the police were waiting outside? That would be the best way to nab me—wait for me to exit with the paper. What if they already had the man in the blue shirt?

'Fuck it,' I said to myself, deciding not to think about all that could go wrong. I was not parting with the money or deviating from my plan, not now the worst was behind me. There was no reason to think it was a set-up. Hell, there had been a police officer in the toilets … And assuming there was no set-up, assuming Harry had not ratted, the police would be unprepared for me. I had to move, and move fast.

I snatched up the newspaper and strolled out with a devil-may-care glare into Shinjuku Station proper. I passed a deli and a small supermarket and continued on towards the Saikyo Line. I hardly took a breath the whole way until I caught sight of something that calmed me considerably. Turning right to descend the broad stairs to Platform Four, I saw the policeman from the toilet. He was not more than five metres away, helping a girl up onto a stretcher with a second, skinnier policeman. The skinny one had a plastic cabinet with him, and from this he pulled a clear mask, expertly placing it to the girl's mouth and pulling the elastic band back behind her head.

'Ambulance,' I said, feeling stupid.

Platform Four rumbled.

I took the stairs three at a time down to the train, slipping in seconds before the doors beeped shut. Only then, heartbeat racing, did I wonder if I had dropped the money. But there was no time to check as the train jolted and started forward. I stood with the folded paper in hand, praying I had not lost it all. It took five tense, clanking minutes to reach Ikebukuro, where I jumped out and again ran to the toilets, locking myself in a cubicle. I pulled the paper open but nothing fell out. I shook it manically and at last a small envelope slipped silently into the drop pit between my legs. Thankfully this was dry. I fished it out with a ball of toilet paper before tearing it open and removing a thin wad of 10,000 yen notes, all of which I stuffed into my wallet before dropping the envelope back in the toilet and stamping on the handle to flush all evidence.

I let myself back out and again took the Saikyo Line, this time to Akabane where I transferred onto the Keihin– Tohoku Line for Nippori. There was probably a faster way of reaching Nippori, but I knew this route well. From Nippori I took the Skyliner to Narita, hopping off well before the international airport at the city itself. With a tourist map and considerable trudging I found the Japanese-style hotel I had booked online.

It was a narrow building jammed between a dentist and a doctor's office. Built in the sixties, it was now beginning to fall apart. Pulling back a heavy, wooden sliding door I let myself in and found a small office, crammed full of paper. There was a calendar with a young Japanese girl in a bikini and a desk piled high with junk. Three filing cabinets were open, revealing yet more documentation, and there was a small orange thermos threatening to fall onto the floor. Someone had slipped a note under the office door and I was about to call for assistance when I realised it was for me. The Japanese script made no sense, but my name was written in a gap with a red permanent marker, and when I lifted the note up I found a key underneath with no tag. I turned it over in my hand. There was a large 403 stamped into it.

Tapping the key on my hip I wondered if I should have taken my shoes off at the front door, but it hardly mattered. No one was around and the corridor was all smooth, green concrete. Whatever this place was, it was not strictly traditional. Concessions had been made. There was a stark cafeteria with colourful plastic chairs, wood-veneer tables and a service counter, as well as a narrow, humming vending machine full of overpriced beer.

There was no noise coming from my room when I finally found it, no indication anyone was inside. But I persisted in telling myself Mami had collected her key and was quietly waiting for me. I had booked for two. Surely they would have put two keys out. I slotted the small, oddly shaped key into the door and fought back disappointment when I found the room empty and untouched, two futons at the rear folded up and waiting. As a room it seemed un-welcoming and depressing. There were no chairs or tables, only an in-built bench and small beige TV. I took off my shoes and stepped onto the tatami matting. The room smelt stale, so I opened its only window.

There was a small, laminated notice written in English sitting beside the television. It told me to make myself at home, fold out my bed when I felt tired and share the bathroom with others. Beneath it was a map indicating the way to this bathroom, which was seemingly back down on the first floor near the cafeteria. I turned on the TV to fill the room with noise, and at that moment a passenger jet, no doubt on its final approach, passed overhead with a thunderous, rolling *shhh*. It set every wall rattling.

Feeling cold, I shut the window.

I sat on the tatami and stared up at the room's only light—one globe with a cheap oriental frame. I could look into it without difficulty and still read the clock. In four hours it would be my birthday. It was an awful place to have a birthday, an awful time for a birthday. To celebrate I paid too much for a beer from the cafeteria vending machine, taking it back to my room and sipping at it. I thought about the money and went so far as to take out my wallet, putting it on the TV. I did not bother to count it. Not caring what happened to it I left it there and, folding out a futon, tried to sleep. There was always a chance Mami was delayed.

Plan B

When I woke the following morning, it was to the sound of the TV. I stared into it, into an ugly, fluorescent studio full of Japanese celebrities. Then, body aching, I stood, turned it off and noticed I was shivering. No doubt it was close to zero outside and I groped for the bar heater, clicking it on. Nothing seemed to happen.

For an hour or two I lay on the futon listening to the rain. Then, still cold, I dressed without bothering to shower and wandered outside. The rich smell of soil and bark, stirred up by the rain, only strengthened as I wandered away from the hotel towards far-off rice paddies. Above me the sky was fogged over and hung low. The trees I passed were all leafless and skeletal, a few with tiny birds on the topmost branches, their wings hugging knot-like bodies. Cars passed, leaving a short trail of white exhaust, though there was little else in the way of people about. For a moment, wholly miserable, I wanted to wrap myself in people. It did not matter who. I wanted to drink, joke and celebrate my birthday with others. In the past it had been my habit to avoid friends on my birthday, to slink off like a cat preparing to die without giving a thought to those who might want to celebrate with me. But this year I wanted to be the centre of an enormous party.

At some point, fed up with walking, I turned and started back towards the hotel. I thought glumly about the future now lying in wait for me. The obvious thing to do was return home, live with my father and enrol in something suitably obscure. Staying in Japan would be foolish. Where would I live? I could not return to Niigata without giving Phillip his share of the cash and I had no intention of doing that. There was always Europe or South America or a hundred other destinations, but to travel alone now seemed a gloomy proposition. The excitement had gone out of loneliness.

Finally the hotel fell into view and something— a movement—caught my eye. I watched as a hefty rat scampered along the top of the front sliding door and slipped in behind a dented airconditioning unit. I wanted to catch it and stomp its skull flat.

To Tuvalu

Slotting the key into my door I did not expect to find Mami sitting on my windowsill in a red tweed coat with white stockings, strands of hair dancing in the cold, wet, midafternoon breeze. She smiled and tossed aside the TV remote.

'So where are we going?' she asked, jumping up and draping herself from my shoulders. Her hair smelt of shampoo and her skin was soft against my face when she kissed me, first on the cheek and then on the lips.

'How long do we have to stay in here for?' she asked, making it clear she did not approve.

'Shit. You're here.'

'I am. Let's get out of Japan as soon as we can.'

'You're serious? You're planning to skip bail?'

I was by now desperately trying to fight off a growing, very physical excitement. This apparition—which was no apparition at all—ran the instep of one soft, stockinged foot up my calf.

'Bail? There is no bail. Not anymore. That was a misunderstanding. My father fixed it. Anyhow, you're the one who suggested I flee.'

'I know, but—'

'You're not backing out are you?'

'No.'

She pointed to my wallet, still atop the TV. 'I didn't peek but it felt heavy. Are you rich now?'

'A little rich.'

She laughed. 'Do we have air tickets?'

'Yes.'

'Then let's go.'

'The flight's tomorrow.'

'Going where?'

'Tuvalu.'

'Tuvalu? Is there such a place?'

'I believe there is.'

Mami laughed. 'Pure madness. What's it like?'

'It's an island. Warm, beautiful.'

She took off the coat, revealing a figure-hugging short black dress with chiffon layers and a lace ruffle, the tweed belt hanging from her hips. Then she unzipped my pants and playfully tugged at them. 'Sounds ideal,' she said.

I had not wanted her to do what she proceeded to do, had not requested it. I had not showered, and I told her to stop, but she would not listen. She told me to shut up and did as she pleased until I climaxed and dropped backwards onto the futon, clutching at my crotch. Unable to speak, her mouth clamped shut in a grin, Mami pointed frantically towards the communal bathroom map and finally shot out the door trying not to laugh.

When she returned she put the tweed coat back on and we went for a walk, leaving my wallet on the TV without fear of theft and heading towards the same sunken, concrete-boarded paddies I had visited earlier in the day. All was white. It had started to snow and we stood at the edge of one of the larger paddies, staring across it.

'My mother grew up in the country, up in Nagano. In the winter, farmers would fill these rice paddies with water and let them freeze over. Then everyone skated on them.'

'I thought she was Korean.'

Mami hesitated. 'Born in Korea.'

'And what, now she lives in Nagoya with your father?'

'No.'

'Where does she live?'

'My stepmother, the Ice Queen, lives with my father in Nagoya. My mother's been dead for years. She died in a plane crash, since you must know. She only ever had me. My sister, the newly married Kaketa, now a Hashimoto, she belongs to the Ice Queen. Thank God I never have to see my family again. I've cut up all my credit cards. There's nothing tying me to any of them.'

'I'm sorry about your mother,' I said, trying to suppress a suspicion I was being lied to. Perhaps Mami read my mind because she suddenly took off her shoes and stepped into the snow-covered rice paddy. Her warm feet melted the ice and dirt became mud, smearing the soles of her white stockings. She took them off, one leg at time, balled them up and walked awkwardly out towards the middle, bare skin bright between the red coat and snow.

'My family will be worried,' she called, turning and

frowning slightly. 'But my sister has her husband to look after her and my father … To hell with him. To hell with him for locking me up with the Ice Queen in Nagoya like that, like some sort of wild, dangerous animal, everyone watching, making sure I'm not going to kill myself. Hakodate was no better. The papers all said I'd run away, but I was abducted more like it. I didn't get a chance to run, not until now.'

'I met your father,' I yelled to her.

'I know.'

'He wasn't very nice.'

'No.'

'What about your stepmother?'

'What about her?'

'Why do you hate her?'

'I don't hate her.'

'You called her the "Ice Queen".'

Mami shrugged, a far-off little movement, like a play of light.

'She's from another planet,' she yelled, 'and since they'll be back for her soon, I've never made much effort. Never seemed worth it.'

'Very funny.'

'I thought it was.'

Mami lit a cigarette and the snowy breeze carried the smell of tobacco to me. She stared about her and then started to walk. In an ambling fashion, she made her way back to the footpath, where we waited for her feet to dry, the mud peeling.

'Why did you take your shoes off?' I asked. 'You should have left them on.'

'No. Without's best.'

Later the same afternoon, framed in the light from the window, Mami was beautiful in her black dress. I kept glancing over at her and smiling. Even when she noticed and told me to quit it I did not. She was intent on smoking as much as possible and thinking about things I could not begin to guess at. She pulled one knee to her neck, rested her head on it and waggled her big toe with her free hand, watching it as if it belonged to someone else. Now and then she sighed and stretched, but mostly she seemed to want to be left alone in the windowframe, as if waiting for something.

'What time do we take off?' she asked, shortly after nightfall.

'Early afternoon. I'll check the tickets.'

'No, don't bother now. We'll check later.' She jumped down. 'I have something for you.'

She reached deep into her bag and tossed my crumpled denim jacket onto the floor.

'You can keep it,' I said. 'Remember, I said you could.'

'No, I don't want it. I was only ever trying it on.'

That night, probably stupidly, I tried to sleep with her, but she told me she felt ashamed and opted just to lie naked.

'Ashamed?' I asked, frustrated.

'I wrote so many of those letters,' she said. 'It's amazing how many I wrote.'

'What letters?'

'Like the one I sent you.'

'You really sent more than one?'

'I had a lot to be ashamed of. For a while, after I was caught stealing, I decided to be perfectly serious about being ashamed. Like most of my feelings it came and went, but not before I posted all those letters. I don't know why I'm ashamed again now, though.'

I removed my hand from her bare hip and flopped onto my back, staring up into the single, dim bulb. When I looked out the window it was snowing heavily and there was a layer of white on the outside ledge.

'You really wrote a lot of letters?'

'Yes,' she said with a laugh. 'I'm embarrassed now that I sent them. I sent them to people I haven't seen since elementary school. Dear so and so, sorry for pulling your hair and breaking your arm. That sort of thing.'

I had to smile. 'Look on the bright side, at least you'll arrive in the South Pacific with a clear conscience.'

At the mention of Tuvalu, Mami's eyes sparkled. She adroitly rolled on top of me. 'I want to save it for then,' she said.

'What?'

'Sex.'

'Okay.'

'We'll save it for this mystery island you won't tell me a thing about.'

'This island I don't know a thing about.'

Cold, I nuzzled into her and felt with sore fingers the warmth of her skin, felt it radiate out, but it was not enough to prevent a shudder.

She whispered in my ear. 'I bet it has bright green

tropical trees, big monkeys, natives and cerulean blue oceans. I bet it has ocean whichever way you look. I bet I won't even need to wear a watch.'

'Probably not.'

'And,' she said, 'there'll be rain storms. Raindrops the size of marbles. We'll wake to the sound of tropical rain, or failing that the sound of waves. I love the sound of waves at night, don't you? They're so calm and regular. We'll lie on a bamboo bed in each other's arms like this and listen, and everything that's here will be left here, left to Japan, to grimy, unfair, sad Japan, with its overcast sky, with its industry and iron and sharp edges.'

A jetliner roared overhead and the hotel walls rattled loudly, then fell silent.

'Goodnight,' Mami said. 'Tomorrow we'll be in Tuvalu.'

I fell straight to sleep then but woke too early, woke when I should have slept. I heard her behind me, trying to cross the dark room quietly, her bare feet causing the tatami to groan. I heard paper slip over material and leather placed carefully back on plastic. When I rolled over, squinting, she was silhouetted in the doorway by fluorescent light.

'Go back to sleep,' she whispered, 'I'm just getting a soft drink from the vending machine.' And I nodded and rolled back, and when she shut the door all I could see was the deathly quiet snow falling outside.

Acknowledgements

Many thanks to Annette Barlow, Christa Munns, Catherine Milne, Ali Lavau and Catherine Taylor for a fantastic edit; to everyone at Allen & Unwin for their great support and patience; to *The Australian* and Vogel's for the ongoing encouragement and opportunity they give new writers; to Soph for her last-minute insights; to the many wonderfully kind and interesting Japanese people who explained so much of Japan to me; to the *gaijin* who were and still are there, especially Eric; to Serendipity Lavender Farm, Nar Nar Goon, for teaching me about lavender lollies and other useful details; and to old friends everywhere who always told me to get on and finish something. All mistakes are my own.